SNAPSHOT
of a
MURDER

ALISON HENDERSON

SNAPSHOT OF A MURDER

DEDICATION

To my daughter Jessica, who loves cozy mysteries
and Carmel-by-the Sea.

CHAPTER ONE

Turning forty was the third-worst thing that happened to Isadora Munro that day.

The first, or possibly second, was spelled out in the note she held in her hand. Izzy stared at the words, but they made about as much sense as a jumble of hieroglyphs. She glanced up from the paper and gazed across the quartz-topped breakfast bar into the living room of the elegant high-rise condo which, until ten minutes ago, she'd believed she shared with her fiancé. Now, the paintings and photos had been removed from the walls, the decorative items packed away in brown cardboard boxes, and the plush area rugs rolled and taped for transport. In the course of eight short hours, the once-welcoming room had been stripped bare, leaving only a blank, impersonal space, devoid of soul or comfort.

In the entry hall sat a forlorn trio of boxes with *Izzy* written on the sides in bold black marker and a stack of

1

her favorite framed photographs on top. With a frown, she returned her attention to the note, as if the true meaning of the words would become clear if she gave them a second chance.

Dear Izzy,

Since I know how much you hate equivocation, I'll get straight to the point. After due consideration, I've decided it is in both our best interests to move ahead separately, rather than together. Once you've had a chance to think about it, I'm sure you'll agree. I want to assure you I don't take this step lightly. My decision has been a long time coming. I know I should have acted sooner – that's on me – but I didn't want to hurt you.

Be that as it may, I have sold the condo, and the movers are coming Friday morning to transport my belongings to Las Vegas, where I will be heading up my firm's new branch office. Your clothes are still in the closet, but the rest of your things are packed and waiting in the front hall. You have until the new owners take possession on the fifteenth to remove them.

Whether or not you decide to remain in San Francisco is up to you, of course, but this might be the perfect opportunity to make a complete life change and move to the house your great-aunt Dora left you in Carmel. Whatever you decide to do, I wish you every happiness.

Bryce

"After due consideration." Izzy crushed the paper in her fist as the implications of her situation sank in. The freaking note was so *Bryce*. Every word reeked of *lawyer*. He wished her "every happiness." The slimy, cowardly, weasel. She threw the wad of paper against the wall as hard as she could, scowling as it fell harmlessly to the floor.

That morning, she had left for work at seven-forty-five, as usual. Her fiancé had been in the bathroom, towel around his waist, perfecting his hair in the mirror, as usual. He'd paused to plant a quick peck on her cheek and told her to have a good day, as usual. He hadn't mentioned her birthday, but she knew he knew, and assumed he had a celebration of some kind planned for this evening.

Shivering in the brisk fall air on the seven-block walk to her office in the Pacific Western Life Insurance building, she'd even allowed herself to hum a few bars of "Happy Birthday."

At ten-thirty, her department was called into the break room, where her boss unveiled three dozen Happy Birthday cupcakes. For the next twenty minutes, she and her colleagues sang, drank coffee, and ate cupcakes before returning to their cubicles.

At eleven o'clock, Izzy's boss had summoned her to his office. As she walked down the hall toward the Executive Suite, she indulged in a bit of optimistic speculation. She and Harold Peabody had always gotten along well. Perhaps he wanted to offer a personal birthday wish, possibly including some recognition of her fifteen years of service in the Claims Department of Pacific Western Life. Even a promotion wouldn't be out of line. After all, she'd been a Senior Claims Examiner for five years. It was time.

But when she knocked on Harold's door and poked her head inside, his droopy features looked even more morose than usual, giving him the appearance of a chronically depressed bloodhound.

He stood behind his desk and motioned to one of the chairs opposite. "Please sit down, Izzy."

Her pulse quickened. Nothing about this meeting suggested celebration. She perched on the front edge of the blue upholstered chair and gripped the smooth wooden arms with both hands, ready to spring up at a second's notice.

Harold turned his back to gaze out the bank of windows behind his desk for several long seconds, and when he turned back, he was pulling on the lobe of one ear, his nervous tell. He dropped his hand suddenly, as if he'd been caught doing something he shouldn't, and cleared his throat. "I've asked you here because I have news that will affect you." He glanced down at his desk and began fiddling with the brass letter opener he'd been given by the president of the company to commemorate twenty-five years of service. "Actually, it will affect many of us in the Pacific Western family."

Izzy lifted her brows slightly and tilted her head, silently encouraging him to get on with it.

Harold cleared his throat again. "The Board of Directors announced this morning that the company has been sold to Amalgamated Federated Life. As so often happens in these situations, many areas of the operation will be combined and consolidated for efficiency purposes. I'm afraid the Claims Department is one of those areas."

Izzy stared at her boss, who avoided eye contact by concentrating on spinning his letter opener in a circle on the leather-bound blotter pad. "What exactly does that mean?"

Harold's hand stilled as he raised his chin and met her gaze. His brown eyes were sad above their deep bags. "I have been asked to move to Amalgamated Federated's Home Office in Indianapolis, and the rest of the department is being let go."

"When?" Her voice croaked like she'd been lost in the desert for a week without water.

"Today, I'm afraid. Now, in fact. You'll be given time to return to your desk and pack your personal items before being escorted from the building."

Izzy collapsed against the back of the chair. She'd given this company more than a third of her life. Now what?

"Don't worry," Harold rushed to reassure her, "Amalgamated Federated will provide three months' severance pay and the services of a search firm to help all terminated employees find a new job. And, of course, you can count on me for a top-notch reference."

She rose abruptly. "Thank you." Then she turned and headed for the door.

As she reached the hall, Harold called after her, "I'm sorry, Izzy. Good luck!"

Hours later, as she stood in the kitchen of her soon-to-be-former condo, gazing at the box that contained her dancing duck pencil holder, her framed photo of Bryce, and the little stuffed armadillo a co-worker had given her for Christmas a few years ago, her boss's parting words rang in her ears.

Good luck.

Izzy had never been a big believer in luck, but she sure could use some now. Today had been such a disaster, she was surprised the dumpster behind the condo building hadn't spontaneously burst into flames. When she shot another glance at Bryce's photo, her back molars clenched at the sight of his slick smile. She'd always been a grounded, sensible person. How had she allowed herself to be taken in by a flashy, smooth-talking ambulance chaser? Maybe the fast-paced life of a rising young personal injury attorney had promised excitement her safe, quiet life lacked. Maybe, at thirty-five, she'd begun to feel she was missing out. For whatever reason, she'd fallen for Bryce Howe fast and hard.

Someday she might thank him for this jolting reality check, but at the moment, her overriding emotion was shock, bolstered by fury. She plucked his photo from the box holding the detritus of her career and hurled it into the shiny, stainless steel trash can at the end of the counter, taking a small measure of satisfaction from the sound of breaking glass.

Now, she had to figure out what to do with the rest of her life. She was a forty-year-old woman with no job and no home. This called for tequila.

It turned out Bryce had not only packed all the dishes, but the selfish louse had also cleaned out the pantry and refrigerator. Izzy made a call, and thirty minutes later, a cheerful young man delivered enough pre-made margaritas and tacos to host a small fiesta. She used that half hour to investigate the remainder of the apartment and discovered the bed had been stripped and her suitcases laid out, ready for packing. Even her bathroom toiletries had been bagged. Clearly, Bryce expected her to leave tonight. The rat hadn't even left her a towel.

When the food arrived, she ate standing at the kitchen counter. For some reason, she'd always thought better on her feet. Her mother used to tease her about the thinner air at her exalted altitude — at five foot eight, Izzy towered over the much shorter Lila Munro. The memory of her mother triggered another thought: *What will Lila say when she finds out Bryce dumped me?* Then again, how would she find out? There was no one to tell her but Izzy, and they hadn't spoken since Lila jetted off to the Greek Isles with her latest has-been rock-star flame several months ago. Izzy took another long swig of her margarita to banish all thoughts of her mother.

By the time she'd eaten her fill, she'd reached one conclusion. She was not leaving the condo tonight — Bryce could go hump a camel. She was emotionally drained, and the unaccustomed quantity of tequila had muddled her brain. Tomorrow, she would decide what to do. With uncharacteristic slovenliness, she abandoned the remnants of her meal and made her way to the bathroom.

Peering into the mirror, she freed her hair from the elastic band that held it in check at the office. With a shake of her head, a flurry of curly brown locks cascaded onto her shoulders. Izzy stared critically at her reflection with its oval face, pointed chin, and ordinary brown eyes. She wasn't a great beauty, but she didn't look forty — at least she didn't think so. She wondered briefly if Bryce was leaving her for a younger woman, then decided she didn't care. If she let herself think about why he'd done this, she might cry, and the man wasn't worth a single tear.

She washed her face and patted it dry with a handful of unused napkins left over from her dinner delivery, then returned to the living room and stretched out on the couch. Hands behind her head, she gazed through the floor-to-ceiling windows at the twinkling lights of San Francisco and wondered whether she should — or even could — stay in the city where she'd lived her whole life. Maybe Bryce was right about one thing, although she hated to admit it. Maybe it was time for a change.

The next morning, the October sun had barely risen above the eastern horizon when it forced its way through the high-rise maze of downtown skyscrapers and blazed against Izzy's closed eyelids. She raised one hand to shade her eyes and blinked a few times, trying to figure out why she was lying on the narrow living room couch instead of the luxurious king-sized bed in the bedroom. When she sat up and sniffed, the stale, lingering odor of tacos brought the memory of yesterday's debacle back with crushing clarity.

However, now was not the time to sit around feeling sorry for herself. Now was the time for decisions and action, both of which required coffee. And coffee, thanks to Bryce, was not happening unless she walked to the café on the corner and picked it up.

Even before coffee, what she really wanted was a hot shower and clean clothes. The clothes weren't a problem, since hers were still in the dresser and closet. The shower, however, presented a challenge. What was she supposed to do without a towel? Even if she'd hadn't used them all last night, she refused to dry herself with paper napkins.

There was only one solution.

The packers had labeled all the boxes stacked around the condo with a brief summary of the contents. Izzy found one marked *Linens* in a corner of the spare bedroom and used her keys to slit the tape. The towels were on top, fluffy and fresh. Bryce — or someone — must have done the laundry before packing the box.

After showering, she braided her hair to restrain the curls and keep the whole mass out of her face, then pulled on her favorite orange turtleneck and jeans before gathering her toiletries. The corners of her mouth tipped up at the sight of the wet towel draped across the shower rod as she turned off the light. It might be only a minor act of rebellion, but it pleased her to know she'd put a small kink in Bryce's tidy moving plan.

She often seemed to do her best thinking in the shower, and this morning was no exception. While working the shampoo into her hair, she'd taken stock of her situation, made a mental list of what she had and what she lacked, and come to a decision. She might not have a job, a fiancé, or a San Francisco condo, but she had savings, a three-month severance package, a car that ran, and thanks to her great-aunt Isadora, a cottage in a picturesque beach town she'd always loved. It was more than enough to start a new life.

Surveying the trio of boxes and pile of photographs in the front hall, she was shocked to realize how few material possessions she actually owned. When Bryce had asked her to move into his glamorous, ultra-modern condo, she'd happily discarded her second-hand furniture and kitchenware, saving only keepsakes with particular personal value. Those were still in the boxes she'd packed them in before the move. Bryce must have brought them up from the basement storage locker. She promised herself to explore their contents as soon as she reached Carmel. Perhaps she would regain some of herself in the process.

Actually, it was a good thing she had so few possessions — she wouldn't have to worry about renting a van or U-Haul. Her boxes and suitcases would fill the cargo area of her trusty Subaru, but they should just fit.

Two hours later, with a Grande Americano and a poppyseed muffin under her belt, Izzy loaded the car and rode the elevator up to the twenty-eighth floor for the final time. After laying her keys on the kitchen counter, she turned out the lights and closed the door on a major chapter of her life. As usual, the elevator ride down to the underground parking garage gave her stomach the wobbles, but an invisible burden seemed to lift a fraction with every floor she passed, so that by the time she reached the bottom, she experienced a lightness she hadn't felt in years.

She drove out of the garage and headed to the 101 Freeway South. Pushed by the breeze off the ocean, chubby white clouds scooted across the sky as she drove through Palo Alto, San Jose, and Gilroy, until she reached the turn-off to the Monterey Peninsula. Forty minutes later, she pulled into the driveway of Aunt Dora's green-shingled cottage in Carmel-by-the-Sea. The little house on Lincoln Street had been a peaceful haven from the chaos of life with Lila while Izzy was growing up and was now her new home...at least temporarily.

The house was small—just a living room, two bedrooms, an eat-in kitchen, and one bath—but it had a cozy fireplace and a garage big enough for her car. Pink climbing roses rambled up and over an arched, gated arbor that led from the driveway to the flagstone front walk.

Izzy barely spared a glance at the house as she parked and searched her purse for the key to the front door. Her first order of business, before moving a single box, was a mad dash to the bathroom. Without a pit stop, every ounce of the Grande Americano screamed for release. When she stepped out of the bathroom feeling much relieved, she heard a voice call from the living room.

"Izzy dear, is that you?"

She rounded the corner from the hallway and spotted a tiny woman with sparkling white hair, dressed in teal-colored jeans and an oatmeal ribbed turtleneck, topped by a darker blue quilted vest. "Vivian!"

"I saw your car and let myself in. I hope you don't mind."

Izzy felt as big and clumsy as a bear as she bent to embrace the petite, older woman she'd known most of her life. Vivian Silver lived in a tidy bungalow across the street and had been Aunt Dora's closest friend for more than half a century. Until she sold her art gallery and retired ten years ago, she had been the exclusive agent for Isadora Munro's critically acclaimed paintings of the local coastline. Izzy remembered Vivian teasing her great-aunt about being exactly ten years younger, which would make her now eighty-five.

After a final squeeze, Vivian stepped back from Izzy's embrace and scanned her up and down with a critical eye. "How have you been, dear? You look tired. And where's that young man of yours — Chance, or Mace, or Fleece, was it?"

Despite the events of the past twenty-four hours, Izzy smiled. "His name is Bryce, as you very well know, and as for where he is — I have no idea."

Vivian raised one carefully-penciled brow. "And I take it from your tone that you don't really care."

Izzy answered with a definitive toss of her head. "Not one iota."

"Then we won't mention him again." Vivian turned and glanced out the open door to the car in the driveway. "Have you come for a visit?"

Izzy headed for the door. "It's more than a visit. I'm here to stay, at least for the time being. I don't have much, but I brought a few boxes and my clothes."

"You're moving in? That's wonderful!" Vivian clapped her hands together and followed Izzy down the front walk. "Dora would be thrilled! She always hoped you'd leave the city and come to Carmel. That's why she left the house to you."

Izzy hauled the first of her boxes out of the back of the car. "And I'm very grateful, especially now. I have wonderful memories of spending summers and school holidays here as a child. It's the perfect place to regroup and sort things out."

"Mmm. I take it that means you're...uh...footloose and fancy free, so to speak."

Izzy set the first box on the floor in the living room and headed back for the second. "In every respect."

"Ah. No further explanations required. Onward and upward, as they say. I'll just add that you've picked the perfect place. People have been coming to this village for decades to reinvent themselves and get a fresh start. It's practically a requirement." Vivian followed Izzy to the car. "Are you sure I can't help?"

"No. I've got it." She nudged the door closed with one hip.

"In that case, I'll go home and fix us some lunch. I'm sure you're hungry after your drive."

With sixteen ounces of coffee now flushed from her system, Izzy realized she was surprisingly hungry. "That would be wonderful. Thank you, Vivian."

The older woman waved over her shoulder as she prepared to cross the narrow street, which was shaded by massive coastal oaks and towering pines. "I'll be back in a few minutes."

Izzy had carried her suitcases inside and hung her clothes in the closet of the small second bedroom that had been hers as a child when she heard a series of knocks on the front door.

Vivian stood on the porch carrying a handled shopping bag. "I've got chicken salad sandwiches, grapes, and peanut butter cookies."

Izzy stepped back and pulled the door open wide. "That sounds delicious!"

Vivian led the way through the living room to the kitchen at the back of the cottage, set her bag on the counter, and began unpacking. "If you'll get plates and glasses, I'll divide this up. I don't know about ice, but unless you turned off the utilities the water should still be on."

"I had the bills switched to my name, but I left all the services running. I always thought I'd make it down here for a weekend, but things kept coming up." Those things largely being the social events Bryce preferred to a quiet weekend in a rustic cottage.

After Vivian finished arranging the plates, they sat across from each other at the well-worn kitchen table which was so small their knees nearly touched. Aunt Dora had always said the cottage was the perfect size for her and her namesake, Izzy. Any more space would have been a waste.

Vivian wiped a dab of mayonnaise from her upper lip with a flick of her tongue. "Feel free to tell me if I'm being a prying old biddy, but what about your job, dear? Will you be able to do it from here, or have you taken a leave of absence from the insurance company?"

Izzy took a drink of water. There was no reason not to share the whole truth of her situation with Vivian. She'd known Aunt Dora's neighbor as long as she could remember, and while the house felt empty without her great-aunt, Vivian's familiar presence was a comfort. "I won't have to worry about working remotely. I was laid-off yesterday."

"Temporarily?" Vivian's tone was hopeful.

"I'm afraid not. The company has been sold, and they're merging departments."

"Aah." Vivian popped a grape into her mouth and pondered while she chewed. "Then this is the perfect time to take stock and decide what you want to do next. I don't suppose you've had any ideas yet."

Izzy shook her head. "It's barely been one day—I'm still processing the news. All I know is, whatever I do probably won't involve life insurance."

"I have to admit, spending one's workday in the company of dead people doesn't sound too pleasant." Vivian plucked another grape from the cluster on her plate.

Izzy's brows tightened in a small frown. "Dealing with death is complex. Determining exactly what happened, and why, can be interesting, but it's always sad to think about the survivors, the family. I think I'm ready to do something more upbeat."

Vivian responded with a nod and a smile. "Good for you. Here, have a cookie."

After her welcoming committee left, Izzy stood at the kitchen sink, gazing out the window into the compact backyard while she rinsed the dishes. There was a pretty stone patio with a wisteria-draped trellis and a flagstone path leading to a separate structure in the back that Aunt Dora had used as her painting studio. She remembered it as being light and bright and smelling of turpentine, and made a mental note to explore it as soon she got settled. With luck, the space might provide some inspiration.

Since the house had been closed up for six months, her first priority was to air it out. After her great-aunt's funeral, Izzy had stayed in town for a week, dealing with paperwork, meeting with Dora's attorney, and wrapping up her affairs. She'd made a stab at cleaning out the drawers and closets, but she'd never intended to use the place for more than an occasional weekend retreat. If she was going to live here full time, she wanted to make the place her own.

With all the windows open, she turned her attention to the main bedroom. Since it was the largest and had windows on two sides, she'd assumed it would become hers. But as she stood in the doorway, taking in the old-fashioned brass bed and antique dresser, she wasn't sure she could do it. The lingering scent of her great-aunt's favorite perfume squeezed her heart, bringing a prick of tears to her eyes.

Izzy didn't believe in ghosts, but she could swear she felt a brief, gentle touch on her shoulder. *It's yours now, child.*

How could she argue? She brushed the back of one wrist across her eyes and got to work.

By five-thirty, she had made a grocery list, moved her clothes into the main bedroom, washed all the linens, remade the bed, and was hanging fresh towels in the bathroom when the doorbell rang. She opened the door expecting to see Vivian—the only person she knew in Carmel—but was confronted by a tall, slender man of about her own age, with medium-brown hair and horn-rimmed glasses. He was wearing a white business shirt with khaki trousers and a maroon figured bow tie, and held a bright red Le Creuset casserole dish in both hands.

At the sight of her, he smiled. "Isadora Munro, I presume?"

Izzy hesitated. He didn't look dangerous, but these days who could tell? And how did he know her name? "Um...yes?"

The man's smile broadened. "Sebastian Larrabee—I live next door." He nodded toward the sprawling,

Spanish Colonial-style, stucco house to the south. "I assumed you'd be busy with moving-in tasks and wouldn't have time to cook, so I brought you a little something to tide you over until you can get to the market. It's Beef Bourguignon, my own take on the classic recipe." He lifted the casserole.

Her mouth began to water. She couldn't not invite the man in. He'd made one of her all-time favorite dishes—one she had never, and would never, attempt on her own. She pulled the door back and stepped aside. "Thank you. It's so nice to meet you."

Sebastian marched in and headed straight for the kitchen as if he'd done it hundreds of times. "Dora was a terrific lady and a great neighbor. She would be so happy to know you're moving in."

Izzy trailed along behind him. "I don't believe we've met before. How long have you lived here?"

"Over ten years, but I used to travel all the time." He set the casserole on the stove. "My life has settled down somewhat since I bought the *Carmel Acorn*."

"You own the *Acorn*? I love the *Acorn*. Everybody loves the *Acorn*!" The weekly rag was famous up and down the coast, and probably around the world, for its beach-going pet column, serio-comic police log, and tongue-in-cheek cartoon.

"Owner and publisher, at your service." He made a small bow, then his expression turned serious. "I'm so sorry I missed Dora's funeral. I had urgent family business matters to attend to in Hong Kong and couldn't get away."

A lump formed in Izzy's throat at the memory of the service, attended by dozens of her great-aunt's longtime friends.

Sebastian frowned and patted her shoulder. "I'm

sorry. I didn't mean to distress you."

"That's okay." She gave him a watery smile. "I just miss her."

"We all do." He gestured to the casserole. "Now, this will keep in a low oven until you're ready to eat, and don't worry about the pot. You can leave it on my doorstep anytime."

"Thanks again for bringing it over."

"That's what neighbors are for." He headed for the door. "I'm sure I'll see you soon. Take care."

Until now, Vivian was the only neighbor Izzy had ever known. Her mother had never had the time or interest for anyone other than herself, and the residents of Bryce's condo building had remained anonymous behind their locked doors. Having a stranger do something nice for her was an entirely new experience.

Sebastian's wine-rich beef stew turned out to be the best she'd ever eaten, and it fortified her to spend the rest of the evening re-arranging the bathroom and kitchen and generally trying to make the cottage feel like home. She collapsed into bed around nine o'clock and immediately fell into a deep sleep.

Hours later, she was jolted awake by a suffocating weight suddenly landing on her chest. When her eyes flew open in alarm, she found herself staring straight into a pair of accusatory golden orbs glowing fiercely in the dark, barely six inches from the tip of her nose.

CHAPTER TWO

Izzy shrieked and jerked upright. The glowing-eyed monster let out a strangled yowl, levitated two feet off the bed, and made a mad, scrambling dash for the doorway, claws skittering on the hardwood floor. With her heart pounding and hand shaking, Izzy switched on the bedside lamp. The room looked exactly as it had when she'd gone to bed.

What on earth was that thing? Yes, the past two days had been traumatic, and she'd been exhausted when she fell asleep, but surely she hadn't dreamed a thing like that. And what if it was still in the house?

She glanced around the room for something — anything — to defend herself, settling on Aunt Dora's antique silver hairbrush from the top of the dresser. Wielding it like a club, she tiptoed across the room and into the hall, where a quick glance showed no intruder. She searched the house, flipping on the lights room by room, but found nothing amiss. It must have been a nightmare — there was no other reasonable explanation. If so, she had one more thing to blame on Bryce. A glance at the clock on the stove told her it was 4:00 a.m. — too early to get up. After awakening with such a start, falling asleep again wouldn't be easy, but she decided to try anyway and trudged back down the hall.

The room was light, though not sunny, when the doorbell woke her. According to her phone, it was seven-thirty, definitely time to get up. The bell rang again, so she padded barefoot to the front door and peeked through the beveled-glass panes across the top. When Sebastian Larrabee greeted her with a smile and wave, Izzy opened the door. Behind him, the early morning fog was so thick, she could barely make out Vivian's house across the street.

"I just wanted to make sure you were all right this morning."

She regarded him with a quizzical frown. "I'm fine. Why wouldn't I be?"

"I saw your lights on at four in the morning and worried you might be having trouble settling in."

His concern left her with mixed feelings. On one hand, it was reassuring to know someone close by was watching out for her. On the other hand, knowing that same someone was observing her windows in the middle of the night bordered on creepy. "I thought I heard a noise."

Sebastian stiffened almost imperceptibly. "What kind of noise? I tried several times to convince Dora to install a security system, but she always dismissed the idea as ridiculous in a safe little town like Carmel."

"I don't think a security system would have helped. It was probably just a bad dream." Izzy lifted her chin and met his gaze straight-on. "I'm surprised you noticed the lights. You're either a real night owl, or a very early riser."

"I have business interests in several different time zones."

"So owning the *Acorn* isn't your only job?"

He laughed. "The *Acorn* is great fun, but it's largely a labor of love. Since you're from San Francisco, you're probably familiar with the Eastern and Trans-Pacific Bank."

Her brows arched. "Oh, so you're one of *those* Larrabees."

He responded with a sheepish grin. "Guilty as charged."

Before she could reply, something soft and warm brushed against one ankle, then twined around the other. She shrieked and jumped back, heart pounding and hand clasped against her chest.

"Good morning, Bogart." Sebastian knelt and reached one hand toward a slinky, sable-colored Burmese cat. "Where have you been keeping yourself?" Bogart head-butted his hand and purred.

"Is he yours?"

"Oh, no. Bogart is his own cat. He adopted Dora about three years ago, but before that, he lived with Anna Carlyle, the head librarian. When Anna got married, her new husband insisted on calling Bogart *kitsums-itsums*, which was intolerable to a cat of his dignity. Anna refused to dump the husband, so Bogart left in a huff. He roamed around town for a couple of weeks, scoping out different accommodations before choosing Dora." Sebastian gave the cat one last head-scratch then pushed to his feet. "Say, I wonder if Bogart was your early morning visitor."

Izzy regarded the feline with suspicion. "I'm sure he

wasn't in the house yesterday evening, and I don't know how he could have gotten in. I have no idea what he's doing here now."

"He probably came to check you out. After Dora passed away, he moved on, but now that someone's living in the house again, he's sizing you up as a possible replacement."

"But how did he get in? I didn't leave any windows open. Does he walk through walls?"

"Didn't you notice the cat flap in the kitchen door? Dora had it installed for him. Come, I'll show you." Sebastian walked past her and headed for the kitchen with Bogart trotting alongside.

She hurried to follow. "Aunt Dora never mentioned having a cat, and I never saw him when I visited."

"Bogart chooses his associates with care. He was probably reserving judgement while he checked you out from a distance." Sebastian squatted beside the door that led from the kitchen to the patio. "See here?" He pushed on a panel in the lower portion of the door, and it swung open, then snapped back into place. "It's very clever — looks like part of the door. Dora had it specially designed and custom-made."

To demonstrate, Bogart butted the panel with his head and slipped outside, only to reappear a moment later. He gazed up at Izzy with golden eyes and meowed.

She had to admit he was a beautiful animal, slinky and elegant, but she had no idea what to do if he decided to move in with her. She had no experience with cats. "What does he want?"

Sebastian regarded the feline with a critical eye. "If I had to guess, I'd say he expects breakfast."

"But I don't have anything to feed a cat. I don't even

have anything to feed myself, except leftovers of your fabulous Beef Bourguignon."

"I'm sure Bogart would love some of the beef minced up, but it sounds like you need to make a trip to the market this morning."

"Yes." She eyed the cat, who was sitting at her feet, staring up at her with an expectant golden gaze. "Although I didn't plan on shopping for two."

"Consider being chosen by Bogart as an honor. He tolerates few people and actually likes even fewer."

Izzy didn't feel particularly honored. She might not have much of a plan for her new life, but she was pretty sure being caretaker to a finicky, opinionated feline wasn't part of it.

Sebastian rubbed Bogart's ears one last time, then straightened and headed for the front door. "You need food, and I have to go to the *Acorn* office this morning, so we can walk into town together. I'll introduce you to my favorite coffee shop and bakery, Taste of Torino. Can you be ready in half an hour?"

She needed few things as much as she needed coffee right now, and the thought of Italian pastry made her mouth water. "Absolutely. That sounds perfect."

Thirty minutes later, after fixing Bogart a gourmet breakfast—which he deigned to eat only after thorough investigation—she was showered, dressed, and had corralled her unruly curls into a tidy braid. When the doorbell rang, she greeted Sebastian with a smile. She slipped on a jacket and locked the door, and they set off on the four-block stroll to the main business district. The residential streets of Carmel-by-the-Sea were narrow and bumpy and lacked sidewalks, so watching one's step, especially at night, was a must. This foggy morning, Izzy barely missed walking head-first into the giant, gnarled branch of an ancient oak that hung out over the road.

During their walk, Sebastian kept up a running commentary on current affairs in the village, which required only an occasional editorial murmur from her. That was a good thing, because she was only half-listening. Her mind was busy wrestling with the big question on this first day of her fifth decade — who did she want to be, and what did she want to do with her life from this point forward?

When they reached Ocean Avenue, the main street of town that ran west from Highway 1 downhill to the beach, Sebastian turned right, and Izzy lengthened her stride to keep up with his longer legs. She might be used to walking the hills of San Francisco, but usually opted for a more relaxed pace. Fortunately, the storefront of Taste of Torino appeared in the next block ahead before she started to breathe hard.

The bakery window was divided into two sections. One side displayed exquisite, hand-made chocolates that were almost too beautiful to eat. However, as much as she loved chocolate, eight-fifteen was too early, even for her. The other half of the window was filled with exotic baked confections with names like *Sfogliatella*, *Maritozzo*, *Bomboloni*, and *Zeppole*. The only things she recognized were *Cannoli* and *Biscotti*, but merely looking at the display was enough to add five pounds.

Sebastian held the door for two young women who were leaving, each with a cup of coffee in one hand and a napkin-wrapped pastry in the other. He nodded to Izzy. "Come on. It's even better inside."

He was right. The moment she stepped through the door, the aromas of freshly brewing coffee and pastries warm from the oven enveloped her in a cozy cocoon of

23

comfort.

While Izzy peered into the glass-fronted cases, overwhelmed by the choices, a brunette in her late thirties, wearing a white apron marked by smudges of flour and something brown that might have been chocolate, spoke to Sebastian. "Good morning, Mr. Larrabee. What can I get you today?"

"Hi, Lorna. The usual, I think—a cappuccino and two biscotti." He turned to Izzy. "What would you like?"

"All of it?"

The corners of his eyes crinkled behind his horn-rimmed glasses, but he simply shrugged. "Whatever you say. The lady will have—"

"One of those." Izzy pointed to a luscious, crescent-shaped confection comprised of dozens of paper-thin layers of pastry. "And a cappuccino."

Lorna nodded and, using a pair of tongs, plucked the one next to the hand-lettered sign that read *Sfogliatella*. Setting each order on a small white plate, she prepared two cups of cappuccino.

As Sebastian paid, he nodded toward a small seating area on the other side of the bakery. "Let's grab a table over there while we can."

Breakfast in hand, they wound their way through the patrons now crowded in front of the display cases and found an empty table next to one of the smaller front windows.

Izzy slid into her chair and scanned the bakery. "This place certainly is popular."

"You'll see why as soon as you taste that." Sebastian tipped his head toward her sfogliatella, picked up his cup, and took a sip.

Izzy regarded the pastry, trying to figure out the best way to approach it. After deciding a fork would probably shatter the delicate layers, she picked it up with her fingers. The first bite was pure sweet, flaky heaven. She glanced up as she chewed. "Mmm."

Sebastian's deadpan expression belied the impish gleam in his eyes. "I told you so."

She finished her bite and took a sip of her cappuccino. "I've never seen a bakery combined with a chocolatier, but I have to say I approve."

"The owner is half-Italian and half-Swiss. This way, he gets to indulge both sides of his heritage, and we all benefit."

"Ah, Sebastian Larrabee, just the man I want to see!"

They turned as a stocky man of medium height approached the table. He had rosy cheeks and a round head topped by thinning, curly blond hair. His accent was too subtle to identify but suggested central Europe.

"Aldo, how are you?"

When Sebastian offered his hand, the man shook it with vigor. "I have a problem to discuss with you — something that deserves the attention of your readers — but this is not the time or place." He acknowledged Izzy's presence with a polite smile. "I do not wish to interrupt your meal or deprive the lady of your company."

When Sebastian glanced her way, Izzy raised her brows in curious inquiry.

"Izzy, I'd like to introduce Aldo Pefferman, the proprietor of this dangerously caloric establishment. Aldo, allow me to present Izzy Munro, Dora Munro's great-niece and Carmel's newest resident."

Izzy offered her hand, and Aldo surprised her by bringing it to his lips. "Delighted to meet you, Ms. Munro." He released her hand and returned his attention to Sebastian. "If you are free Wednesday evening, I intend to present my concerns at the City Council meeting. You will be able to get the details at that time, as well as ask questions."

Sebastian sat back in his chair. "That sounds intriguing. You've piqued my interest, Aldo. I'll put it on my calendar."

Pefferman dipped his chin in an abbreviated bow. "Seven o'clock at City Hall."

"I look forward to seeing you there."

Izzy followed the man's quasi-military gait as he left the table and marched through a stainless steel swinging door that presumably led to the kitchen, then turned back to Sebastian. "He's an interesting character."

Her breakfast companion dunked one of the biscotti into his cappuccino and bit the end off, washing it down with the frothy brew. "You wouldn't know it to look at him, but Aldo Pefferman is one of the most powerful and influential men in town. In addition to the bakery, he owns two other restaurants, as well as numerous commercial buildings. He's been on the City Council for six years, and rumor has it, he plans to run for mayor in the next election."

"You're right—I wouldn't have guessed. He seems like just another eccentric Carmelite."

Sebastian's gaze was faraway and contemplative. "Aldo can be very charming as long as you don't cross him." Then he focused on her face with a smile. "But I can't see you getting mixed up in any of his business or real estate deals."

Izzy scoffed. "I don't think there's much chance of that. For one thing, I don't have the money."

"Carmel real estate is a very high-stakes game." Sebastian dunked his biscotto again. "Have you had any further thoughts about what you might want to do, now that you're here?"

She sighed and glanced out the window at a family of tourists with a pair of school-aged children and a toddler in a stroller who had stopped to peer at the goodies in the main plate-glass display window. "Not yet. I'm going to take my time, settle in, and explore the town. Something will come to me." *I hope.*

"An excellent attitude. Carmel is an inspiring place. I'm sure you'll find your answer." He took another sip of coffee. "In the meantime, you should come with me to the City Council meeting Wednesday evening. Local politics is a fascinating introduction to any community. It will give you an opportunity to meet people, and we'll find out about Aldo's big issue. Aren't you curious?"

"I have to admit, I am."

"Good. I'll stop by to pick you up, and we can walk over to City Hall together."

After they finished eating, they parted ways — Sebastian heading to the *Acorn* office, and Izzy back home to pick up her car for a trip to the grocery store. There was a small market within walking distance of the cottage if she only needed a few items, but for her first major stocking-up expedition, the big supermarket down the highway would be more efficient.

She was home and had everything put away by eleven. Now, to get down to business. She'd always loved visiting Aunt Dora in the quirky little house, but this time was different. The cottage was now hers, and with each passing hour, she felt more at ease, more at home, and more convinced that this was the place she was meant to be. It was time to make it official.

She set her laptop on the kitchen table, then found the box labeled *Desk and Papers* and began the arduous task of changing her address with every official entity she could think of—bank, credit card company, utilities. She had just finished sending her former boss an email telling him where to mail her severance check when she realized she should probably let her mother know, too. It might be months before Lila was back in the country, so a brief email would suffice for her, as well.

By the time she finished, Izzy was exhausted and starving, but she felt lighter, both in body and spirit. She had always been a logical person, and logic told her she should be anxious and apprehensive. The entire foundation of her life had been swept out from under her in a single day, and everything else had to change along with it. It was scary, but at the same time, surprisingly liberating.

The aroma of Sebastian's Beef Bourguignon must have wafted outside as she reheated it, because the moment she took the casserole from the oven, Bogart barged into the kitchen through the cat flap, meowing loudly as he head-butted her leg.

"All right. I'll cut some up for you, but this is the last time I'm sharing my dinner. I bought you four different kinds of cat food at the store today. If you don't like any of them, you'll just have to freeload somewhere else."

Her announcement prompted a series of multi-tonal feline vocalizations that, based on Bogart's posture and expression, appeared to express a combination of annoyance, impatience, and inherent superiority.

She shook her head as she diced a tender chunk of meat for the cat, then set it on the floor before fixing her own plate. Pulling out a chair, she sat at the kitchen table and savored Sebastian's take on the traditional French beef stew while watching Bogart devour his meal like a famished tiger. After he finished, he sauntered over, twined himself once around her legs, purring loudly, then headed to the cat flap and disappeared into the darkness. Izzy sat for a moment, staring at the closed door, feeling like a servant who had just been dismissed.

This business of living with such an independent, yet demanding, creature would take some getting used to. She knew she could avoid the issue by nailing the flap in the door shut, but she suspected she would be the loser. Bogart wouldn't care—he would find someone else to cater to his needs—but she would be depriving herself of the company of a singular and unique feline. As Sebastian had said, Bogart was his own cat, and Izzy had to admire him for that. In fact, now that she'd been cut loose from every anchor in her old life, she might just emulate his approach.

Her own woman. She liked the sound of it.

That night, she stood in front of the bathroom mirror, examining her face with a critical eye as she brushed her teeth. The basic bone structure was okay—high cheekbones tapering to a slightly pointed chin—and her skin was holding its own against the onslaught of time. She could probably slow down any incipient crows' feet if she remembered to wear sunglasses more often. But the heavy mass of curls pinned on top of her head looked, and felt, so *yesterday*, unchanged since childhood, visible baggage of the old Izzy.

She rinsed and spit, then regarded the pile of mud-brown ringlets with a frown. She'd never liked her hair, her mother's hair. Lila had always reveled in the whole hippie persona. She still did. Wild and free, that was Lila Munro. But Izzy was nothing like her mother, and now, more than ever, it felt important to prove it. She'd battled her hair her whole life, never claiming better than a draw. It was time to change that. Forty years was enough. She intended to begin her life as a new woman with a win.

The next morning, Bogart hadn't deigned to show up for breakfast, so Izzy was alone in the kitchen, drinking a cup of coffee and researching local hair salons on her phone when the doorbell rang. She carried her coffee cup to the door and peeked through the bank of glass panes at the top. It was Vivian. She opened the door to her smiling neighbor.

Vivian raised a foil-covered plate. "I baked a coffee cake this morning and brought you half."

"How sweet of you!" Izzy ushered her into the living room. "First Beef Bourguignon, now coffee cake. Between you and Sebastian, I'll be waddling like a hippo in no time."

Vivian waved off her comment and headed for the kitchen. "Nonsense, dear. You inherited your great-aunt's tall, willowy figure, along with her name. No matter what she ate, Dora never seemed to gain an ounce. During the last few years, her appetite faded, so Sebastian and I engaged in an informal competition to see whose cooking could tempt her the most. Sebastian usually won—he's a marvelous cook."

When Izzy peeled the foil cover from the coffee cake, the luscious aroma of cinnamon made her mouth water. "I have to say, this smells wonderful. Will you join me for a slice? I have plenty of coffee."

"That sounds lovely." Vivian slipped off her down vest and draped it over the back of one of the chairs before taking a seat.

Izzy served them each a generous slice of the still-warm, cinnamon-and-sugar-covered cake and poured two cups of coffee before joining her neighbor at the table.

Vivian cut off a small bite of coffee cake with her fork. "I have a garden club meeting this afternoon. What's on your agenda for today, dear?"

"I'm thinking of getting a haircut."

The older woman regarded her with interest. "A minor trim or a major makeover?"

Izzy shook her head, sending the cascade of long, tight curls swaying. "I want something completely different. My life has been stagnant for years, but now that everything is changing, I want a new look to reflect the new me."

Vivian responded with a crisp nod. "An excellent idea, and I know just the woman to help you, Chantal Costas. She owns a salon downtown, and she's a true artist, a miracle worker." She tossed her stylish white bob. "If Chantal can make an old lady like me presentable, she'll have you fit for the red carpet. Hand me your phone, and I'll call her to see if she can fit you in."

Izzy placed her phone in Vivian's outstretched hand. After a brief conversation, she handed it back. "She can take you at one-thirty. I'll walk you there and introduce you, then head to my meeting. How does that sound?"

Accustomed to weighing every decision carefully and thoroughly, Izzy's brain was slow to respond. She'd had the same look her whole life. Was she really ready to make such a drastic change, and at the hands of a total stranger? Then her inner rebel poked her...hard.

Be bold. Now is the time. Besides, what's the worst that can happen? It's only hair. It will grow out.

She straightened her shoulders and smiled. "That sounds great."

"Perfect. I'll pick you up at one-fifteen. Now, let's finish our breakfast before the coffee gets cold."

Izzy tried to put the upcoming appointment out of her mind as she spent the rest of the morning working on bringing the living room into the twenty-first century. She rearranged the furniture and ordered new curtains and slipcovers for the sofa and armchair online. Aunt Dora had some wonderful old volumes in the built-in bookcases that flanked the stone fireplace, but there were also a number that could be donated to the library to make room for Izzy's personal collection. She packed the discards in an empty moving box and set it beside the door, then surveyed the walls. Her aunt's spectacular stormy seascape of Big Sur had to remain over the fireplace, where it had hung as long as Izzy could remember, but a few of the others could be moved to other rooms to accommodate the best of her own framed photographs.

Shortly after they'd begun dating—probably in an effort to impress her—Bryce had given her a top-quality camera for her thirty-fifth birthday. It had opened a whole new world and allowed her to see the city of her birth through fresh eyes. Most photographers liked to depict San Francisco's most celebrated sights like the Golden Gate Bridge or the "Painted Ladies," the famous row of colorful Victorian houses. Instead, Izzy chose to explore the city's minutiae, details like a single red leaf from a Japanese maple resting on a smooth, dark rock in a stream near the Tea Garden in Golden Gate Park, or an abandoned toy car in the concrete stairwell leading down to a dingy basement flat.

She experimented with several arrangements for the photos until she was satisfied, then stood back and surveyed the room, envisioning it with the new slipcovers and window treatments. It was still the cozy sitting room of her childhood memories but with a touch of modern flair. There was only one thing lacking. Aunt Dora had never owned a television, preferring instead the nature outside her door and the company of good books. While Izzy was looking forward to twilight walks on the beach, she wasn't sure she could survive without her favorite British murder mysteries. A trip to the big electronics store in Marina tomorrow should solve the problem.

At one-fifteen, Vivian appeared on the doorstep, as promised. "Ready to go?"

Izzy grabbed a jacket, locked the door, and followed her friend down the flagstone walk to the street. She'd brushed her hair but left it loose so the poor stylist could see what she was getting into.

"You'll love Chantal." Vivian slipped on a pair of dark sunglasses to ward off the hazy October afternoon sun. "She's a real firecracker."

Izzy wasn't sure "firecracker" was the best recommendation for a hairdresser.

Her neighbor must have read her expression, because she laughed. "Don't worry. She's petite and energetic, with a real artist's eye. She grew up in Monterey, the fourth generation in a large family of Portuguese fishermen. Her father and uncles operate one of the biggest seafood markets on the wharf, and her mother and older brother run Francisco's Deli here in Carmel. You'll have to try it. Their homemade crab chowder is the best on the Peninsula."

The mention of chowder brought a sudden pang of homesickness. On Friday evenings, Izzy used to stop at a neighborhood bistro on the way home from work to pick up a quart for dinner. Bryce always said it signaled the beginning of the weekend. The thought of her former fiancé caused a brief pang of loss, but much less than the memory of the crab chowder.

As they turned right on a side street at the edge of the business district, Vivian continued her endorsement. "On top of everything else, Chantal is a great source of gossip. She knows everyone in town, and she's an excellent listener, the kind of person people naturally want to talk to. She hears all the juicy stuff. Here's the shop." She pointed to a sign on a cute, Tudor cottage-style building that read Cece's Salon. "The name comes from her initials—C.C., or CeCe, for Chantal Costas." When she opened the Dutch door, a tinkling bell overhead announced their arrival.

A brunette with waist-length, auburn-streaked hair, turned to face them. Perched atop thick platform sandals designed to make her appear taller, she grinned at Izzy with a wide, dazzling smile and flashed a wicked-looking pair of scissors. *Snip, snip.*

Izzy swallowed. Hard.

CHAPTER THREE

A thin veil of nervous sweat dampened Izzy's chest as she sat in the stylist's chair, covered in a nylon cape. She couldn't remember the last time she'd been in a hair salon.

CeCe's owner, Chantal Costas, gave her a perky smile in the mirror and fluffed her curls. "So, what can we do for you today? Vivian said you were ready for a new look...something about a big birthday."

Izzy grimaced. She'd never mentioned her birthday — Vivian must know more about her than she realized. "I've had long hair all my life. It's time for a change."

Chantal lifted a long, tight ringlet and considered it with a practiced eye. "How do you feel about your curls?"

Izzy could still hear the boys in grade school calling out "Frizzy Izzy" and "Kinky Munro" on the playground at recess. "It's a love/hate relationship, at best."

Chantal pursed her lips. "Let's see if we can make it love/love. Of course, we'll have to take off quite a bit of length to give the curls some bounce. What do you say?"

Izzy struggled to imagine how she'd look without her signature tresses, but if she wanted a new look for her new life, there was no point in going half-way. "Let's do it."

"Good for you! Now, what about the color?"

The question threw her for a loop. Even though a few gray hairs had popped up around her hairline in the last year or two, she'd never considered changing the color. "What would you recommend?"

"I'd like to bring out your lovely golden undertones."

Izzy squinted at the mirror, but all she saw was plain brown.

The stylist lifted a curl to demonstrate. "We'll do something I like to call honeylights, like normal highlights but softer and warmer. They'll accentuate the curls and give the style movement."

Izzy was smart enough to recognize when she was out of her depth. "Whatever you think."

Chantal laughed. "Don't look so worried. You'll love it, I guarantee."

Two hours later, Izzy felt like she'd known the other woman all her life. While the stylist clipped, snipped, and applied various potions, she chatted about her family, including her rat of an ex-husband, and Izzy surprised herself by sharing her resentments about her mother and the details of Bryce's betrayal.

When Chantal finally stepped back, Izzy stared at her reflection in wonderment. She'd been transformed into someone she barely recognized. This woman was chic, modern, and confident. The stylist had lopped off at least a foot of hair, added layers and golden highlights, conditioned it within an inch of its life, and styled it into big, soft curls instead of frizzy coils.

She gave her head a gentle shake. "It does bounce."

Chantal grinned. "I told you. You look fabulous!"

Izzy smiled back in the mirror. "Vivian was right — you are an artist."

"That stupid ex-fiancé of yours would never know you now."

He wouldn't. Her own mother might not recognize her. She felt a rush of excitement at the idea of starting fresh, free of anyone's expectations but her own.

When she stepped out of the salon, she drew a deep breath of crisp autumn air. No place else smelled quite like Carmel. The sun was shining brightly in a clear blue sky, and yellow leaves from the few deciduous trees decorated the sidewalk. It was only three-thirty, and she wasn't ready to go home yet, so she decided to walk the few blocks to Ocean Avenue and indulge in a cappuccino and a chocolate or two from Taste of Torino.

The same woman who'd waited on her and Sebastian was working behind the counter again and greeted her with a brief flash of recognition. "It's nice to see you. What would you like this afternoon?"

Izzy pointed out two delicately molded candies, one decorated with a tiny sail of piped dark chocolate and the other with swirls of white. "I'll have one of each of those and a cappuccino to go, please."

As the woman was placing the chocolates into a small white paper bag, the owner, Aldo Pefferman, came out of the back. He walked up behind the clerk, slipped one arm around the back of her waist, bent his head, and murmured in her ear.

When Aldo straightened, he spotted Izzy and broke into a wide smile. "Ah, Ms. Munro, you're looking exceptionally beautiful this afternoon. Unless I'm mistaken, I believe I recognize the handiwork of Chantal Costas."

Izzy couldn't suppress a grin as she shook her head gently, sending her curls swaying. "You're not mistaken."

He kiss his fingertips. "*Bellissima!* You were lovely before, but Chantal is a true magician. What can we do to make your day even better?"

Izzy pointed to the bag in the woman's hand. "Your chocolates have been on my mind since yesterday morning. If they're half as good as they look, I may become an addict."

Aldo threw back his head and laughed—a big, round, rolling sound. "A happy addiction, indeed! I predict we'll be adding you to our roll of regulars before the week's out. And, of course, as a regular you'll want to get to know our manager, Lorna Ferris. Lorna, this is Izzy Munro, Dora's great-niece. She's just moved to town."

The manager acknowledged her with a nod. "Pleased to meet you."

"I'll leave you two to finish up." Aldo gave Lorna a lingering pat on the back, then returned to the kitchen.

Izzy watched his broad back disappear through the swinging steel door. "Mr. Pefferman certainly is friendly."

Lorna shot a quick glance toward the door. "Oh, he's great. Everybody in town loves Aldo." She turned back with a smile. "I'll get you that cappuccino, now."

Five minutes later, Izzy stepped onto the sidewalk with a lidded paper cup in one hand and the bag with her chocolates in the other. Before she'd gone two feet, a dark-haired man dressed all in black, standing outside the shop next door, accosted the late-middle-aged woman walking in front of her.

"Excuse me, madam. How are you doing today?" He held up a small blue bottle. "We could all use a lift, couldn't we? And I have the perfect thing for you. A few dabs of this cream applied around your eyes every night will take twenty years off your appearance. Come with me, and I'll show you how." He clasped her upper arm and turned to lead her into the shop.

"Let go of me. I'm not interested in your cream or anything else you have to sell." The woman wrested her arm from his grasp with a scowl and marched off, muttering under her breath.

Izzy sidestepped the sidewalk barker and headed for the tranquil courtyard park around the corner. Nestled between two buildings and shaded by several massive oak trees, it was the perfect place to sit and watch the stream of people go by. As she sat on a bench, sipping her coffee and nibbling her chocolates, a tall, blond couple with two tall, blond teenagers walked by, carrying on an energetic conversation in some Nordic language, followed by a young Asian couple pushing a baby in a stroller and discussing the latest development at their employer, a prominent Silicon Valley tech firm.

A few minutes later, Lorna Ferris rounded the corner, deeply engaged in a call on her cell phone. She was talking fast and gesticulating vigorously with her free hand. As she passed the entrance to the park, she tossed a handful of crumpled paper in the general direction of the squirrel-embossed wooden trash receptacle and continued down the sidewalk, deep in conversation.

Izzy took her time finishing her coffee and enjoying

the cool, ocean-scented air. Despite — or possibly because of — the bustle around her, she felt remarkably relaxed and at ease. By the time her cup was empty, the afternoon freshness had turned chilly, and she was ready to go home. As she approached the trash can with her empty cup and bag, she spotted a wad of used napkins on the ground next to the bin. That must have been what Lorna was trying to throw away, but missed.

When Izzy bent to pick them up, she noticed something metallic about the size of the ring-tab from a soda can lying in the bed of ornamental succulents and picked it up, too, intending to discard it along with the rest. However, as she straightened and held the item closer, she realized it wasn't the tab of a can at all — it was a key.

After dropping the paper into the barrel, she raised the key to the light and examined it more closely. It was small, but sturdy and beautifully-made, with a hand-carved filagree design on the end, the sort of key that would have opened an old-fashioned jewelry or music box. She hated to throw it away, so she slipped it into her pocket. It might make an interesting detail in one of her photographs.

That got her thinking. Carmel was such a quaint, picturesque town, with its storybook architecture and stunning natural beauty. She would love to explore it with her camera. As she strolled back toward the cottage, she focused her attention on her surroundings, looking for small vignettes that embodied the unique ambiance of the village. It was getting late, however, and the shadows were too deep for a photo excursion this afternoon. Remembering how much she'd enjoyed watching the sun set over the bay with Aunt Dora, she decided to stop at home and pick up her camera, then take a walk along the beach before dinner.

Half an hour later, she was strolling down the nearly-deserted crescent of white sand. With the sun low in the sky and a band of thin clouds hanging over the horizon, the light was perfect, and she was able to snap a number of dramatic sunset shots before it got too dark. When she arrived back at the cottage, she found Bogart sitting imperiously beside his empty food bowl.

"Don't give me that look. If you don't show up for breakfast, you go hungry. House rules."

Mrowr. The feline rammed his head into her calf.

"All right, all right." She peeled back the top of a small can of cat food, forked it into his bowl, and set it in front of him.

Bogart purred so loudly while he ate, Izzy was afraid he might choke. When she rubbed the thick, mink-like fur on the back of his head, he mumbled a warning growl but continued eating. She straightened and regarded him with her hands on her hips. "Lucky for you, you're so beautiful. Your attitude leaves a lot to be desired."

After the cat finished eating, he surprised her by stretching out on the floor in front of the back door, where he watched her with hooded eyes and periodically flipped his tail.

Izzy shrugged. "I guess if you're going to stay, you're going to stay. Far be it from me to cramp your style."

Working around him, she fixed herself a quick stir-fry for dinner and ate it at the kitchen table under the feline's watchful eye. When she'd finished eating and cleaned up the dishes, he rose and sauntered into the living room, where he hopped up on the end of the sofa next to the lamp and waited expectantly.

"Hey, bud, you're in my spot."

She lifted his furry bulk and set him aside before settling back against the pillows in the corner and propping her feet up on the coffee table. Bogart immediately climbed onto her lap and stretched out along the length of her thighs before she could object.

"Okay, if that's the way it's going to be." She reached for the book she'd left on the end table and began to read.

They stayed that way for the next two hours, with Bogart purring while he kneaded her legs with his fully-clawed paws, and Izzy occasionally rubbing his velvety ears. Around nine o'clock, he flexed his muscles and sprang off her lap onto the floor, prompting the sudden realization that while she'd stocked up on cat food, she'd completely forgotten about a litter box. She jumped up and followed him to the kitchen, uncertain what to do if he started to relieve himself on the floor, but unwilling to ignore the possibility. Bogart simply paused in front of the door, then turned with a look of disdain, pushed open the cat flap, and disappeared into the night.

There was no sign of him in the morning, so Izzy assumed he had another favorite breakfast hangout, which was fine, because she had a busy day planned. She wanted to be at the electronics store as soon as they opened to buy a TV. When she'd moved in with Bryce, his entertainment system was already in place, and she'd never paid much attention to the specifics of how everything worked. She figured it might take most of the afternoon to set up her own equipment and select the proper streaming services to ensure she didn't miss her favorite shows. The process might not be speedy, but one way or another, she would figure it out.

She did, in fact, figure it out and was happily

engrossed in a baking competition show — although she could barely tell a spatula from a stand mixer — when the doorbell rang. After spotting the top of Sebastian's head through the glass, she turned off the television and went to open the door.

He raised his cell phone. "We need to exchange numbers so I don't keep showing up on your doorstep uninvited."

Izzy smiled and stepped aside. "You're always welcome, but that's a good idea."

"I love your hair short like that — it makes you look younger. Oh...was it rude of me to say that?"

She laughed. "Possibly, but I forgive you. I'm getting more comfortable with my age every day, but that doesn't mean I want to look it."

He followed her into the living room and glanced around. "I see you've made a few other changes." He nodded. "Dora would approve. She would want you to make the place your own."

"Since I didn't bring any furniture, I'll be using what's here for the time being, but I've tried to add a few of my favorite things."

"Like these photographs?" He stepped closer to examine an atmospheric, black-and-white view of the San Francisco docks at night. "They're really quite good. Did you take them?"

"I did. I'm looking forward to expanding my skills while I'm here."

Sebastian nodded again. "Carmel's the perfect place for that. Spectacular scenery and buckets of charm. A person could drown in the stuff if they're not careful." He turned to face her. "But I have another idea I'd like you to consider. The *Acorn* always needs photos of local people and events, and you have a knack for highlighting details most people would overlook. I'm sure our readers would appreciate a fresh, more artistic, perspective, something more interesting than the standard news shots."

Izzy hesitated. In pondering her new life and how she might make a living away from insurance, the possibility of photojournalism had never occurred to her. "I don't know…"

His eyes twinkled. "We pay good money for top quality."

"Well…"

"How about giving the idea a trial run Saturday afternoon? In addition to being Halloween, it's also the birthday of the village of Carmel-by-the-Sea. There are activities for the children, and everyone in town turns out for the pumpkin roll and costume parade down Ocean Avenue. The *Acorn* always has a big spread, and I'd love to see something more interesting than the usual photos of the high school marching band and the mayor driving an antique car."

It sounded like fun, and she had nothing to lose. If she didn't produce any stellar shots, no one would ever know, because they wouldn't appear in the paper. "I'd like that. It will give me a chance to participate in a town tradition, as well as stretch my artistic muscles."

"Great!" Sebastian beamed. "The festivities begin in the park at one o'clock, and the parade starts at four." He turned to leave, then stopped. "I almost forgot why I came over in the first place. I wanted to remind you about the City Council meeting tomorrow night, and I was serious about the phones." He handed Izzy his phone. "Put your number in for me, unless, of course, you'd rather not."

Although one could never be absolutely certain,

Sebastian seemed trustworthy, and she felt safer knowing she could reach someone in case of an emergency. She accepted his phone. "I agree, it will be much more convenient." She tapped in her contact info, and handed it back with an expression of mock suspicion. "And if I start getting barraged with spam texts or calls, I'll know who to blame."

He laughed and reciprocated the action when she gave him her phone. "Now, about tomorrow evening— I'll stop by and pick you up around six-thirty. We'll want to get there early to get seats in the front. Since Aldo Pefferman made the effort to invite me in person, I anticipate fireworks of some kind." He opened the front door and hesitated at the threshold. "Oh, and don't forget to bring a flashlight and your camera. If the meeting gets lively enough, you might be able to start your career with the *Acorn* early." He flashed his brows and was gone.

****

The next evening, Izzy threw together an early dinner of raw vegetables, hummus, and pita and was ready and waiting when Sebastian rang her bell. She draped the strap of her camera bag around her neck, flicked on her flashlight, and followed him down the stone walk to the street. In an attempt to maintain the original character of the village, the non-commercial areas of Carmel-by-the-Sea had no streetlights, so a strong, reliable flashlight was a must if one wanted to avoid a broken ankle.

On the way to City Hall, which was only a few blocks away on a quiet residential street at the edge of the business district, they talked in more detail about the specific Halloween day events Sebastian wanted photographed. They arrived well ahead of the seven o'clock starting time for the meeting, but people were already climbing the steep steps from the street up to the quaint, red-brick building.

Sebastian scanned the line at the door with a grimace. "I warned you there might be a crowd. I hope we'll be able to get decent seats. The Council Chamber isn't very large."

Fortunately, as often happens in public gatherings, people seemed reluctant to sit in the front row, so they were able to snag a pair of seats against the wall at the far end, which turned out to be an excellent observation point.

As the room filled, the din grew louder, to the point where Izzy practically had to shout to make herself heard. "I'm surprised by the crowd. I wouldn't have expected so many people to be interested in a City Council meeting."

Sebastian raised his voice to match. "You'll find that in a town this small, everyone has a strong opinion about everything, and they don't keep those opinions to themselves."

Finally, the Council members filed in and took their seats at the long table at the front of the chamber, and Mayor Celia Stanley called the meeting to order. The first order of business was a report from the Chief of Police about the installation of new traffic cameras to capture images—including license plate numbers—of cars entering and leaving the city limits. The cameras were expected to help identify and track the perpetrators behind a recent spate of smash-and-grab robberies that had been plaguing downtown jewelry and high-end clothing and leather goods stores. Next on the agenda was a citizen complaining about the City Forester, who had fined the contractor building an addition on his house for cutting the roots of a large pine tree. That brought lots of loud boos and cheers from the assembled citizens.

Izzy leaned toward Sebastian and whispered, "I see what you mean about strong opinions."

After the mayor quieted the group, Aldo Pefferman rose, his cheeks reddened and his hair unruly. "Your Honor, I would like to bring an important issue before the Council. I have in my hand," he raised a fist full of papers, "twelve formal complaints filed by visitors and citizens alike against the scourge of high-pressure, over-priced—sometimes even fraudulent—so-called skin care shops that have come to plague our city. There are currently four within five blocks on Ocean Avenue alone! These establishments have slick young salespeople stationed on the sidewalks, handing out samples and engaging with passersby, often to the extent of physically guiding them into the stores, where they are pressured into buying outrageously priced skin creams which cannot be returned, even unopened. As a city, we cannot continue to turn a blind eye to this outrage. We need to work with the landlords to decline to renew the leases of these blights on our town, or direct the Police Department to cite them out of existence."

A man who appeared to be in his early forties, with a swarthy complexion and thick, slicked-back black hair, jumped to his feet, waving a fist. "Sit down and shut up, you old dinosaur!"

Izzy stretched to whisper in Sebastian's ear. "Who is that?"

He turned with one hand cupped around his mouth.

"Christos Getz. He owns one of the skin care stores Aldo is complaining about, and it happens to be right next door to Taste of Torino."

Aldo glared at Getz. "Three of these complaints indicate the jars were empty when the purchaser got them home, and they were unable to get a refund. One woman swears she will never visit Carmel again after her experience with one of these shops." He glanced around the packed room. "This is the last thing we want in our city."

"You're just trying to shut down legitimate businesses because they're in competition with your wife!"

"His wife?" Izzy whispered to Sebastian.

"Serena Pefferman is a partner in a rejuvenation spa. That's her over there." He gestured with a nod to a woman with thick black eyelashes, unnaturally smooth skin, and long, silver-colored hair. "The man sitting next to her is Dr. Marcus Holder, her business partner."

Izzy's brows rose. There was something almost cartoonish about the duo. Mrs. Pefferman reminded her of an anime character, and the doctor, with his perfectly coiffed dark hair and square jaw, would have been right at home in tights and a cape. All he lacked was a big red "S" on his chest.

"You leave my wife out of it," Aldo yelled. "You're nothing but a huckster and a charlatan!"

Red-faced, Christos Getz charged up the aisle toward the Council table.

The mayor stepped to the podium and spoke into the microphone. "Take your seat, Mr. Getz, or I will have the Sergeant-at-Arms remove you from the chamber."

Sebastian leaned toward Izzy. "Get your camera ready."

She had just removed the lens cap when Aldo Pefferman rounded the table, heading straight for his adversary. When the combatants collided directly in front of the podium, the mayor shouted for the off-duty officer stationed near the doorway. In the meantime, Izzy snapped away, capturing the moment Getz's right fist connected with Pefferman's jaw, as well as the councilman's answering head-butt. The officer broke up the fight within seconds, but both men were nursing bloody lips as he hauled them from the room.

As the mayor called for order and the crowd settled down, Sebastian sat back in his folding chair, looking pleased with himself. "Normally, I send one of the reporters to cover Council meetings, but I'm glad Aldo invited me to this one in person. This will be front page news unless something more dramatic happens before we go to press tomorrow night. I hope you got some good shots."

"It all happened so fast, but I think I managed to capture the action." Izzy showed him the images on her camera.

"Three or four of those are terrific — it will be hard to choose one. Can you edit the best ones and get them to me by tomorrow afternoon?"

"Of course." She smiled to herself. If Sebastian used one of her photos in the *Acorn* and paid her for it, it would be her first baby step toward a new career.

As soon Mayor Stanley restored order, she called the next speaker on the agenda. A late middle-aged man with an angry scowl rose from the audience and strode to the podium. He represented a citizens group opposed to the design of a new house to be built on the site of a century-old cottage near the beach. The proposed design was much larger and starkly modern, and a sizeable group of vociferous neighbors objected to every aspect of it. The architect and a representative of the city planning department were on hand to answer questions, but no one was interested in what they had to say. Voices were raised, lawsuits were threatened, and eventually nothing was settled.

The remainder of the meeting was short and uneventful. When it wrapped up, Sebastian and Izzy joined the slow-moving line of people exiting the chamber.

As they neared the door, Sebastian wrapped a Burberry plaid cashmere scarf around his neck to ward off the late evening chill. "What do you think of your introduction to small-town politics?"

"It's pretty boring...until it's not."

He laughed. "That's a good way to put it. By tomorrow morning, everyone in the village will be talking about tonight's incident and taking sides, though I predict a much larger turn-out for Team Pefferman than Team Getz. None of the locals are very happy about the recent invasion of slippery skin care hucksters from L.A."

"That doesn't surprise me. I saw one of those high-pressure sidewalk salesmen in action a few days ago, and his potential customer's reaction was pretty hostile. I'm surprised they get any business with those tactics."

Sebastian took her elbow as a man jostled her from behind. "It's probably a lot like telemarketing robocalls. If you pester enough people, a few are bound to succumb."

Before Izzy could reply, a woman's voice rose above the murmurs of the milling crowd in front of them. "Well, that was exciting, although I'd love to have seen Christos Getz knock Aldo Pefferman flat on his fat posterior—the pompous, self-important, power-crazed—"

The naked hatred in her voice sent a shiver up Izzy's spine. She rose on tiptoe, craning her neck until she identified the source—a trim, gray-haired woman pushing a man in a wheelchair.

"Not me," the man interrupted. "I wish he'd killed him."

She turned to Sebastian, eyes wide. "Apparently not everyone in town is on Team Pefferman."

CHAPTER FOUR

The next morning, Bogart was back for breakfast. Izzy shot him a side-eyed glance as she forked canned food into his bowl. "You know, it would be a lot easier to provide the level of service you expect if you'd maintain a more predictable schedule."

He flipped the end of his tail in disdain before diving, nose-first, into his dish.

After her own breakfast, she downloaded the photos she'd taken at last night's City Council meeting and went to work editing them on her laptop at the kitchen table. She hoped Sebastian would be pleased. He'd said he didn't want everyday, run-of-the-mill news photos — which was a good thing, because these were anything but. She'd been perfectly positioned to capture the moment Christos's fist had connected with Aldo's jaw, sending spittle flying into the air, as well as Aldo's charging head-butt, complete with trickles of blood.

Sebastian had included his email address when he'd

entered his contact info into her phone, so she chose the three best pictures and sent them off. The moment she hit the button, she felt energized, yet antsy. Would he get back to her, and if so, how quickly? Or would she have to wait for the *Acorn* to come out to see if any of her photos had made tomorrow's edition? In the meantime, she needed to do something productive, something to move her life forward.

Although the cottage had a second bedroom, it had occurred to her that she might be able to convert Aunt Dora's painting studio in the backyard into an office/photography studio, but she had no idea of its current condition. Aunt Dora had always painted in natural daylight, so Izzy wasn't even sure the building had electricity — a must for setting up lighting for photo shoots and a computer station for digital editing. It was time to investigate.

Dressed in worn jeans and a ratty old Cal Bears sweatshirt and armed with a flashlight, just in case, she headed out the back door and across the flagstone patio to the wooden structure that looked like an oversized shed with floor-to-ceiling windows in one wall and an array of skylights. A rusty old padlock held the door closed, but the set of keys she'd received from Aunt Dora's attorney included one with a tag that read Studio. She inserted it into the lock, and with a firm twist, the shackle swung free.

The door creaked as she pushed it open, and dust motes floated in the broad beams of filtered light coming through the dirt-streaked windows and dingy skylights. The sight and smell instantly whisked her back to the carefree summer days she'd spent playing in a corner while Aunt Dora painted. Leaving the door open to air out the lingering odor of oil paint and turpentine, Izzy regarded the space with grown-up eyes. It was roughly fifteen feet by twenty feet and open to the rafters, with plain board walls and a paint-stained concrete floor. If she decided to use the space, she would have to decide whether to spruce it up or leave it in its current condition as an homage to its previous life. At the moment, she was leaning toward the latter.

A close inspection revealed that not only did the studio have a pair of hanging overhead light fixtures wired to a switch beside the door, but there were three — count them, three — wall sockets! That sealed the deal. There was work to be done, but the natural light would be wonderful when the glass was clean, and there was a lovely view of the garden. The place was unheated, so unless she wanted to work in a fleece onesie during cool weather, she would need to buy a space heater.

However, the first order of business was a serious scrubbing. She headed back to the house for cleaning supplies.

It took all afternoon and the next morning to remove months of grime and prepare the studio for its new purpose. At twelve-thirty, Izzy stood in the center of the room, stretching her back and surveying her handiwork. Her skin was damp under her sweatshirt, her cuffs were wet, and she'd split one knee of her jeans, but the results were worth the hard work. The place now smelled of lemon-scented cleanser instead of the pungent tang of turpentine, and although it was a cloudy day, light flooded the building through sparkling clean windows. She'd even found a ladder and climbed onto the roof to wash the skylights. When she locked the door and headed inside for lunch, she was filled with a sense of satisfaction and accomplishment unlike any she'd felt in her fifteen years at Pacific Western Life.

She tossed her dirty clothes into the laundry basket and washed at the bathroom sink before returning to the kitchen. A quick scan of the refrigerator turned up a take-out container of tomato basil soup from the small market a few blocks away, so she dumped it into a pot and set it on the stove. While she stirred the warming soup, it occurred to her that without the income or time constraints of a full-time job, she needed to actually learn how to cook. Perhaps she could ask Sebastian for a few pointers.

She had finished her soup and was washing out the bowl when the doorbell rang.

Vivian grinned and held up a folded newspaper. "You made it—the front page of the *Acorn!*"

Sebastian had sent a one-word reply to her email with the photos—*Thanks*—so Izzy wasn't sure what to expect. When she accepted the paper, her gaze went straight to the lead story about the fisticuffs at Wednesday night's City Council meeting. Accompanying the text was her photo of Christos Getz's fist connecting with Aldo Pefferman's jaw, and there beneath it, in small, but legible, type: *photo credit, Izzy Munro.* Not Isadora, which some might confuse with her great-aunt, but Izzy. Excitement bubbled through her at the sight of her name in print. It didn't matter that she hadn't yet been paid. She was now a professional photographer.

Vivian interrupted Izzy's train of thought by enveloping her in as big a hug as someone eight inches shorter could manage. "Congratulations! Dora would be so proud. She always hoped you'd eventually discover your creative side."

"I'm not sure there was anything particularly

creative about being present with a camera when two grown men decided to act like schoolboys, but I have to admit, it's fun to see my name in the *Acorn*."

Vivian's lips pressed into a firm line. "Don't disparage your own work, Isadora Munro. You snapped the shot. You chose the crop. You adjusted the lighting. And the result is a dramatic image that does much more than merely describe the event. It captures a real sense of what happened."

Izzy glowed inside. "Thank you. I don't know what to say."

"There's nothing else to be said. Now, I also stopped by to tell you I ran into Chantal yesterday, and she asked if you could come to the salon for a few minutes this afternoon. She has a proposition for you."

Izzy was intrigued. "A proposition?"

"She didn't tell me anything more. Maybe she wants to fix you up with her older brother, Luis. I've met him—he's pretty cute." Vivian flashed her brows suggestively.

Izzy groaned. She would rather stick a needle in her eye than go on a date with Chantal's brother, or anyone else.

"Oh, for heaven's sake." Vivian rolled her eyes. "I was just teasing. Chantal said you told her about your break-up with Bryce, and she's very sensitive. Whatever she wants, I'm sure it has nothing to do with dating her brother. Promise me you'll go see her."

"Okay, okay. I'll go. Maybe she'll give me a quick refresher course on how to handle these curls." Izzy pulled the end of one tress, then released it like a spring.

"I'm sure she'd be happy to. Now, get going. I'll see you later."

Izzy had to admit she was curious about Chantal's

proposition. If the stylist had taken *before* and *after* photos, she might want to hang them in the salon to demonstrate her skills, but she hadn't. Izzy put her lunch dishes in the dishwasher, grabbed a sweater, and strolled the few blocks to Cece's. One of the best things about living in a town that occupied a single square mile was having nearly everything she needed within walking distance. Her car rarely left the garage.

When she opened the salon door, Chantal glanced up from a customer who was getting a root touch-up and smiled. "Izzy, I'm so glad you came! If you'll take a seat over there, we can chat while Sally's color cooks."

Izzy wandered over to a chair by the window and chose a fashion magazine from the rack on the wall. The long-legged, barely post-pubescent models in their cutting-edge designer clothes made her feel old and frumpy, but she couldn't help noticing that several had hairstyles similar to what Chantal had done with hers. Maybe she was more chic than she realized.

A few minutes later, Chantal approached, peeling off her disposable gloves. "Can I get you something? Water or tea?"

"No, thanks. I'm fine. Vivian said you wanted to talk to me."

Chantal perched on the chair beside Izzy and crossed her legs. "I'm hoping you might be able to help me out."

"Um…sure. What can I do?"

"I know you said you moved here to start a new life, and I don't want to infringe on that in any way, but while you're getting that new life started, what would you think about working here part-time? Vivian showed me your photo on the front page of the *Acorn* — congratulations, by the way — and told me about your interest in becoming a professional photographer, but that takes time. Every artist I know had some kind of side gig at first, and Vivian said you didn't have anything lined up yet."

Izzy had briefly considered that, but she'd thought about a bookstore or gallery, not a salon. "Are you sure? As my hair can testify, I have no training, experience, or talent in that area."

Chantal laughed. "No worries. My receptionist suddenly abandoned me to move to Alaska with her boyfriend, and I'm in a bind. I can't answer the phone if I'm in the middle of a shampoo, and if I don't answer the phone, I lose business. It would only be half-days for a few weeks, until I can find a full-time replacement. And since you're new in town, the salon's the perfect place to meet people. What do you say?"

Izzy was anxious to dive into her new life. Did she really want to tie up half her time answering someone else's phone? "Well, um—"

"I can't pay what you're used to, but I can pay you what I paid my former receptionist." Chantal's grin was both infectious and disarming. "You know what they say—every little bit helps."

Izzy opened her mouth to decline, but hesitated while her brain did some quick math. She would be getting three months' severance pay from Pacific Western, but only three months. After that, she would go through her savings fast unless she found another source of income. As Chantal had said, establishing a photography business would take time, and even if it was ultimately successful, she had no idea how much money she could realistically expect to make. Chantal's offer might be exactly what she needed to help span the gap and give herself some financial breathing room.

She smiled. "You're right—every little bit does

help—and it sounds like fun. I appreciate the offer."

"Great! Can you come in Monday morning at nine o'clock and work until one? The daughter of one of my clients, who's a student at the local community college, has agreed to work afternoons for the rest of the semester. With luck, I'll be able to find a permanent replacement by January."

After starting work at eight o'clock for the past fifteen years, nine sounded positively laid-back. "That will be fine." Izzy rose and offered her hand. "I'll see you then, and thanks again."

She left CeCe's with a bounce in her step and headed for Taste of Torino for coffee and a pastry. Aldo was right—his wares were definitely habit-forming. Pretty soon she'd have to start watching her calories, as well as her pennies, but today she wanted to celebrate her newly-employed status. She'd barely been in Carmel a week, and it was already starting to feel like home.

****

Saturday morning, Izzy was awakened by a solid weight on her chest and a pair of gold eyes staring straight into hers, but this time she didn't panic. She lifted the hefty cat with a groan and set him on the bed beside her. "Bogart, I think you need to go on a diet."

Rowrr.

She glanced at the clock on the bedside table. "At least you waited until after seven. I guess I should be grateful for small favors." With a yawn, she threw back the covers, stuffed her feet into a pair of fuzzy blue slippers, pulled on her old flannel robe, and followed the hungry feline to the kitchen.

After breakfast, she showered and dressed, then

headed out the back door to her studio, smiling as she unlocked the door. Her studio. The words, even unspoken, gave her a happy glow. She spent the rest of the morning choosing and preparing her equipment for the afternoon's festivities. She didn't have a wide array of lenses, but for candid shots of people enjoying the Halloween parade and other activities, her two favorites should work fine. Since she always made a point of keeping her gear in good condition, the only thing the lenses needed was a touch-up cleaning, and she was ready to go.

While she was gathering her equipment, her phone buzzed. She pulled it out of her pocket and was surprised to see the name. "Sebastian, hi. I was just getting everything together for the photoshoot this afternoon. What can I do for you?"

"I have a huge favor to ask." He sounded frazzled, not his usual urbane self at all. "I hate to lay more on you, but do you think you could possibly write up a short article about the Halloween festivities to go with your photographs? The reporter I'd assigned to cover the parade has come down with the flu, and I'm stuck in San Francisco for the weekend. It doesn't have to be long—just hit the highlights. I'd be forever grateful."

Izzy hesitated. Could she? She hadn't written anything except business memos and reports since college. But Sebastian had been so kind and generous since she'd moved to town. The least she could do was help him out in an emergency. "I'd be happy to give it a shot. I'll try to get the basics down, and you can whip it into shape before you print it."

"That's great! Just send it along with the photos. Sorry, I've got to go now. Thanks again."

With a shake of her head, she slipped the phone back

into her pocket. Since she would be attending the celebration anyway, and keeping an eye out for anything interesting or unusual, it shouldn't be too hard to write up a brief description of what she saw.

Although the parade didn't begin until four o'clock, Sebastian had asked for photos of the preliminary events, so shortly after one, she packed up her gear and walked the few blocks to the center of town. It was cool and overcast, but the gloomy weather hadn't put a damper on the youngest residents' enthusiasm, and they were out in force.

Izzy's first stop was the city park in the center of town that served as the equivalent of a village green, where she got several cute shots of costumed children having their faces painted by volunteers from the library. One little tiger, who looked to be about three, shrieked with glee when he saw his new stripes and whiskers in a mirror provided by the artist. He proceeded to run around the small park, growling at everyone in his path, until his frightened baby sister began to cry in her stroller and his mother distracted him with the prospect of trick-or-treating.

The Halloween parade marked the only occasion when businesses were allowed to have representatives out on the sidewalk, and nearly each establishment had someone handing out treats to costumed passersby. Although Izzy wasn't the only one in street clothes, she felt drab and out of place as she moved through the boisterous crowd. She might be working, but she wished she'd taken a few minutes to throw together some sort of colorful outfit.

As she strolled up and down the streets of the main commercial district, snapping photos of outrageous or unusually clever costumes, she passed several people dressed as the Grim Reaper. They weren't walking together in a group, but were scattered throughout the crowd, about one per block, on both sides of the street. They didn't appear to be handing out candy or actively engaging with the revelers. Instead, they just walked up and down the street, holding their tall, silver scythes like flagbearers. Izzy sensed a story there, although she had no idea what it could be. For all she knew, the Reapers might play an integral part in the Halloween celebration later, so she photographed several of them. If they turned out to be important, she could include a picture and description in her submission to the *Acorn*.

The crowd numbers increased all afternoon. At three o'clock, police officers began moving the remaining cars parked along the parade route and placed barricades across the streets leading into the business district. As people staked out their viewing positions along the main drag, Izzy looked for an advantageous spot to take photos of the action. She decided the curb in front of Taste of Torino offered a perfect view, as well as the opportunity to grab a quick cup of coffee to help chase away the afternoon chill.

When she stepped inside, she quickly discovered she wasn't the only one with that idea. The line at the counter was more than fifteen minutes long, even though Lorna Ferris had several additional helpers that afternoon to deal with the crowd. After paying for her latté, Izzy made her way back outside, where she encountered Aldo Pefferman, greeting pedestrians on the sidewalk with a plate of his fancy handmade chocolates. The councilman smiled cheerfully, despite sporting a bandage on his forehead above an impressive black eye.

She was a little surprised to see him in public, since

the news of his recent skirmish had been splashed all over the front page of the *Acorn* yesterday. But his candy was very popular, and based on their friendly smiles and comments, people didn't seem bothered by the altercation at the City Council meeting.

A moment later, Christos Getz stepped out of his shop next door. He also bore the marks of Wednesday's sparring match—a neat row of black stitches centered between his eyebrows, a swollen lower lip, and a dark bruise on the corner of his jaw. Both men froze, as if daring the other to back down first. Then Aldo took a step forward, and Christos followed suit. Curious pedestrians turned to look as they veered to avoid the pair.

Before either man could speak, Serena Pefferman marched out of Taste of Torino carrying a fresh plate of chocolates. Her long, silvery-white hair was pulled back in an elaborately braided style that could only have come from some social media influencer, and her nails resembled giant, ruby-colored claws. With a frown at the two men facing off on the sidewalk, she reached for her husband's elbow and yanked him back.

"Aldo, you're almost out of candy for our friends. I brought you a fresh plate." Her voice was sharp with unspoken rebuke.

He blinked and turned. "Huh? Oh, yes." He traded platters with her. "Thank you, my dear."

His wife's lips curled in a condescending smile. "Try to remember why you're here." Then she spun on her spiky black stilettos and strode back inside.

Aldo's face reddened, but he faced the crowd with a jovial smile and began handing out chocolates again. Christos Getz returned to his shop.

"Izzy!"

She spotted Chantal on the sidewalk about ten feet away, waving and jumping up and down as she tried to see over the army of taller parade-goers. She waved back but was reluctant to abandon her prime spot at the curb. Five minutes later, the petite stylist elbowed her way to Izzy's side.

She turned sideways just enough to allow Chantal to squeeze in beside her. "I'm surprised to see you. I thought you'd be busy, since it's Saturday afternoon."

"I always close the salon at noon on parade day. Most of my clients are here, and besides, there isn't an empty parking space anywhere near the shop.

"There's a good turnout, even though it's cloudy and cool."

Chantal rubbed her hands together, then stuffed them in the pockets of her jacket. "Everyone comes to the parade. It's the biggest local event of the year and gives us a chance to reconnect with neighbors and friends we don't see very often."

Izzy tipped her head toward Aldo. "You just missed a near show-down."

Chantal followed her glance. "You mean our illustrious city councilman almost got into it again with Christos Getz? I saw your photo in the *Acorn*. Those two *really* don't like each other."

Their conversation was interrupted by the blare of trumpets, the booming of bass drums, and the *oompah* of tubas as the high school marching band appeared at the top of Ocean Avenue, signaling the beginning of the parade. As the band advanced and other groups of marchers followed, Izzy snapped pictures of small, evocative vignettes, like the expression on the tuba player's face as she blew a big breath into her mouthpiece and the man dressed as a French mime, in white make-up, a striped shirt, and a red beret, handing out candy to costumed children along the edge of the route.

Sebastian would probably only have room for two or three shots in next week's edition of the paper, but Izzy hoped to hang a number of the other pictures in her studio to show to prospective clients as examples of her work, assuming she managed to attract prospective clients.

"Ms. Munro, Ms. Costas!" A resonant male voice called out over the band's unique version of *The Skeleton's Ball*.

Both women turned to find Aldo Pefferman directly behind them, offering his platter of chocolates.

"Have one, ladies...please." He thrust the plate forward.

After Izzy and Chantal each chose a beautifully crafted piece and thanked him, he picked one up and admired it. "My wife never lets me enjoy my own creations, but what she doesn't know won't hurt her, and we won't tell, will we?" With a grin, he popped the chocolate into his mouth and savored it with obvious pleasure.

Izzy turned back to the parade just in time to snap a shot of the mayor trying to hold a towering headdress of artificial fruit upright while riding in the back of a bright yellow vintage Studebaker convertible. Her car was followed by two fire trucks from the Carmel-by-the-Sea Fire Department, periodically hitting their lights and sirens.

When the clamor died down, she heard the unmistakable sounds of an argument behind her and turned around. Aldo and Serena Pefferman were standing nose-to-nose against the side of the building, half-hidden behind the open door. If they were trying to keep their voices down, they were failing.

Serena poked her husband's chest with an accusatory finger. "Aldo, have you been eating chocolate again? Don't try to deny it — I can see it on your lips! You know what the doctor said." She tried to yank the plate from his hands, but he refused to relinquish it.

He glanced at the curious faces in the crowd and hissed, "Keep your voice down and go inside. I'm fine."

"You are not fine. I can tell just by looking at you. I hate to think what your blood sugar is right now. I'm going to get your insulin." She hurried back into the shop and disappeared.

Watching Serena's angry progress, Chantal shook her head. "You have to hand it to the Peffermans — they're never boring."

Moments later, they heard Aldo protesting and turned back. His wife had a firm grip on his upper arm with one hand, and was holding a syringe in the other.

"Get away from me, woman. You're creating a scene."

"This is for your own good." Serena jabbed the needle into the back of his arm through the knit of his sweater, and pushed the plunger.

Aldo yelped and tried to jerk away, but she didn't release him until she'd delivered the full dose. "There. Now at least I don't have to worry about you killing yourself today." Tossing the syringe into the trash container at the curb, she turned and marched back inside.

Izzy turned to Chantal. "That was interesting."

Her friend nodded. "I'm almost sorry it ended so quickly. It would have made a great incident report for the *Acorn* police log."

Since the sidewalk drama seemed to have wrapped up, they returned their attention to the parade. A group of children dressed in costumes of various sea creatures and carrying a banner that announced them as the Ocean Explorers Club from the local elementary school was passing, and Izzy got a couple shots of a striking blue jellyfish with sparkly silver tentacles.

At a tap on her shoulder, she turned.

"Here, have another."

A smiling Aldo thrust his platter of chocolates in her face. He had obviously refilled it, and she was unable to resist, though to be honest, she didn't try very hard. She wouldn't have any appetite for dinner, but his silky, melt-in-your-mouth confections were worth every calorie. As she opened her mouth to thank him, she noticed he didn't look well. His face was pale, and a tiny muscle near his hairline was quivering visibly.

"Mr. Pefferman, are you all right?"

"No…I feel dizzy…double vision." He swayed, and his voice had taken on a hoarse quality.

As the plate in his hands tipped precariously, Chantal grabbed it before it fell to the sidewalk. She leaned toward Izzy and whispered, "Look at his eyes."

Aldo's eyelids were drooping, and his cheeks had gone slack. Alarm bells went off in Izzy's head. She might not have formal medical training, but in her line of work she'd read enough medical records to recognize certain symptoms. "I think he might be having a stroke."

He reached out and grabbed both her arms, eyes wide with fear. "Help…can't…breathe."

His chest heaved as his lungs labored to move air in and out in harsh, rasping breaths. Then his eyes closed, and he slowly crumpled. Izzy and Chantal leapt to catch him before he hit the pavement. Izzy lifted his shoulders a few inches and scooted under him to cradle his head, while Chantal squatted beside them.

Chantal's eyes were round with panic. "Is he dead? What do we do?"

When Izzy placed one hand on Aldo's chest, she felt movement, minimal but definite. "He's alive, but he needs help quickly. Ordinarily I'd say, call 911, but it would probably be faster to chase down that fire truck." She pointed to the truck that had passed several minutes earlier and was now headed down the street toward the beach parking lot.

"Right." Chantal jumped up and pushed her way through the tight crowd that had gathered around them. She burst into the street and took off down the hill as fast as her chunky-heeled boots would carry her.

Izzy glanced at Aldo's ashen face, now beaded with sweat, and a paralyzing fear gripped her. She barely knew this man. What if he died in her arms? Right or wrong, she felt somehow responsible, and all she could do was will him to live.

CHAPTER FIVE

The Halloween parade continued down the avenue, its participants oblivious to the emergency on the sidewalk, but Izzy tuned out the cheerful din. She checked Aldo's pulse — it was weak and thready. Where was the ambulance? Surely Chantal had caught up to the fire engine by now.

After another minute that felt like an hour, there was a disturbance in the street as the parade participants stopped marching and stepped aside to make way for the Fire Department ambulance. The vehicle stopped in front of Izzy, and four firefighters hopped out and rushed to her side. One who was carrying a medical bag seemed to be in charge.

The woman checked Aldo's pulse, then listened to his chest with a stethoscope. "What happened here?"

"He said he felt dizzy, and his eyelids and face drooped. Then he seemed to have trouble breathing before he collapsed. I thought he was having a stroke."

The paramedic signaled her colleagues to bring the gurney from the back of the ambulance before turning back to Izzy. "Do you know anything about his medical history?"

"I think he might be diabetic. Shortly before he collapsed, his wife scolded him for eating chocolate candy against doctor's orders. She gave him an injection of what she said was insulin."

"How long was it between the injection and the onset of his symptoms?"

"I'm not sure. Not long...maybe ten minutes?"

When the woman turned to say something to another member of her crew, Chatal appeared at Izzy's side, flushed and breathing heavily. "I ran as fast as I could. Is Aldo okay?"

Before she could reply, a shrill female voice shrieked above the clamor, "Where is he? Where is Aldo? Where is my husband?"

Izzy twisted to see Serena Pefferman shoving her way through the crowd.

Serena knelt beside her husband. "What happened? Is he dead?"

The paramedic pushed to her feet and gestured to the other firefighters for the gurney. "No, ma'am. Now, if you'll please stand back, we're getting ready to take him to the hospital."

Serena rose but continued to carry on. "Did he have a heart attack? I told him a thousand times to take better care of himself and stop eating all those sweets."

"Are you his wife?" the paramedic asked.

Serena bristled. "Of course, I am. Don't you know who this is?"

"The woman who flagged us down gave us his name—Aldo Pefferman."

The firefighters lowered the gurney and lifted Aldo onto it. The second his head left her lap, Izzy scrambled to her feet while the crew rolled him to the ambulance and loaded him on board.

When Serena looked like she might try to climb in, too, the lead EMT held out a restraining arm. "Ma'am, we'll be taking him to Community Hospital. You can follow in your car."

Serena disappeared into the crowd on the sidewalk — presumably to retrieve her car — and the ambulance pulled away from the curb, blue lights flashing. The driver gave short blasts of the siren to clear the remaining parade participants from the road as they rolled up the hill toward Highway 1, en route to the Community Hospital of the Monterey Peninsula, known to the locals as CHOMP.

Chantal shot one last glance at the disappearing taillights of the ambulance, then wrapped her arms across her chest and shivered. "That was pretty scary. Do you think he'll be all right?"

"I don't know. If his collapse was related to his diabetes, the hospital should be able to stabilize him quickly." Izzy didn't add that she would be surprised if that turned out to be the case. Aldo's symptoms didn't match those of any claims she'd investigated resulting from diabetic emergencies, and in any case, the insulin injection should have prevented such an extreme reaction.

After the disruption of Aldo's medical situation, the parade splintered and disintegrated, so Izzy decided to head home. Since Chantal needed to pick up her car, they walked together as far as the salon.

After the two parted ways, Izzy continued to ponder Aldo's sudden attack. His symptoms were baffling.

Based on her admittedly limited knowledge, facial drooping and difficulty breathing weren't common signs of either abnormally high or low blood sugar. She could only hope the doctors at CHOMP would figure it out and get Aldo back on his feet quickly. Although she barely knew the man, his collapse had created an odd sort of bond between them.

When she got home, she found Bogart waiting in the kitchen, looking seriously put-out.

Mrrow! He twined around her legs, butting his head into her calves and voicing his complaint at the top of his lungs.

Izzy glanced at the clock. It was five-thirty— probably time to think about food for both of them. She fed Bogart first because he was insistent, and his dinner was the quickest. While he munched and slurped noisily at her feet, she boiled some pasta for herself and whipped up a simple topping of garlic-sauteed vegetables. After dinner, he followed her into the living room and fell asleep on her lap while she channel-surfed, trying to find something to take her mind off the events of the afternoon. She gave up around nine and went to bed with a book, while Bogart slunk out through the cat flap to do whatever a debonair feline-about-town did at night.

The next morning, she planned to go through the photos she'd taken of the parade, edit them, and write up a short, descriptive article to send to Sebastian before the deadline for Friday's *Acorn*. The day before, she'd found a check for her photo of the fireworks at Wednesday evening's City Council meeting on the kitchen floor. Sebastian must have slipped it through the cat flap. The amount was more than she'd expected, boosting her hopes of one day being able to support herself as a photographer.

Since it was Sunday, she was still in her pajamas, lounging at the kitchen table with a second cup of coffee when the doorbell rang. The unexpected sound startled her, causing her to slosh coffee down her chin and onto the table. Cursing, she grabbed a napkin and blotted herself and the table top before heading for the living room.

Since she only knew three people in Carmel, and didn't want to growl at any of them, she forced a smile before opening the door.

The man in front of her wasn't among her three local acquaintances, and his appearance on her front porch was so out-of-context, it took several seconds for her brain to identify and process the sight of him. He was tall, but not unusually so — perhaps four or five inches taller than her own five foot eight — and had thick, dark brown hair with a sprinkling of silver at the temples, cut fairly short. Dark brows and a square jaw gave his face an unyielding, no-nonsense air. He belonged to a life that felt light years away.

"Joe? Joe De Rossi? What are you doing here?"

Recognition flared in the man's eyes, but he didn't smile. "I might ask you the same thing." He scanned her face with the dispassionate thoroughness of a seasoned investigator. "You've changed in the past year."

Izzy touched her shorter curls with a nervous smile. "It's the hair. I'm still getting used to it."

He took his time then nodded. "It suits you. When I saw the name 'Isadora Munro' listed as a witness in the paramedic's incident report, I told myself it had to be a coincidence. What would Izzy Munro be doing in Carmel, involved in a suspicious death?"

"Suspicious death?" Her heart sank. This wasn't the

news she'd been hoping for. "Mr. Pefferman is dead?"

Joe nodded. "He died early this morning. I'm sorry to show up on your doorstep like this, without warning, but no one at the Police Department had your phone number."

Izzy was still distracted as she struggled to accept the reality of Aldo Pefferman's death. "I just moved to town last week. This was my Aunt Dora's house, and I had the landline disconnected last summer, after her death."

Joe nodded. "I need you to come to the station to answer some questions and make an official statement about what happened yesterday."

She straightened, gathered her thoughts, and regarded him with a slight frown. "That begs my earlier question — why are you here? Why would I come to the Carmel police station with you? The last time I saw you, you were an SFPD detective with the Homicide Division."

He raised one brow. "And you were a Senior Claims Examiner with Pacific Western Life."

She glanced away. "I guess we've both had some major life changes."

"Which we can discuss on the way to the station."

She surveyed her t-shirt and loose, draw-string pants. "I can't go anywhere like this. I'm still in my pajamas."

Joe's expression remained stolid. "I'll wait."

She hesitated. It felt rude to ask him to wait on the porch but uncomfortably familiar to invite him in while she dressed. Although Joe De Rossi had always seemed like a stand-up guy, their previous relationship had been purely professional.

He seemed to sense her discomfort and glanced at his watch. "How long do you need to get ready? I'll pick us up a couple of coffees and be back in twenty minutes."

Izzy flashed a quick smile of relief. "That would be great. I'll hurry."

As soon as he left, she raced to the bathroom, took a quick shower without washing her hair, and threw on a clean pair of jeans and a burgundy sweater. She was just slicking on a coat of lip gloss when the doorbell rang again. She grabbed a jacket and opened the door. Joe held up a large paper cup topped with a plastic lid, which he handed to her as she stepped outside.

As they strolled down the front walk, her mind buzzed with questions. She decided to jump right in. "I realize your reasons for leaving San Francisco are none of my business, but can I assume you're now working for the Carmel PD?"

He shook his head and took a sip from his cup. "Last year, when I reached my twenty-year mark with the SFPD, I decided to retire. My wife made the decision easier by divorcing me to marry my partner."

Izzy cringed. Why hadn't she kept her mouth shut? "I'm sorry."

"Don't be. I'm adjusting, but you can understand why I wanted a change of scenery. Someplace with more open space and a slower pace of life sounded good. There was an opening for a Senior Investigator with the Monterey County District Attorney's office, so I applied and got the job. I've been here six months."

"Then you're not with Carmel PD."

"No. The DA has a Bureau of Investigation with wide-ranging duties, one of which is to assist local jurisdictions with major cases. Since CPD only has one part-time detective, and she doesn't have much experience with suspicious deaths, the chief requested our assistance."

"Which brings us back to Aldo Pefferman."

He shot her a side glance as he took another sip. "I'd rather not discuss that until we're at the station."

Izzy nodded. "I understand. Everything by the book."

"You know me—I'm a by-the-book kind of guy."

She did know that. She also knew he was a tenacious investigator with solid police instincts. In the past few years, they had worked together on at least a half dozen high-profile cases in which she'd suspected the beneficiaries of large life insurance policies of having had a hand in the insured's death. In each case, Joe had helped prove her suspicions correct.

He stopped at a stop sign and looked both ways, even though there wasn't a vehicle in sight. "So, since we can't discuss the case, you can tell me what you're doing here." He glanced at her left hand, holding her coffee cup. "The last time I saw you, you were working for Pacific Western Life and engaged to that lawyer."

"Bryce Howe, yes." She side-stepped a cantaloupe-sized pothole. "Well, I must have offended the universe big-time, because both Bryce and the insurance company dumped me on the same day." To head off any expression of sympathy or pity, she added, "I'm fine. Happy, really. The move here allows me to change course and do something different with my life."

Joe regarded her with raised brows. "You're through with insurance, then?"

She sipped her coffee while she debated whether to mention her photography, but if he happened to pick up a copy of the *Acorn*, he might notice her byline on the front page. She drew a deep breath. "I'm hoping to turn my photography hobby into a new career."

He considered her statement and nodded. "I can see

that. When we worked together, you always had an eye for noticing small, telling details. Your instincts and photos helped us catch a killer more than once."

"I'm sure my methods seemed idiosyncratic—if not silly—to an experienced detective, but taking pictures of the setting in which someone died helped me visualize and understand the death. When you're looking at a multi-million-dollar claim, you want to be sure the company doesn't pay the proceeds to a murderer. It's better to let a judge decide who gets the money."

"Well, you did a great job. I'm sure Pacific Western will miss your talents."

Izzy couldn't keep the tinge of bitterness from her voice. "Apparently, they disagree."

"That's their loss, but I hope you're not planning a career as a crime scene photographer in a town as small as Carmel-by-the-Sea. The locals tell me nothing ever happens here."

"No. The publisher of the *Carmel Acorn* is my next-door neighbor. He's asked me to take pictures of local events and, in a pinch, write a short article for the newspaper. I won't make a living doing it, but it's a start."

They had reached the plaza in front of the police station, and Joe hesitated at the base of the steps. "I don't suppose you were taking photos at the parade yesterday."

"Actually, I was."

He glanced at her purse. "You don't have your camera with you."

She frowned. "No. Why would I?"

"I'd like to see the photos you took yesterday. They might contain something useful."

"Are you going to tell me what's happened?"

He reached for the handrail. "After I take your statement. Let's go inside."

After tossing their empty cups in the barrel outside the station, Izzy followed him inside, and the desk sergeant directed them to a windowless interview room in the bowels of the building. After they settled into a pair of uncomfortable wooden chairs, Joe laid a notebook and pen on the narrow table. Then he leaned back and rested one ankle across the opposite knee. "I know you're a careful observer. Tell me about the parade. Did you see anything noteworthy or unusual?"

He scribbled occasional notes while she walked him through the pre-parade activities at the park and her observations of the crowd, taking time to describe everything she'd found worthy of a photograph, including the unsettling Grim Reapers. When she got to the point of meeting Aldo outside Taste of Torino, Joe lowered his leg and leaned forward in his chair, resting one elbow on the table.

"And you ate the candy he was handing out?"

Izzy nodded. "I had a piece. Lots of people did. His bakery was one of the most popular stops on the parade route. Mr. Pefferman even ate three or four pieces himself, although his wife came charging out to scold him. Apparently he's diabetic and not supposed to have sweets."

"How did he seem after eating the chocolates?"

Her brows pinched in a tiny frown. "Fine. He was quite cheerful. Why?"

Joe ignored her question. "What happened after that?"

Izzy closed her eyes and ran through the afternoon's events to make certain she reported them in the correct order. "A short time later, Mrs. Pefferman came back outside with a syringe. Based on their earlier conversation, I assumed it contained insulin. Aldo resisted, but she injected him in the back of the arm then returned to the bakery."

"Did she take the syringe with her?"

Izzy thought a moment. "No, she threw it into the curbside trashcan."

"And when did he start experiencing symptoms?"

"Ten…maybe fifteen minutes later." She narrowed her eyes and sharpened her gaze. "Joe, what happened to Aldo Pefferman? Do you think his wife made a mistake with his insulin dosage?"

He sat back and ran a hand through his hair, sending it upward in short, spiky bristles. "It wasn't insulin that killed him. Based on the results of his bloodwork, the doctors are convinced Mr. Pefferman died of botulinum toxin poisoning. We're awaiting the final ruling from the ME which should come later today."

Izzy's frown deepened. "Botulism? I thought that was a form of food poisoning. There couldn't have been anything wrong with the chocolates—I feel fine, and I didn't see anyone else get sick."

"We have a team taking samples from all the ingredients and equipment in the kitchen of Taste of Torino as we speak, but based on the cursory research I was able to do this morning, I don't think he died from anything he ate yesterday. The symptoms usually take longer to develop and are not rapidly fatal."

"I guess that's a relief, but I wonder what the source of the toxin could have been."

"We can't speculate at this point. We have a lot more people to talk to—including Serena Pefferman—and more testing to do. I'll have Forensics look for that discarded syringe. Since it's Sunday, the trashcan probably hasn't been emptied yet."

Izzy had spent years unraveling the complexities of untimely deaths, but this conversation felt unreal. Aldo Pefferman wasn't some abstract insurance client she knew only on paper. She'd met him multiple times. She'd been talking to him just before he collapsed, and now he was dead. "Be sure to put Christos Getz on your interview list. He owns the shop next to the bakery, and from what I've seen, the two men despised each other. They got into a physical fight at the City Council meeting Wednesday night and looked like they might start up again yesterday afternoon shortly before Aldo became ill."

The intensity of Joe's gaze sharpened. "Do you know anything about the source of their animosity?"

"Based on their shouting match, it sounded like Aldo wanted to severely restrict or shut down Mr. Getz's business and others like it after the city received a slew of complaints about high-pressure sales tactics and fraudulent business practices."

"Hmm, interesting. A promising line of inquiry." Joe scribbled something in his pad then glanced up. "What can you tell me about Serena Pefferman?"

"Not much, I'm afraid. I've never met her, and I've only seen her twice—once at the Council meeting with her business partner, and then again yesterday afternoon at the parade."

"As you can imagine, she's in no condition to talk to the police today. But I have an appointment to interview her tomorrow afternoon, and I'd like to get as much background on her husband and their relationship as possible. How did she seem to you yesterday?"

Izzy took her time. "If I had to describe her behavior, I guess I'd say concerned. Aldo didn't appreciate her nagging, but she seemed genuinely worried about his health."

Joe nodded and glanced down at his notes. "You mentioned her business partner. Do you know what business she's in?"

"According to my neighbor, Sebastian Larrabee, she's part-owner of a rejuvenation spa, whatever that is."

"I'll see what I can find out about it before I talk to her. Thanks. Is there anything else you know that might help me?"

"Not that I can think of at the moment."

He flipped his notebook closed. "Thanks. I guess that'll be all for now, although I'd still like to see the photos you took at the parade. Is there a time we could get together, maybe tomorrow morning before I interview Mrs. Pefferman?"

Izzy started to agree, then shook her head. "I almost forgot—I'm starting a new job in the morning."

"Oh? That was quick. I thought you'd only been in town a week."

"I'm filling in half-days as the receptionist at a friend's salon for a few weeks. She thinks it will be a good way to meet people."

Joe nodded. "She's right. In my experience, even in a big city like San Francisco, the neighborhood barber shop or hair salon can be the best place to get a feel for the local community. What time do you get off?"

"One o'clock."

"I've got an idea. Why don't I pick up some lunch and meet you at your place at one-thirty? We can look at your photos while we eat. I'm not meeting with Serena Pefferman until three."

"And maybe you can fill me in on any new

developments before your meeting."

He raised a brow. "Maybe. *If* there's any information I can share."

"Understood."

"Good." Joe closed his notebook and pushed to his feet. "I've got a meeting with the CPD detective in a few minutes, but I'll see you tomorrow afternoon. Thanks for coming in." He offered his hand, and Izzy shook it. "I'll walk you back to the front desk so you don't get lost."

The jumble of thoughts churning through her mind distracted her, causing her to nearly miss the bottom step in front of the police station. She grabbed the railing to steady herself, then glanced around. A car rolled past, but the sidewalk was deserted. If she had to be a klutz, at least it was on a Sunday morning when there were few people on the street.

The air was chilly, but the sun had come out while she was inside, so she decided to take the long way home, down Ocean Avenue all the way to the beach. She clambered down one of the long stairways to the sand, then walked the length of the beach, watching the gulls and curlews poke around in the foam left by receding waves before she returned to the house. She was still struggling to accept that a man she'd seen alive and well less than twenty-four hours earlier had died so suddenly, and of something as rare as botulism poisoning. How often did that happen? In all her years at Pacific Western, she couldn't recall a single instance.

Her first instinct was to dive into researching the condition, but she stopped herself. Examining untimely deaths was no longer her job. She'd put that, along with everything else in her old life, behind her. She was a photographer now, and she owed Sebastian a short article along with a nice selection of pictures from yesterday's celebration. If she happened to spot a detail that might help Joe De Rossi's investigation, that was simply a plus.

She set up her laptop on the kitchen table, inserted the memory card from her camera, and began working her way through the photos.

Sebastian was going to be very happy. The face-painting booth in the park had produced several shots of adorable, costume-clad tots that would be perfect for the *Acorn*, and the expression on Mayor Stanley's face as her Carmen Miranda headdress slid down her forehead was priceless. However, when Izzy got to the photos she'd taken near Taste of Torino, her attention sharpened.

There were several of Aldo smiling, conversing, and interacting with the crowd — some people in street clothes and others wearing costumes — as he handed out his chocolates. She hadn't noticed at the time, but one of the Grim Reapers hovered behind him in one shot. It might be nothing, or it might be significant — she would leave that to Joe to decide. She jotted down the image number before moving on.

She had nearly reached the end of the photos when something else caught her eye. She enlarged the image, adjusted the lighting, and tightened the focus. In the foreground, Aldo was bending over, offering a chocolate to a young girl wearing a dinosaur costume and carrying a big plastic sword, and behind him, in the window of the seating section of the bakery, was a face. A woman's face. A familiar face. And she looked furious.

CHAPTER SIX

Izzy had finished her review of the photos, eaten a BLT minus the bacon for lunch, and was lying on the sofa, scribbling notes for the article to accompany her pictures while Bogart dozed on her stomach, when the doorbell startled them both. Bogart dug his claws into her flesh, then sprang up and raced from the room. Izzy sat up with a sharp yelp and was still rubbing her stomach as she opened the door. Sebastian stood on the porch wearing a look of concern.

Her brows knit in a puzzled frown. "What are you doing here? I thought you were in San Francisco."

"As soon as I heard what happened, I came back early. How are you doing?"

"I'm okay. I've finished going through my photos from yesterday, and there are several I think might work well in the *Acorn,* assuming you're still planning a big spread on the parade."

"We are. The parade is newsworthy on its own. We'll

do a separate story about Aldo Pefferman's death. Are you still going to be able to write the article?"

Izzy nodded. "I haven't written anything yet, but I've started jotting down some notes. Come on in, and I'll show you what I've got."

He followed her into the living room. "I can't wait to see the pictures, but that's not why I'm here. After Aldo collapsed on top of you during the parade, then died hours later, are you sure you're all right?"

"I'm fine. It was a shock, though." She gave a nod toward the kitchen. "I was about to fix a cup of tea. Would you like one?"

"That would be nice. Thank you."

She led the way to the compact kitchen. "Have a seat while I put the kettle on."

He settled into one of the small chairs and draped one long leg elegantly across the other, showing a couple inches of dark blue sock adorned with tiny mallards. "Aldo's death was a shock to everyone who knew him. He was such a robust man. I guess that just goes to show, appearances can be deceiving. Someone said it looked like a stroke."

"That's what I thought at the time." Which was true.

"I'm surprised the local grapevine doesn't have the full story by now, but I checked with the hospital on behalf of the newspaper, and there isn't an official cause of death yet."

She took the steaming kettle from the stove and poured boiling water into a pair of Aunt Dora's Art Deco-style porcelain cups. "I expect the police will issue a statement either later today or early tomorrow, after the Medical Examiner's report is complete."

Sebastian pinned her with a sharp gaze. "That sounds like you have inside information." When she hesitated, he pressed further. "Come on, Izzy, spill. Aldo Pefferman's death is one of the biggest stories of the year in Carmel. If you know something more about it, don't hold back."

There was no real reason to keep her conversations with Joe De Rossi secret. He was officially assigned to the case by the District Attorney's office, a fact that would soon be public knowledge, if it wasn't already. "I was interviewed this morning by an investigator from the DA's office, who turned out to be a former SFPD detective I'd worked with in the past."

Sebastian uncrossed he legs and leaned forward. "So you have inside information. That's excellent! What did he say?"

She considered sharing Joe's preliminary suspicion of botulism, but decided against it. That could wait for official confirmation. "That he expected a formal determination of the cause of death from the ME within the next twenty-four hours."

Sebastian settled back, picked up his tea, and took a sip. "Then I suppose we'll have to wait. But since you know the investigator, I hope you'll remain in touch with him over the course of the investigation and keep me in the loop. I might even have to designate you as the *Acorn's* official investigative reporter for the case." His quick grin made him look about nine years old.

"I'll see what I can do." She didn't mention her appointment with Joe tomorrow to review her photos. "Now, would you like to see the pictures of yesterday's festivities? There are several I think might work well in the paper."

"Absolutely!"

Sebastian selected a half-dozen, and she agreed to email the images to him, along with the article as soon as she finished it.

After downing the last of his tea, he pushed back from the table. "I want to use at least three of these on the front page. I'll make the final selections and cut you a check as soon as I've read the article. Or perhaps you'd prefer to set up direct deposits to your bank account, since it looks like this is going to become a regular occurrence."

The sudden rush of giddy pleasure surprised her. The money itself might only feed her and keep the lights on for a week or two, but Sebastian's suggestion of an ongoing business relationship felt like a major step on the road to a new career.

She grinned in response. "Let's do it."

****

The next morning Izzy was waiting outside the salon when Chantal arrived a few minutes before nine. Some might consider the receptionist's job at a hair salon to be a step backwards, career-wise, but Izzy was pumped. To her, it represented one more piece in the puzzle.

Chantal fumbled in her purse for her keys as she approached. "I should have known you'd beat me in today." Finding them, she unlocked the door and flipped on the lights.

Izzy followed her inside. "I'm looking forward to it. I'm used to being around people all day, and it's pretty quiet being home alone."

Chantal's brows shot up. "Quiet? I wouldn't call what happened Saturday quiet. Having Aldo collapse on you like that was scary enough, but then to find out he died..." A dramatic shudder shook her slender frame. "I was standing next to you, and I can hardly believe what happened."

Izzy shrugged off her jacket and hung it on a peg near the front desk. "I agree. The whole incident was surreal."

Chantal bent over the desk and turned on the computer, scrutinizing the screen as it went through its start-up routine. "Prepare yourself. In about five minutes, we're likely to hear more about Aldo Pefferman than either of us ever wanted to know." She clicked a few keys and brought up an electronic calendar. "My first appointment is with Dottie Cartwright, town gossip extraordinaire."

She barely had time to demonstrate the basic functions of the scheduling system before a heavy-set woman in her fifties pushed through the front door.

"Good morning, Dottie."

Dottie unwrapped a long, knitted scarf from around her neck. "Hi, Chantal." Then she noticed Izzy sitting at the front desk. "Who's this?"

Chantal shot Izzy a smile. "This is Izzy Munro, Dora's great-niece. She's just moved to town and has agreed to help out for a few weeks until I find a replacement for Josie. Izzy, this is Dottie Cartwright, one of my most loyal clients."

Dottie beamed at Izzy. "So nice to meet you. We were all so sad when Dora died. Everyone just adored her!"

Izzy doubted that. Although she'd loved Aunt Dora without reservation, she would be the first to admit her great-aunt could be prickly and particular, especially in her later years.

Without waiting for a response, Dottie followed Chantal to the sink and settled in to have her hair washed, chattering away the whole time. Izzy tuned them out while she worked on familiarizing herself with the salon's computer system. When a new client called for an appointment, she felt a small surge of satisfaction after she entered the information, hit Save, and it worked.

Dottie was back in the styling chair when her voice pierced Izzy's concentration. "I'm sure you heard about Aldo Pefferman."

Chantal murmured in assent as she deftly separated a section of Dottie's wet hair with the tip of her comb and secured it with a clip.

Dottie continued her monologue. "We're all upset, of course, but I'll tell you who was hit the hardest — that manager of his, Lorna Ferris. Everyone knows they've been having a flaming affair ever since she arrived in town."

Her comment piqued Izzy's interest. The first time she'd met Aldo and Lorna, she'd noticed his attentions seemed more personal than might be considered appropriate from an employer, and Lorna's response had appeared ambivalent, at best.

Dottie pulled a piece of hard candy from her purse, unwrapped it, and popped it into her mouth, but it barely slowed the stream of words. Izzy had never heard someone so adept at talking with their mouth full.

"And Serena Pefferman can play the grief-stricken widow all she wants, but mark my words, inside she's jumping for joy."

That didn't jibe with Izzy's impression of Aldo's wife. Her concern for her husband had appeared genuine, both before and after his collapse.

"All you have to do is look at that *partner* of hers, Dr. Holder, to know they're at it hot and heavy."

Chantal stopped mid-snip. "Now, Dottie, we don't know that."

Dottie jerked her head around with a petulant expression, yanking her hair from Chantal's fingers. "Those of us who pay attention do."

When her client bent her head to search her purse for another piece of candy, Chantal met Izzy's gaze in the mirror and rolled her eyes.

Dottie's head popped back up, her mouth full again. "I'll tell you what else I know..."

The fact that Chantal was able to finish Dottie's haircut without chopping off an ear — or one of her own fingers — and style the woman's bushy mop into a smooth bob, in spite of her non-stop talking, was nothing short of a miracle. Izzy was in awe.

After confirming Dottie's next appointment in the computer and sending her on her way with a smile, Izzy turned to her new employer. "I don't know how you do it."

Chantal grinned, brandishing her finishing comb. "Experience, skill, and superior powers of concentration."

"I'll say!"

"Selective deafness helps, too." They both laughed.

Over the course of the morning, several more customers came and went, and Izzy was amazed at how quickly her four-hour shift passed. At one o'clock, she picked up her purse, grabbed her jacket from the peg, and left with the promise to see Chantal in the morning.

She'd only been home a few minutes when Joe arrived, bearing two bags from a taco restaurant in Seaside.

"I didn't know what you like, so I brought fish, chicken, and vegetarian."

She ushered him in and led the way to the kitchen. "They're all great. We can mix and match. Thanks."

He set the bags on the counter and slipped off his jacket while she got plates and glasses from the cupboard. "Unless you're the kind of person who eats tacos with a knife and fork, we should probably hold off looking at your photos until we're done and can wash our hands."

Izzy laughed. "I'm definitely not that kind of person." To prove her point, she slapped a pile of paper napkins on the table between them.

They split the six tacos between them and dug in.

She started with the fish, which turned out to be much better than she expected. "This is really good, and I'm particular about my fish tacos."

Joe wiped his mouth with one of the napkins. "I'm glad you like it. The restaurant is kind of a dive, but they do know how to make tacos."

Izzy finished hers off in a few more bites, then hesitated before moving on to the next. "I don't know how you feel about talking shop while you eat, but — "

He raised one thick, dark brow. "I've got an iron stomach. After more than ten years as a homicide detective, nothing much bothers me."

"I was wondering if you'd received the final report from the Medical Examiner yet."

He hesitated, as if weighing a decision. "I suppose I can tell you, but this is strictly off the record."

"Of course."

"The final verdict was botulism poisoning, as the doctors suspected. It's a nasty way to go, starting with paralysis of the cranial nerves, then moving on to the voluntary muscles, before ultimately progressing to respiratory failure. The hospital was getting ready to put him on a respirator when he died."

Izzy's chest tightened as she remembered Aldo's

drooping eyelids and labored breathing. "That's scary. Do they think it was from something he ate?"

"It's possible, but the concentration of toxin in Pefferman's blood was unusually high to have come from naturally contaminated food, especially since no one else reported having symptoms. The doctors think it was most likely ingested directly or injected."

She pictured the insulin syringe in his wife's hand. "You don't think Serena —"

Joe shook his head. "Not Saturday afternoon, anyway. The ME said symptoms wouldn't appear for twelve to thirty-six hours, no matter how the poison was administered."

"That's a pretty broad time window."

"Which complicates the investigation." He took another bite and chewed thoughtfully. "He did give me a good place to start, though."

She tipped her chin and raised her brows, but kept eating.

"According to the pathologist, the botulinum in this case is related to Botox, the same toxin dermatologists and plastic surgeons use to reduce wrinkles. Only this stuff was a lot stronger, even more highly concentrated than a neurologist would prescribe to treat severe muscle spasms. The doc thinks it's likely Mr. Pefferman was killed by an unlicensed, foreign-made version of the substance that was twenty-eight-hundred times the estimated lethal dose."

Izzy choked at the number and reached for her water glass. Eyes still watering, she asked, "Why would anyone manufacture a product like that?"

"Beats me, but the ME said to look for a vial or box marked *For Research Purposes Only.*"

"Do you think Aldo's death could have been

accidental?"

Joe replied with a skeptical frown. "It's unlikely — but possible, I suppose — if the provider was shady enough and prone to cutting corners."

"I wonder who would have access to counterfeit Botox, and where they would get it."

"That's what we have to find out."

She continued eating while her mind sifted through various options, then she considered Dottie Cartwright's claims. "You were right about hair salons being tuned in to the pulse of a town. Aldo's death was all anyone talked about this morning. It might be baseless gossip, but Chantal's customers seem convinced that Serena Pefferman is romantically involved with her business partner, Marcus Holder. They also said Aldo was notorious for having numerous affairs, including with the manager of Taste of Torino, Lorna Ferris. I don't know any of them well enough to judge the validity of those claims."

"It's worth looking into. People love to talk, and you have to take gossip with a hefty grain of salt, but there's often at least some truth behind the stories."

After finishing the last of the tacos, they washed their hands together at the kitchen sink before sitting down to review Izzy's photos of the Halloween parade. Izzy got out her laptop, and Joe moved his chair so they could both see the screen at the same time. At first, the simple act felt oddly intimate, but the sensation quickly passed. She moved through the photos, slowing when she reached the shots taken outside the bakery.

"Who's that behind Mr. Pefferman?" Joe pointed to the shadowed figure of one of the Grim Reapers.

"I don't know. There were several people dressed in the same costume roaming through the crowd. When you first told me Aldo had been poisoned, I thought they might have been involved, but now that we know the poisoning occurred earlier..." She shrugged.

"I'll ask around and see if anyone knows who they were. They might belong to some club or civic group."

"And then there's this." She clicked on the final image.

He leaned forward, squinting. "Who is that?"

Izzy adjusted the photo as she had earlier.

"Is that Lorna Ferris, the bakery manager?" He peered closer. "She doesn't look very happy."

"To put it mildly."

"And this was before Pefferman collapsed?"

"Yes. It's the last shot I took."

"I wonder who she's so mad at."

Izzy had been asking herself the same question since she'd first seen the picture. "Aldo had confronted Christos Getz on the sidewalk just before this photo was taken. If Lorna was in love with her boss, as the gossips suggest, maybe she was still angry about the fight Wednesday night. Or maybe she and Aldo had just had an argument. Possibly the mere sight of him with Serena infuriated her. Who knows?"

"I think I need to do some background investigation on Ms. Ferris."

Izzy closed the file of photos and sat back. "You have your work cut out for you. The circumstances surrounding Aldo's death are murky and confusing."

"Murder is rarely easy." Joe pushed to his feet. "Thanks for sharing your pictures and the beauty shop gossip. You've given me several avenues of inquiry to pursue."

She walked him to the door. "Thank you for lunch, even if the conversation was a little morbid."

His solid features lightened in a rare, brief smile. "Death seems to be our common ground...so far, anyway." He stepped outside, then paused on the front walk and turned. "I've always appreciated your observations and input. Would you be willing to help again if I find I need some extra-departmental assistance?"

"Off the record?"

"For the time being, at least." He frowned. "Who would you tell, anyway? You've only been in town a couple of weeks."

"Since I witnessed Aldo's collapse firsthand, Sebastian suggested he might want me to write an article for the *Acorn*."

Joe rolled his eyes. "Great. Just what I need — the press on my case."

Her brows rose in wounded innocence. "Hey, it's me we're talking about here, not some nameless member of the press."

"All right. I'll be sure to let you know when I have something you can share with the readers of the local rag."

"And I'll be sure to keep asking."

He sighed. "I'd expect nothing less."

****

Her next opportunity presented itself the following afternoon.

The morning was busy at Cece's. When Izzy wasn't on the phone, she was greeting customers and making sure the coffee maker never ran dry. The part-time manicurist was on duty, and Vivian came in to get a pedicure, so she took a break for a short chat. By now, everyone in town had heard that the police were treating Aldo Pefferman's death as suspicious, so naturally it was the hot topic of conversation. Each client seemed to have her own opinion of the most likely scenario and culprit.

By one o'clock, all Izzy wanted was the quiet of her little green cottage on Lincoln Street, but her peace was short-lived. She was slicing an apple for lunch when her phone rang. She glanced at the screen, then wiped her hands before answering.

"Hi. What's up?"

Joe De Rossi's response was direct and to-the-point, as usual. "Are you busy at three?"

"This afternoon?"

"Yeah. When I interviewed Serena Pefferman yesterday, she gave us permission to search Aldo's office above the bakery. She gave me the key from her husband's ring, saying the office was Aldo's private domain and she hardly ever went there. Unfortunately, she was a lot less cooperative regarding a search of their home, so I've had to request a warrant for that."

Izzy thought about Serena's claim that she rarely visited her husband's office, then remembered how close-lipped Bryce had been about his cases and clients, refusing to discuss them even in general terms. "A lot of people prefer to keep their business dealings private."

"True, but Pefferman has no need for privacy or secrets now, and we owe it to him and the rest of the community to find the truth. Anyway, the regular police photographer is on the scene of a multi-car collision on Highway 1, and I was hoping you could bring your camera to record anything we find."

She hesitated. She'd consulted with Joe in the past, but never immediately after the death had occurred, and then only in an unofficial capacity. "Sure, I guess. Will the Carmel detective be okay with that? I'm happy to help—I just don't want to step on anyone's toes."

"I've already run it past her, and she's open to any assistance we can get. I know the situation is unconventional, but you have some experience photographing crime scenes after the fact, and you *see* things."

Joe had investigated dozens, possibly hundreds, of homicides in his years with the SFPD. If he thought Izzy could help solve Aldo's murder, she wouldn't say no. "I'll do my best."

"I know you will. I'll meet you in front of Taste of Torino at three."

****

When she arrived at the bakery, a long line of patrons snaked out the door and onto the sidewalk. Either half the town was starving for pastry, or morbid curiosity drew them to the late councilman's place of business. Izzy stood on tiptoe and peered over the cluster of heads to Lorna Ferris, who was working behind the counter. The woman's face was ashen, and her hair looked like a goat had chewed it.

A finger tapped her shoulder. "Izzy."

She lowered her heels and turned to Joe, who had walked up behind her. "I'm surprised they're open. Poor Lorna looks miserable. I would have expected Mrs. Pefferman to close the shop, at least until after the funeral."

Joe's upper lip curled slightly. "During our interview she seemed more annoyed by the legal formalities than grief-stricken at her husband's death. I imagine she wants to cash in on the increased public interest while it lasts."

"That surprises me, based on her behavior Saturday afternoon, but maybe the gossip is true."

"Today wasn't the time to ask the widow straight out if she's having an affair, but I'll be pursuing that angle, along with anything else we turn up." He put a hand on her back to urge her through the crowd. "Oh, by the way, I found out about the people dressed in the Grim Reaper costumes at the parade."

"I assume they weren't a gang of pickpockets or members of a Satanist cult."

Joe chuckled. "Nothing so dastardly. They were members of the local Kiwanis Club who volunteered to help the police with crime suppression and crowd control." He gestured to a door tucked between Taste of Torino and Christos Getz's skin care shop next door. "Let's go up. Detective Nolan is waiting for us."

As Joe led the way up the narrow flight of stairs to the second floor, he turned and glanced back over his shoulder. "You'll like Michelle. She's a little older than you—early forties, I'd say—and very professional. Carmel PD isn't big enough to have a full-time detective, so the officers volunteer to take turns. Michelle's been filling the post for the past year or so. She's a whiz at tracking down jewelry store burglars and out-of-town hit-and-run drivers, but she's never investigated a homicide before. That's why the chief called the DA for help."

One flight up, they reached a landing with a door on each side. One was closed, but the door on the right stood open, revealing a spacious room with two windows overlooking the street. It was outfitted as an office with a desk and computer, bookcases filled with three-ring binders, and a small refrigerator. A comfortable-looking sofa sat against the far wall. A large, framed photograph of the Bixby Bridge in Big Sur had been removed from the wall beside the desk, revealing a wall safe, and stood propped up on the floor. A pair of uniformed CPD officers were in the middle of a conversation, but stopped and looked over when Joe and Izzy entered.

Joe stepped forward. "Michelle, I'd like you to meet Isadora Munro, the woman I was telling you about. Izzy, this is Detective Michelle Nolan."

Detective Nolan was a fit-looking woman of medium height with brown hair cut in a low-maintenance pixie style. Izzy smiled and shook her hand. "I hope you don't mind my being here. I promise not to touch anything."

Michelle returned her smile. "Joe says great things about you, and we can use all the help we can get on this one." She gestured to her colleague, a good-looking, dark-haired man of around thirty. "This is Officer Lopez. He'll be working with us on this case."

After Joe and Izzy shook hands with the young man, Detective Nolan turned to Joe. "Did Serena Pefferman give you the combination to the safe?"

"She says she doesn't have it. Hopefully, we'll find it in the desk or one of those binders. Let's get started."

"What about a password for the laptop?"

He shook his head. "If we don't find it here, the forensic IT specialist with the DA's office should be able to access the hard drive."

While the others donned blue latex gloves and began searching the desk drawers, Izzy walked around the office, trying to get a feel for the man who'd worked there. The décor was European and expensive. The desk appeared to be antique, with an inlaid top and carved, gilded legs—possibly a nod to his Italian heritage—and the dark green, button-tufted leather chair behind it radiated an aura of money and power. A gilt-framed mirror hung on one wall, opposite a grand oil painting of a nude woman lounging on a tasseled sofa that would have been at home in any museum. The rug covering the wooden floor was thick and plush and woven in a classic Persian design. The only anomaly in the room was the brown corduroy sofa. It looked like a refugee from someone's grandma's basement.

Except for the sofa, everything was of the highest quality, and Izzy had to wonder what it was doing there. Always fascinated by objects that appeared out of place with their surroundings, she removed her camera from its case and snapped a few pictures. Joe had asked her to focus on the details of the scene, and the photographs would help prod her memory later.

She was working her way around the room, taking shots of each item and every nook and cranny, when Officer Lopez called out to Joe and Michelle.

"I think I found something." He had opened the small refrigerator and was holding up a glass vial. "There are five of these, and the label says it's insulin. I also found an empty one in the trash."

Joe inspected the vial. "Bag them all. We'll send them to the lab to confirm the contents and look for prints."

Michelle Nolan's brows knit in a thoughtful frown. "If they are insulin, and Mr. Pefferman was diabetic, it would make sense for him to keep a supply in his office."

Izzy remembered Serena's actions on Saturday afternoon. "When Mrs. Pefferman caught him eating chocolate at the parade, she ran back inside and returned a few minutes later with the syringe. It probably came from this office. It's unlikely Aldo would have kept diabetic supplies in multiple places in the same building." She glanced at Joe. "I wonder how she got in if he had his keys with him."

"That's a question I'll ask her when we serve the search warrant on the house."

While Officer Lopez loaded the glass vials into an evidence bag and Joe and Michelle paged through the binders from the bookcase, Izzy continued her photographic survey. She was standing by the far end of the sofa, next to the window, when a glint of gold caught her eye. She bent to get a better look and spotted a few links of chain peeking out from behind the front leg of the sofa. After photographing it in place, she called to Joe. "There's something over here."

He laid the binder he was examining on the desk and joined her.

"I took a picture but didn't touch it."

He nodded, then reached under the sofa's brown corduroy skirt and withdrew a gold locket necklace. When he straightened and turned it toward the light from the window, Izzy craned her neck to get a better look. The heart-shaped locket had a floral design carved on the front and a tiny catch on one side. Joe pressed the catch with his thumbnail, and the locket opened, revealing a miniature photograph of a young man. He had longish blond hair and a narrow face with high cheekbones. On the other half of the heart, opposite the photo, was a carved inscription — *From I.A. to K A., my wife, my heart.*

"It's pretty. I wonder who it belonged to. Based on where we found it, someone must have lost it in here." Izzy regarded the necklace closely.

Her mind hummed with possibilities. The man in the

photo clearly wasn't Aldo Pefferman. Who were *I.A.* and *K.A.*? The locket might have belonged to one of Aldo's reputed paramours, or it could have been dropped accidentally by one of the cleaners. It might be nothing—or it could be the key to solving the murder.

CHAPTER SEVEN

That night, Izzy lay in bed, sifting through mental images of Aldo's office. The furnishings and artwork, the contents of the refrigerator, the locket. What did it all mean? What did it say about the man? Joe was counting on her observations and insights, but she had nothing.

The next day, she awoke late and fuzzy-headed. She barely had time to feed Bogart before dashing out the door without breakfast. Fortunately, the coffee maker was brewing at CeCe's, and Chantal had brought in a plate of her mother's Portuguese pastries. After a busy morning at the salon, Izzy decided to give her brain a rest and get some fresh air.

The sun was shining, and since she hadn't received any specific requests from Sebastian, it was the perfect afternoon to explore the town on her own. She'd had the idea of putting together a series of photos for an exhibition, or possibly even a book, featuring the nooks and crannies of Carmel-by-the-Sea. Something identifiable and evocative of the quirky hamlet, yet different from the usual tourist fare. She decided to start at the east end of town, where Ocean Avenue began its downhill march from Highway 1 to the sea.

She took several shots from different angles of a patch of late-season wild poppies blooming at the foot of the stone World War I Memorial Arch. The scene had a wistful air Sebastian might appreciate for Friday's Veteran's Day issue of the *Acorn*. Moving into the main business district, she found herself intrigued by several window displays and snapped photos of a pink-clad fairy offering a pair of dangling diamond earrings, a series of hand-painted miniature enameled teapots, each with an image of a different rooster, and a large oil painting of a forlorn-looking blue dog wearing a red collar.

By four o'clock, she'd worked her way down several blocks of Ocean Avenue. Taste of Torino was just ahead, and she could hear a cappuccino calling her name. The shop was busy, but not to the point of being crowded, and Lorna was behind the counter, as usual.

When Izzy reached the front of the line, Lorna smiled. "It's nice to see you again—Izzy, isn't it? You're becoming a regular."

Izzy returned her smile. If the woman was mourning the loss of her boss and rumored lover, she showed no sign of it today. Her eyes were bright and her expression unburdened.

Izzy ordered her coffee, then took it outside where the afternoon light was beginning to gather over the ocean in preparation for what promised to be a spectacular sunset. When she glanced across the street, she was struck by an imposing building set on a rise above lush gardens that appeared to be enveloped in a golden glow. She had to get pictures.

Keeping a close eye on the out-of-town drivers who might not be keeping a close eye on her, she crossed the wide, divided street at the corner.

Built in the 1920s in the Territorial adobe style, the town library had always been one of Izzy's favorite places. During her childhood visits, Aunt Dora had taken her every week to check out a new selection of books. Bright blue trim and an orange-tiled roof accented the white stucco exterior, and the main floor reading room was lit by an enormous, two-story arched window.

Izzy was trying to figure out how to operate her camera without setting her coffee on the sidewalk when a woman's voice interrupted her fumbling.

"You can set your cup here, dear. We'll keep an eye on it for you."

Startled, she glanced up. A couple who appeared to be in their seventies were seated on a park bench a few feet away.

"Oh, thank you." Izzy walked over to them.

The woman reached for her cup. "Are you visiting from out of town?"

"No, I've recently moved here." She transferred her cup to her left hand and offered her right. "Izzy Munro."

"I'm Dina Korman, and this is my husband Kurt. Welcome to Carmel."

"Thank you." As Izzy handed the woman her coffee, something familiar about the pair niggled at her memory. "Did I see you at the City Council meeting last week?"

"We were there, all right," Kurt Korman grumbled. "What a fiasco."

"It was rather…dramatic."

"I wish Getz had taken that blasted Pefferman down a notch or two."

His wife placed a gentle restraining hand on his arm. "Now, Kurt..."

He shook it off. "I mean it. And I'm glad someone finally stepped up and took care of him. This town is better off without him."

His vehemence took Izzy aback. "Obviously, you weren't a fan of Aldo Pefferman."

Kurt waved his cane. "You're darn right, I wasn't. He's the reason I can barely walk."

"What happened?"

When hot color rose in Kurt's face and he began to sputter, Dina patted his thigh. "Don't upset yourself, dear." She glanced at Izzy. "We live across the street from the Peffermans, and last year we were involved in a legal dispute with Aldo. Kurt built a beautiful enclosure at the end of our driveway to hold our trash barrels, and Aldo objected, saying it was too close to the street." A grim look came into her eyes. "I guess he preferred the sight of big blue plastic bins."

"That self-important peacock took his complaint to the Planning Commission and pressured them to make me tear it down," Kurt interjected.

Dina squeezed her husband's hand. "The stress gave Kurt a stroke, and he's only now starting to recover."

Since Izzy had barely known Aldo and had just met the Kormans, all she could do was nod sympathetically. "I'm so sorry."

Kurt grunted. "Aldo Pefferman may have enjoyed being a big fish in a small pond, but believe me, a lot of people in this town are glad to see the last of him."

Izzy had no response to that, so she snapped a few quick shots of the library, then retrieved her coffee from

Dina and took her leave.

The Kormans' story troubled her all evening. Despite his celebrity and jolly manner, Aldo had clearly had enemies. The next morning, Izzy decided to mention the meeting to Chantal and get her take on the situation.

After the stylist settled her first customer under a heat lamp to accelerate her color processing, Izzy joined her at the coffee maker. She described the encounter and repeated Kurt's final comment.

Chantal sipped her coffee and nodded. "That doesn't surprise me, and it sounds like Dina was restraining herself. You should hear the things she says about Aldo when she gets wound up—blames him completely for her husband's stroke. Kurt's a retired aeronautical engineer and was always super sharp and very active. He used to play golf or tennis nearly every day, and now he can barely stand. I'm sure it's difficult for Dina. As a neurologist, she treats stroke victims all the time, but she can't do anything to speed up her own husband's recovery."

"That is sad. I can see why they have so much animosity toward Mr. Pefferman."

"Animosity is too tame a word. More like outright hatred. Still, Kurt's an invalid, and I can't imagine Dina Korman killing anyone. She's a doctor."

Izzy remembered one of her more sensational claims at Pacific Western, in which she determined that an elderly woman had been murdered by her doctor son who couldn't wait for his inheritance. "Being a doctor doesn't necessarily disqualify someone from being a killer, but in this case, I think you're right. Kurt is dependent on his wife, and she seems devoted to him. I doubt she'd risk being arrested and leaving him to fend for himself, no matter how much she hated Aldo

Pefferman."

Chantal leaned back and rested her elbows on the counter next to the coffee maker, taking some of the weight off her feet. "He wasn't a very nice man. When you think about it, there are a lot of reasons somebody might have wanted to kill him."

"I'm far from an expert, but in my experience, there are a limited number of motives for murder, assuming the killer isn't a psychopath. It's usually desire, hatred, jealousy, greed, or revenge." Izzy took a sip of her coffee while the random bits of information she'd gleaned thus far about Aldo's death coalesced into a single impression. "This case feels like greed or revenge."

Chantal shivered inside her leopard print sweater. "That was impressive, if creepy. I've never known anyone who had personal experience with murder. How did you come to that conclusion?"

Izzy reached around her friend to freshen her coffee with a splash from the pot. "It's not complicated. You start with the basics. Aldo was killed by an overdose of an unusual type of botulinum toxin, which isn't easy to obtain. His death couldn't have been a crime of passion or opportunity. It had to have been planned in advance."

Chantal's heavily fringed eyes widened. "Botulinum? As in Botox?"

Izzy nodded as the hot brew warmed her from within.

"Then the police don't have to look any further than Serena." Chantal's tone left no room for indecision or doubt.

"Why is that?"

"She and her partner spend half their time at their rejuvenation spa injecting people with that stuff."

"I'm afraid that doesn't help much. According to the pathologist, Aldo wasn't killed with the same substance that's used for cosmetic procedures in this country. He was injected with a highly-concentrated, illegal variety, probably manufactured in Mexico."

"Who would have something like that?"

"Mostly illegal back-street clinics, not upscale spas in places like Carmel."

Chantal appeared unconvinced. "Still, you have to wonder…"

"You do," Izzy agreed. "Money was the primary motive in most of the insurance claims I investigated that turned out to be murder. Serena Pefferman probably had the most to gain financially from her husband's death, although there might be others with a big stake, too. There might be someone who owed Aldo a lot of money, or a business partner who stood to take full control of a joint venture at his death. The police have a lot of digging to do."

The kernel of an idea began to form in Izzy's brain. Joe hadn't said anything about requesting a search warrant for Serena Pefferman's business yet. Maybe she could do some preliminary reconnaissance to save him time. "I think I might stop by Mrs. Pefferman's wellness spa for a consultation about my crows' feet."

Chantal snorted. "What crows' feet? You don't have crows' feet."

"Sure I do. Right here, see?" Izzy turned the side of her face and pointed above her cheekbone.

Chantal leaned forward and squinted. "Nope. Don't see a thing."

"What about the forehead?" Izzy raised her brows as high as they would go.

"Maybe a line or two, but very faint."

She heaved a dramatic sigh. "Those faint lines are ruining my body image and self-esteem. I'm sure a concerned professional would urge me to do something about them right away, before I'm so traumatized I become a recluse."

Chantal burst out laughing. "Well, we can't let that happen. It would be tragic."

"I'd better call for an appointment as soon as I get home."

"Why wait? If you want to avert catastrophe, you should call now."

Izzy suppressed a grin. "I'm lucky to have such an understanding boss."

"Yes, you are." Chantal checked her watch. "I've got to get Mrs. Handley out from under that lamp before her hair turns orange. If you visit Serena Pefferman's spa, promise me you'll be careful. The woman might have killed her own husband. Who knows what she'd do to a stranger?"

"Don't worry. I'm not going to question or confront her. That's up to the police. I just want to take a look around, check the place out."

Izzy returned to the front desk and placed a call to Beauty by the Bay Rejuvenation Spa. She explained her concerns and made an appointment for the following afternoon. After she hung up, her body thrummed with nervous energy. She had never participated in an active investigation to the point of personally interacting with a suspect. Was that smart? Was it safe? Was she interfering where she didn't belong? She didn't want to make things more difficult for Joe and the police. She just wanted to help find Aldo's killer.

When she arrived home and checked her phone, she discovered an email from Sebastian, asking if she had any photos to submit for this week's issue of the *Acorn*. He was in San Francisco but was working with the staff in Carmel to finalize the layout. She opened her laptop and forwarded the shot of the World War I Memorial Arch, and by the time she'd stuck a couple slices of leftover pizza in the microwave, she'd received an acceptance and a notice of a direct deposit from her bank.

She smiled as she read the email. Although a weekly photo or two and the occasional short article for the local paper wouldn't pay the bills, every little bit helped.

****

At two-twenty-five the following afternoon, Izzy stood in front of Beauty by the Bay, waffling about her decision. The spa was located on the top level of a two-story, outdoor shopping mall on Ocean Avenue that was home to some of the most exclusive retailers in town. Several decorative jars of facial and body creams were artfully arranged in the window in front of a black curtain. After a few minutes of mental back-and-forth, she drew a deep breath and opened the door.

The main room was decorated in minimalist luxury — cream walls, pale wood floating shelves, a bare hint of sandalwood aroma, and some kind of peaceful mood music playing softly in the background. Everything was designed to foster calm and relaxation...as well as loosen a client's grip on her purse strings.

Serena Pefferman rose from behind a simple, blond wood desk with a smile. If she recognized Izzy from the scene of her husband's collapse, she gave no sign. "Ms. Munro? Good afternoon. It's lovely to meet you. I'm

Serena Pefferman. Please have a seat." With a graceful sweep of her hand, she indicated a blush-colored upholstered chair on the other side of the desk.

"Thank you." Izzy's fingers brushed the fabric. Raw silk. She hated to think what the prices for products and treatments at this place must be. Serena and her business partner had clearly spared no expense creating a lush environment.

The woman across the desk showed no signs of recent bereavement. Her appearance was composed, clear-eyed, and professional. Izzy decided to prod a little to see if she could break through that perfect exterior. "Serena Pefferman? Are you the wife of the late city councilman? I'm so sorry about your husband's death. You must be devastated."

Serena clasped her hands in front of her on the desk. "Thank you. It was very sad."

It was the least-devastated devastation Izzy had ever seen. Chantal might be right in her assessment of the merry widow.

Serena tapped her nails on the desk in a subtle signal to return to business. "Now, I understand you have concerns about your skin. How may we help you?"

Izzy stared in fascination at the woman's lips as she spoke. They were so smooth, sharply defined, and unnaturally plump, she might have been carved from a block of wax. After a few seconds, she realized Serena had asked her a question and pulled herself back into the conversation. "I turned forty a few weeks ago, and I'm afraid the years are starting to show."

Serena's perfect brows quivered but didn't budge as she regarded Izzy's face. "I'm glad you came in...and not a minute too soon." She reached for what appeared to be a giant magnifying glass on a stand. "I'll need to examine your skin to see what we can do."

Izzy leaned forward as Serena used the glass to inspect every tiny line and pore. She felt like a rare insect being examined by an entomologist.

Finally, Serena sat back and slid the magnifier to the side of the desk. "I'm happy to say, it's not too late. I believe we can help you."

Izzy refrained from telling the woman what she could do with her help and smiled politely. "I'm so relieved."

Serena rose from the desk and took a small jar from the shelves behind her, then offered it to Izzy. "If you use this cream twice a day to repair the sun damage and reduce the fine lines, you should begin to see results in three to four weeks."

Izzy examined the jar and checked the list of ingredients, then unscrewed the lid and sniffed. The scent was a light floral mix. "How much does this cost?"

"Only three hundred thirty-five dollars. I think you'll agree that's a bargain to erase ten years from your appearance."

Three hundred thirty-five dollars? Did some women actually pay that much for a few ounces of fancy cold cream?

Izzy returned the jar to the desk. "Will it also take care of the frown lines in my forehead?"

"I'm afraid not. Those will require an injection with botulinum toxin."

Izzy's instinctive reaction must have shown, because Serena hastened to add, "But don't let that scare you. You'll barely feel a thing. Dr. Holder is a wizard with a needle. If you like, I can see if he's free for a quick, preliminary consultation."

"Thank you. That would be helpful."

Serena excused herself and headed for a doorway beneath a sign that read *Treatment Rooms*. As soon as she was out of sight, Izzy rose and slipped behind the desk. While Serena had been examining her face, Izzy's gaze had been drawn to the products displayed on the shelves behind her. She particularly wanted to check out one pyramid of small white boxes with purple printing that were about the size of a vial used for injections.

Sure enough, the boxes proclaimed BOTOX in bold letters. As she scanned the array, she noticed three boxes with slightly different lettering. The colors were the same, but unlike the others, these did not feature the name of the manufacturer, and something was written down the side in words too small to read from this distance. She reached for one to take a closer look, but heard voices approaching in the hall. In a matter of seconds, she pulled out her phone, snapped several pictures, and was back in her chair by the time Serena returned, accompanied by the man Izzy had seen with her at the City Council meeting.

"Ms. Munro, I'd like to introduce Dr. Marcus Holder, the Medical Director of Beauty by the Bay. He'll be happy to address any concerns you might have about our treatments."

Izzy took his offered hand. If Serena had been cheating on her husband with this man, she was inclined to give the woman a pass. Even from across the room, she'd been able to see that he was handsome, but up close, Marcus Holder was positively dazzling, with lightly curling black hair, sea blue eyes, and a magnetic smile. On top of that, his flawless complexion was a walking advertisement for the spa.

"Ms. Munro, I'm delighted to meet you. Serena tells me you're interested in Botox treatment but have a few concerns."

Izzy had prepared several questions in advance. The only challenge was remembering them in the face of the doctor's blatant charm. "Um, yes. I have to admit, the thought of being injected with a deadly toxin makes me nervous. How safe is it?"

"Let me put your fears to rest. Our procedure is completely safe. The concentration we use is fully approved by the FDA and is much too low to cause any health problems to the patient." He walked behind the desk and took a box from the display on the shelf.

Izzy's attention sharpened when she noticed it was one of the boxes with different markings.

"If you look closely, you'll see —" He peered at the box, and his smooth forehead almost puckered. He thrust it at his partner as if it were a live grenade. "Serena, how did this get here? Get rid of it immediately!"

Izzy's stomach fluttered, then tightened. "Is there a problem?"

Dr. Holder's reassuring expression returned. "It's nothing to worry about. Our supplier must have made an error with our last shipment. We would never have used it. I assure you, we take every precaution to safeguard the well-being of our clients. Now, how soon would you like to make an appointment?"

Izzy rose so abruptly, the elegant chair wobbled on the smooth wood floor, and she had to grab the back to keep it from falling. "I'm...um...not quite ready to take that step." She scurried toward the door with Marcus and Serena in hot pursuit. "I'll call you."

"Don't you want the cream?" Serena called after her, holding up the jar. "It works wonders on aging skin! Or how about fillers for your lips?"

"Next time, maybe." Izzy dashed out the door and scurried down the elevated sidewalk, dodging clusters of window-shopping tourists.

When she reached Ocean Avenue, she crossed the street before pausing to glance over her shoulder. Assured she wasn't being pursued by a face cream-waving assailant, she stopped for a moment to catch her breath and allow her nerves to settle. Serena and her partner might not accost potential customers on the sidewalk like Christos Getz's employees, but their approach was just as high-pressure.

Anxious to share the results of her visit to Beauty by the Bay with Joe, Izzy stepped off the busy sidewalk into a quiet courtyard and pulled out her phone. The call went straight to voicemail, so she left a message, asking him to call her.

When she got home, she found Bogart curled up on the sofa, fast asleep. He looked so cozy, she made herself a cup of tea, picked up a book, and joined him. The feline bestirred himself just long enough to resettle on her stomach and remained there without moving for the next two hours. When he finally awoke, he stretched until his front paws tickled her chin and his tail brushed her knees.

Izzy smiled and stroked his chin with a single finger, earning a rumbling purr. "I see you're awake just in time to eat. Remind me to come back as a cat in my next life."

Bogart merely blinked. When she tried to pick him up under the arms, he went limp, like a giant, overcooked noodle.

"Come on, get up. I need to start dinner or we'll both starve." She set him on the floor, swung her legs over the side of the sofa, and headed for the kitchen.

The cat followed, meowing loudly, and kept it up

while Izzy pulled a saucepan and a stockpot from the lower cabinet next to the stove.

When he rammed his head into her hand, causing her to drop the pot lid, she frowned. "What's up with you? Knock it off."

The cat walked to the door and head-butted the cat flap.

"You want to go outside? So go. I'm not stopping you."

He marched back and twined himself around her ankles, meowing the whole time, then nudged her leg.

"What? What is it?"

Bogart nudged her again, then walked to the door.

Izzy frowned and followed him. Maybe the cat flap was stuck. But when she bent and pushed it, the panel swung open freely. "See? No problem."

He meowed again and nudged her leg, then returned to the door.

"What?" Did he want her to open the door?

She unlocked the back door and held it open with a flourish. "There you go, Your Highness."

The cat meowed again, but didn't budge.

"Do you want me to come outside with you?"

He nudged her leg.

"Okay, but just for a minute. It's starting to get dark." She stepped out onto the stone patio, muttering under her breath. "I don't know why you suddenly can't take care of business on your own or use the litter box in the laundry room."

Bogart headed behind a bush then reappeared a moment later and meowed.

"Fine. I'm going back inside now. You can come or not, your choice." When she turned and opened the door, he meowed again, louder than ever. "Stop yelling at me. The neighbors are going to think you're being murdered and call Animal Control."

He responded with a blasé blink and howled again, then turned and headed around the side of the house toward the front yard.

Izzy was tempted to let him go. After all, he wasn't really her cat. He wasn't anybody's cat. But when she heard him yowl again, she decided to follow. What if there was something truly wrong and she needed to take him to the vet?

When she rounded the side of the house, she spotted him standing in the street, regarding her with an expression of impatience. She marched down to join him. "If you think I'm going to—"

He strolled down the road a few feet, then stopped and turned, as if he were waiting for her to catch up. As she walked toward him, he took off again.

Izzy picked up her pace until she was within three feet, but the cat kept marching ahead. "Wait a minute. Are you trying to get me to take you for a walk? We don't have a harness or a leash, and besides, people don't take cats for walks."

Bogart ignored her complaints and continued walking until he reached the entrance to a large city park that had been left largely untouched—a strip of wild, natural pine forest in the middle of town.

"Don't go in there! I don't have a flashlight."

Too late. He followed the stone-dust walking path about twenty feet before darting into a clump of bushes.

Izzy stopped and peered into the gathering gloom of the park. Wisps of Spanish moss hung from the branches of the tall pines and overgrown, gnarled oaks, giving the place the spooky air of a New Orleans graveyard. She refused to take another step just to indulge a feline whim. "Bogart, get out here now."

There was a rustling in the bushes where he'd disappeared.

"This is your last chance. I'm going home." She silently counted to ten. "Okay, you're on your own."

She turned, but before she could take a step, an otherworldly, snarling scream directly overhead ripped through the dusky silence. The sounds of fluttering and flapping filled the air as every bird in the forest took flight. Bogart shot out of his hiding place, scaled Izzy's jeans like a salamander with claws, and tried to climb inside her shirt. When the scream sounded again, her heart rate stuttered then soared. Clutching the cat to her chest, she raced from the park as if the hounds of hell were at her heels.

She didn't slow down until she was safe in her kitchen with the back door locked. Heart pounding and chest heaving, she released her death grip on Bogart, and he leapt to the floor. With shaking hands, she filled a glass at the sink and drank most of it before setting it on the Formica counter with a thud.

Meow!

Izzy eyed the annoyed feline at her feet in disbelief. "Don't look at me like that. This is all your fault. What *was* that thing?"

He ignored her accusatory tone and nosed his empty food dish.

With a sigh, she filled his dish and refreshed his water before fixing a bowl of chicken rice soup for herself. She'd planned to actually cook tonight but no way was that happening now. She barely had enough energy to open the can and dump it into the pot.

After dinner, she retired to the living room, where she stretched out on the sofa and turned on the TV.

Bogart decided to join her instead of heading back outside to do whatever it was he usually did at night, and made himself comfortable on her stomach. As Izzy watched Miss Marple poke around a small English village that looked a lot like Carmel-by-the-Sea, but with a duck pond, she stroked his mink-like brown fur, marveling at its lush softness. She must have fallen asleep sometime before ten, because when she awoke, Bogart was snoring on her chest, and Miss Marple had solved the mystery. She set him on the floor with an admonishment to stay out of trouble and went to bed.

Five hours later, a loud hissing sound woke her with a start. She opened her eyes to the sight of a pair of glowing golden orbs. "Bogart, I thought I told you — "

He hissed again, arching his back until his fur stood on end like a gelled Mohawk. Then he hopped to the top of the dresser and pressed his nose against the slats of the closed blinds. Tossing the covers aside with a frown, Izzy climbed out of bed, parted the blinds, and peeked out.

A dark figure stood in the street facing her house, silhouetted by the light over Vivian's front porch. Suddenly, the person raised one hand, and a flash of light hit Izzy in the eyes, temporarily blinding her. When she opened her eyes, the light — apparently a flashlight beam — had dropped to illuminate a spot in her front yard.

A guttural growl issued from deep in Bogart's throat, and Izzy gasped. There on the lawn, not fifteen feet away, lay a full-grown mountain lion, staring back at her and flicking its long, thick tail. Between a pair of huge paws lay something that must have been the big cat's dinner. Slowly, its lips parted in a silent snarl, displaying an impressive set of fangs..

CHAPTER EIGHT

Heart pounding, Izzy snapped the blinds shut and jumped back from the window. Her gaze dropped to Bogart, who stood frozen on the dresser in full alert mode.

There's a mountain lion in the front yard.

She took several deep breaths to slow her pulse, then ventured back to the window and peeked out. All was still. Moonlight shone through the trellis, casting a grid of shadows across the grass. Something small, square, and white lay abandoned in the yard, but the cougar was gone. Had she imagined it?

Then she had another, even more disturbing, thought. What if the creature had followed her scent from the park? It would have ended up at the back door. All cats were notoriously flexible. Could a hungry, resourceful mountain lion fit through Bogart's cat door?

What if it's already in the house?

Izzy shot a frantic glance around the room, looking for something to use as a weapon. She'd be cougar kibble before she could get close enough to whack it on the nose with Aunt Dora's silver-handled hairbrush, so that was out. She could try throwing books at it, but that might only make it angry. Then she spotted the small wooden chair tucked beneath her great-aunt's dressing table. Lion tamers used chairs, didn't they? She grabbed the chair and ventured into the hall, brandishing it in front of her.

Calling out, she turned on the light, hoping to startle the cat into fleeing if it was inside, but the house remained silent. The spare bedroom, living room, and bathroom were empty and undisturbed. Only the kitchen remained. Screwing up her courage, she raised the chair as she flipped the light switch.

Nothing.

Pent-up breath hissed from her lungs like air from a punctured tire.

Mrrow!

Izzy glanced down to find Bogart, his courage returned, standing at her feet with his eyes trained on the door.

"Oh, no you don't!" She beat him to the door and shoved the back of the chair under the knob. The rungs between the legs effectively blocked the cat flap. "You're not going out tonight, and if you want to continue this relationship, you're going to have to curtail your nocturnal activities."

He regarded her with a look of sheer disdain.

She crossed her arms. "Sorry, but it's non-negotiable. First thing in the morning, I'm going to the hardware store to buy a lock. The cat flap closes at dusk. You will not be eaten by a mountain lion on my watch."

The cat sat on the floor, staring at her and swishing his tail back and forth. After a short time, he gave up and stomped out of the room with both his nose and tail held high in the air. Izzy checked the security of the chair under the door knob, then stumbled back to bed, where she found Bogart lounging on her pillow with his butt where her nose would go. She lifted him—depositing him at the foot of the bed—flipped the pillow, and tried to go back to sleep.

When she awoke, light was streaming around the blinds. In a panic, she grabbed her phone to check the time. *Ten-thirty!* The first thing she did was run to the window and check to make sure her nocturnal visitor hadn't returned. The square white object, which in daylight appeared to be a piece of trash, still lay on the grass, but there was no sign of the lion. Izzy's pulse slowed from its adrenaline-charged rate to something approaching normal.

She pulled on a robe and headed for the kitchen. Shooting a glance into the laundry room as she passed, she noted with satisfaction that Bogart had used the litter box overnight. Maybe he would adjust to the new routine, in spite of himself. When she stepped into the kitchen, she found him sitting beside his empty bowls wearing a look of dissatisfied expectation.

Izzy picked up both bowls. "Okay, okay, Your Lordship. Breakfast is on the way."

After washing and refilling his bowls, she removed the chair from the back door. The imperious feline ate half his food, took a long drink, and then bolted out through the cat flap.

"Remember, curfew's at dusk," Izzy called after him.

She fixed herself a plate of scrambled eggs and

toast, and washed it down with two cups of coffee. She was heading for the shower when her phone rang.

"Hello?"

"Izzy? It's Joe De Rossi. I'm sorry I didn't call yesterday, but I got tied up."

"That's okay." With her phone wedged between her shoulder and ear, she kicked off her slippers and hung her robe on a hook in the tiny closet. "Yesterday afternoon, I paid a visit to Serena Pefferman's wellness spa, Beauty by the Bay, and saw something that might be useful to your investigation."

"I can't stop you from visiting a business as a private citizen, but I wish you'd talked to me first." His voice had a sharp edge of disapproval. "I hope you were careful."

She padded into the bathroom. "You know me. I'm always careful—naturally risk averse."

"That might be the perfect temperament for insurance, but this isn't the same."

"Sure it is. A man's dead, and we're working to figure out how and why." She leaned over and turned on the water in the tub. "I took some pictures, if you want to see them."

Joe muttered something under his breath. "You know I do. What are you doing this evening?"

"Nothing that I know of."

"How'd you like to go to dinner, and you can fill me in?"

"If you promise to share the results of the search of Aldo's office."

He hesitated. "I guess I can do that."

"You'd better. You're the one who invited me to be part of this investigation, remember?"

"Yeah, I know."

Izzy could picture him running a hand through his hair. She'd witnessed the gesture frequently when he was stumped by a case.

"How's seven o'clock? I'll pick you up."

"Fine. What should I wear?" She tested the water for heat, then pulled up the diverter on the tub spout, sending a loud spray from the shower head.

"How should I know? Anything you want. This is Carmel."

She stifled a laugh at his growing frustration. "Okay. See you then."

That meant she had several hours to focus on converting Aunt Dora's backyard painting studio to photography use, and put last night's scare out of her mind. After her shower, she went outside to pick up whatever was lying in the front yard and found a foam tray of the kind grocery stores use to package meat. The tray was torn and had several large puncture marks. Maybe the mountain lion had raided a neighbor's trash during the night. With her thumb and forefinger, Izzy picked the thing up and carried it to the garage to deposit in her own bin.

After a quick trip inside to wash her hands, she headed to the studio to make a list of things she needed from the home center, including a lock for the cat flap. First on the list was a space heater, since the large, open room was too chilly to work in comfortably. She had also decided to hang drywall on one wall. It would make a more neutral, and flexible, backdrop than the current bare boards if she decided to branch out into portraits or still life compositions at some point. Drywall required screws, tape, plaster, and paint, and she would need some basic tools.

She scanned the final list with a grimace, but told

herself if she wasn't willing to invest in her new life, she didn't deserve to have it. She went back inside to grab her purse and keys, then hopped into the car and headed for the highway.

An hour later, she was back in her driveway, staring through the open liftgate of the Subaru, trying to figure out the best way to haul the materials back to the studio.

"Can I help?"

She turned with a smile. "Sebastian! Your timing is perfect."

Dressed in an oatmeal cable-knit sweater, pressed khakis, and polished loafers, he looked like a Brooks Brothers model. She wondered if the man owned anything as plebian as a sweatshirt or jeans.

He bent and peered into the back of the SUV. "The drywall's on top, so we'll take that first. Is it going into the house?"

"No. I'm doing some minor updating to the building out back. I want to repurpose it into a photography studio."

"Dora's painting studio? That's wonderful! She would be thrilled to know it was being used for creative pursuits again."

He carefully slid the top sheet of drywall out. "If you grab that end and back up slowly, I'll get the front. Is it too heavy?"

"I don't think so." Izzy had asked an employee at the home center to cut the sheets in half so they would fit in her car. She figured that would help with the weight, too.

She held her breath as they carried the unwieldy load around the side of the house to the studio, afraid she would drop her end or bump into something and risk damaging the material. When they finally stood the sheet upright against the wall where she intended to hang it, she breathed a sigh of relief.

Sebastian dusted off his hands and cast his gaze around the room. "This will make a perfect work space for you. Would you like some help? I'm pretty handy."

"That would be great, but you're clearly getting ready to go somewhere nice."

He glanced down in surprise. "What? These are my work clothes."

Of course, they are. "In that case, I'll take all the help I can get."

His expression brightened, and he smiled. "All right, then. Let's get busy."

By one o'clock, all the materials were in place in the studio, the space heater was plugged in, and the drywall was screwed into place with the first coat of mud on the seams.

Izzy stood back, wiping her hands on an old towel she'd borrowed from the kitchen as she surveyed their work. "I'm impressed. You weren't kidding when you said you were handy. I wouldn't have expected a member of the San Francisco Larrabee banking dynasty to know a screwdriver from a putty knife."

Sebastian took the towel to flick the dust from his loafers. "I am a man of many talents."

"You certainly are."

"And I have to wonder how an insurance claims examiner picked up such practical skills."

"Bryce, my former fiancé, used to watch a lot of DIY home improvement shows, although I never understood why. The man wouldn't pick up a hammer for something as simple as hanging a picture."

Sebastian returned the towel and straightened the

sleeves of his sweater. "You don't sound too bitter about the break-up."

"I was angry at first, but mainly because it derailed my tidy plans for the rest of my life. After a couple of days, I realized I didn't miss Bryce himself much at all — a sure sign I never really loved him, not the way I should have, if I planned to marry him."

Sebastian nodded. "A sensible conclusion. As long as you have no regrets."

"None. Now that I have some distance, I can see that life with Bryce would have been hollow and frustrating. My new life might be a work-in-progress, but at least I'm making my own choices."

"Good." He gave her shoulder a light pat. "I'll stop by tomorrow to sand the compound and apply a second coat."

"Thanks, but I think I can take it from here. I really appreciate your help. I'm days ahead of where I would have been on my own, assuming I managed to get everything out of the car and moved in here in one piece. I owe you one — actually a lot more than one — for this."

"Nonsense. What are friends for?"

With a cheery wave, he turned and walked out the door, leaving Izzy to contemplate the question — *What are friends for?* For the first time in her life, she was beginning to get an idea.

Her stomach reminded her she hadn't eaten for hours, so she locked the studio and returned to the house. She sliced a tomato and a log of fresh mozzarella and put together a simplified version of her favorite caprese sandwich from the deli near the San Francisco condo. While she ate, she scanned through her email on her laptop and watched a video on drywall finishing to refresh her memory, but found it hard to concentrate with the free-swinging cat flap taunting her from across the room.

After rinsing her dishes and loading the dishwasher, she got out a screwdriver and the lock she'd bought and set to work. Fifteen minutes later, she was satisfied that no one was going in or out through that door unless she wanted them to. Bogart might object to having his freedom curtailed, but he could either get used to it or choose another person. They'd only known each other a couple of weeks, but she was already too fond of him to risk finding tufts of bloody brown fur in the yard one morning.

The roving feline returned for dinner around five o'clock. After he finished eating, he made a beeline for the living room sofa, where he remained until Joe rang the bell at seven.

Izzy met him at the door dressed in slim black jeans and a French blue cashmere sweater, along with a pair of black flats. She never wore heels, partly because of her height, and partly because she hated them and wasn't vain enough to be miserable in the name of fashion.

In brown slacks, white shirt, and plaid sport coat—even minus the usual tie—Joe looked like a cop. A cop with a fresh shave, but a cop, nonetheless. It was a good thing he'd never tried to go into undercover work. She had a feeling Joe De Rossi would look like a cop even if he was working as a carnival barker.

After a quick, assessing glance, he smiled. "You look nice."

Izzy didn't know what to say. Should she respond in kind? That would sound weird. She settled for a simple "Thanks."

She hadn't been sure what to wear since this was more a meeting than a date, and he hadn't said where they were going. But after washing away the drywall dust and grime from her morning's efforts, she'd taken extra pains with her hair, doing her best to copy the loose curls Chantal had created.

Joe waited while she locked the front door, then they walked down the front path side by side. An unfamiliar car she assumed was his was parked in the driveway—a standard, colorless, four-door sedan that screamed *unmarked police car*. It wouldn't hurt the man to add a dash of color and creativity to his life.

When he opened the passenger door for her, she slid inside. "Do you mind if I ask where we're going, assuming it's not a big secret."

Joe climbed in and started the car. "It's not a secret at all. I wasn't sure where we could get in on a Saturday night on such short notice until I'd made a few calls."

"And…?"

"It turns out the manager of one of the best seafood restaurants on Fisherman's Wharf in Monterey is a friend of a friend, and he was happy to accommodate us."

"That sounds lovely." It also reminded her of something a movie mobster might say, but she kept that observation to herself. She didn't know Joe well enough to judge his sense of humor.

They drove up Ocean Avenue to Highway 1, then north three exits to Munras Avenue and turned left toward downtown Monterey and the ocean. Joe parked in the ramp across the street from the tourist area of Fisherman's Wharf, and they strolled down the boardwalk. The restaurant occupied an unassuming building with a plain white clapboard façade, but when they stepped inside, Izzy saw that the back wall was made entirely of glass.

While the hostess led them to their table, she glanced around the large, open room. The decorating style could best be described as *nautical rustic*, with rough wood walls hung with fishing nets, glass floats, and carved wooden pelicans, but the view was spectacular. The sun had set, and she could see the lights of Santa Cruz twinkling on the water across the bay.

They decided to start with the house specialty, clam chowder. Joe ordered locally caught halibut, while Izzy chose the crab cakes. They made small talk until the food arrived, but as soon as the server left, Joe pounced.

"So tell me what you were doing at Serena Pefferman's place of business, and what did you find?"

Izzy raised her brows. "Nice segue."

He shrugged. "I'm a cop. Polite conversation isn't my strong suit."

Something in his tone made her laugh and eased the hint of tension. "I went for a consultation about my wrinkles and sun-damaged skin."

He tipped his head from side to side, examining her face. "I don't see anything."

"That's because it's too dark in here. According to Serena, I'm a decrepit old hag who desperately needs their help."

Joe choked on his chowder and reached for his water glass.

Izzy grinned. "Actually, I went to see her to save you time and effort."

He blotted his mouth with his napkin. "How do you figure that?"

"Since you said you were working on getting a search warrant for the Pefferman house, I figured you wouldn't have had time to do anything about Beauty by the Bay yet. I thought I'd check it out and see if I could spot anything that warranted closer inspection."

"I see." He downed another spoonful of chowder. "And did you?"

"Maybe." She reached into her bag on the floor and took out her phone. Pulling up the photo she'd taken at the spa, she offered it to him.

Joe regarded it with a frown. "What am I looking at?"

"That's a decorative display of boxes of injectable botulinum toxin. Do you notice anything different about them?"

"One of them appears to have a different label. Is that significant?"

"Enlarge it."

He did, peering closely at the printing on the box. As he read it, his frown deepened. "The colors and style are similar, but there's only one licensed manufacturer of Botox in the U.S., and this box doesn't have their name and logo. I don't suppose you noticed if it said *For Research Purposes Only*."

"I didn't have time, but when Dr. Holder saw it, he snatched it off the shelf and told Serena to dispose of it immediately. He sounded angry."

Joe's lips thinned. "I suppose she did as he ordered."

Izzy nodded. "I assume so. I took off at that point."

"I'd like to have taken that box to the lab for analysis."

"There were two more like it in the display that the doctor didn't notice. If you can get a warrant quickly enough, they might still be on the shelf."

"I'll put in a request ASAP."

The conversation was put on hold while the server removed their empty soup bowls and presented their dinners.

Izzy cut a small bite off one of her perfectly crusty crab cakes and dipped it in the accompanying dish of spicy aioli before popping it into her mouth. She nearly moaned aloud in pleasure at the blend and balance of flavors. "These are fantastic."

Glancing up from his halibut, Joe smiled. "Good. Now, back to business. What was your impression of Serena Pefferman and Marcus Holder? There's been a lot of innuendo tossed around about them being romantically involved, which might be a motive to remove her husband from the picture. Did they seem cozy?"

She thought back to the previous afternoon. "Mrs. Pefferman was almost dismissive when I offered my condolences on her husband's death, but I can't say I noticed any particular warmth between her and the doctor. Their relationship appeared to be professional, at least on the surface."

"What about under the surface? You always struck me as being good at reading people, as well as situations."

She stared out the window at the cluster of lights across the bay. "My main impression of Serena is that she's cool and controlled. I don't see her allowing her actions to be governed by emotion."

"And Dr. Holder?"

"He's more animated, more of a hot reactor."

Joe nodded. "Sometimes opposites attract."

"Sometimes. And if they are having an affair, I wouldn't expect them to slobber all over each other in front of a potential client."

"Good point. Maybe their financial records will give us more information." He speared a bite of fish with his fork.

Izzy took another sip of her wine. "Okay. I've shown you mine — you show me yours."

He jerked back as if she'd bitten him. "What?"

"I told you what I found at Beauty by the Bay. You promised to tell me the results of the search of Aldo's office."

"Oh. Right. The contents of the desk and safe were a bust — nothing there but routine business records. Just to be sure, I've asked a forensic accountant with the DA's office to look them over, but everything appeared to be in order."

"What about the insulin vials in the refrigerator?"

"They were clean — regular insulin."

Izzy considered this new information as she finished the last of her crab cakes. "It's important information. I'm just not sure what it tells us. Serena likely got whatever she injected into Aldo before his death from his office, but it couldn't have been the poison because of the time frame. Did you get any useful fingerprints?"

"We got three sets, including Aldo's. We don't have Serena's yet for comparison, but I expect they'll match the ones taken from the door handle of the refrigerator. We'll run the third set through the database as a matter of routine, but we probably won't be able to identify them until we have someone to compare them to. I'd like to rule out Christos Getz, but at this point I have no grounds to request a warrant for his prints."

"He might volunteer them if you put it to him that way."

Joe released a breath with a skeptical snort. "In my

experience, people don't volunteer to give their prints to the police."

"Detective Nolan is female. Maybe Mr. Getz would be more inclined to cooperate if she asked him."

"I'm surprised at you for making such a stereotypically sexist suggestion."

Izzy lifted one shoulder in a casual shrug and smiled. "Whatever works. My mother didn't teach me much, but she did teach me that most men are basically pretty simple—present company excluded, of course."

"Of course." Joe had the grace to look disgruntled as he attacked the remainder of his halibut.

When they finished eating and the server brought the check, Izzy reached for her purse, but Joe stopped her. "Dinner's on me. I'm the one who invited you."

She wasn't sure how to respond. This dinner wasn't exactly a meeting, but it wasn't a date, either. "I know, but—"

"I can always say you're an informant and submit the receipt for reimbursement."

She noted the suspicious glint in his eyes. "You're joking, right?"

His face relaxed into a smile. "Yeah, but I could probably work something out for you if we need to."

"I'm fine. I think I'll stick with being an unpaid civilian consultant, thank you."

"Unpaid civilian consultant. I like it. It has a nice ring." He pulled several bills from his wallet and laid them on the table with the check. "Are you ready?"

In response, she pushed her chair back from the table and stood. Together they strolled out of the restaurant side by side, close enough to converse but not so close as to accidentally brush against each other.

When they arrived at Izzy's house, a pair of

glowing eyes met them at the front porch.

"Bogart!" She bent and snatched the cat up before he could escape. "What are you doing outside?" Then she remembered that in her rush to get ready for dinner she'd forgotten to lock the cat flap before she left. She was going to have to work harder to make that a part of her evening routine.

Joe kept his distance, regarding the feline with a wary gaze. "I didn't know you had a cat."

"This is Bogart. He came with the house...sort of. He had a close call with a mountain lion a couple evenings ago and isn't supposed to be out after dark."

Joe stepped back onto the flagstone walk. "Well, I'll let you deal with him. Thanks for the tip about the boxes at Serena Pefferman's spa. I can't encourage you to investigate without telling me, but I appreciate the information."

"Thank you for dinner. The food was delicious, and I enjoyed the company."

Joe dropped his gaze to his feet before raising it to meet hers. "Maybe we'll do it again sometime...when we need to compare notes."

She smiled. "Sounds like a plan." Still clutching Bogart in the crook of her left arm, she fumbled in her purse until she found her key and stuck it into the lock.

Joe was halfway down the walk when he stopped. "It's good to be working with you again."

"Likewise."

"I guess I'll see you around."

"I'm sure you will." With a quick wave, she went inside and locked the door before setting Bogart on the floor. "What do you make of our friend, Joe De Rossi? If I didn't know better, I'd almost think the rough, tough police detective was shy around women." She laughed at the idea and followed her furry roommate into the house.

CHAPTER NINE

Since the next morning was Sunday, Izzy allowed herself to take her time and enjoy a second cup of coffee while she checked the news before heading out to work on the studio. She gave the drywall joints a final sanding, then pried open the can of paint she'd bought at the home center and poured it into the roller tray. The warm, creamy white wouldn't add much color to the otherwise wood toned room, but it would reflect more light into the interior and make a good backdrop for studio photography.

Two hours later, she returned the roller to the empty tray and stood back to assess her work with a critical eye. What she lacked in experience, she made up in painstaking precision, and the final result wasn't half bad. She might have added a few drips to the accidental abstract on the floor, but the wall was smooth and the color even. With no rain in the forecast, she left the windows open to air the place out and help the paint dry. Picking up her supplies, she headed for the house to clean up in the ancient utility sink in the laundry room.

As soon as she stepped outside, a rhythmic snipping sound caught her attention. Curious, she surveyed the yard and spotted Sebastian, neatly trimming the hedge on her side of the wall that separated their properties.

"Sebastian!"

He turned and waved his pruning shears. "Good morning, Izzy. How's the studio coming?"

She walked over to join him. "Pretty well, I think. I just finished painting the new wall."

"I'm sure it looks great. You've got those famous Munro painting genes, after all."

Izzy snorted. There was polite, and then there was absurd. "You can hardly compare painting a plain white wall to Aunt Dora's landscapes, and the mere smell of paint makes my mother woozy."

Clipping an errant branch that was spoiling the perfect symmetry of the hedge, he frowned. "I don't believe I've ever met your mother."

"I'm willing to bet you never will. Lila's rarely in the States, and she never comes to Carmel."

"That's a shame." His gaze held a hint of sadness.

Izzy refused to be pitied. Her relationship with Lila was what it was, and she'd accepted it long ago. "Not really. My mother and I get along best with plenty of distance between us."

After a pause, Sebastian returned to his trimming with a nod. "In that case, I'm glad Dora was there for you."

"So am I." She suddenly remembered something. "I forgot to ask—why are you trimming my bushes? You don't need to do that. I might be a novice when it comes to gardening, but I'm not helpless."

"Of course you're not, but I like to work outside, especially on a beautiful morning like this. The fresh air helps me think. I've been taking care of this property, as well as my own, since I moved in. Dora used to bring me coffee, and we'd chat when I finished."

Izzy still struggled with the idea that the multi-millionaire heir to a storied banking fortune was clipping her hedge. "I could bring you coffee. Would you like some?"

He smiled broadly. "That would be nice. After I finish this, I want to cut back your hydrangeas. When I'm done, we can visit on the patio for a while."

She had no idea which of the assorted plants around the house and yard were hydrangeas, but nodded. "That will give me time to clean up. Shall we say in about an hour?"

"It's a deal."

He went back to trimming, and she returned to the house.

An hour later, she stepped onto the patio carrying a wooden tray with two mugs of coffee and the sugar bowl and cream pitcher from Aunt Dora's best china set. Sebastian was already lounging in one of the chairs.

She set the tray on the small round table and took the seat across from him. "I hope the hydrangeas didn't give you any trouble."

He poured a splash of milk into one of the mugs. "I hacked them into submission. You should begin to see new growth in a few months."

"I'm sure they'll be lovely, whatever they are."

"They're the bushy shrubs under the living room windows — the ones with the big clusters of blue flowers in the summer."

She nodded, remembering the showy blooms from her long summer visits. "Ah. Gotcha."

"Izzy? Are you home?" a female voice called from the side yard.

"We're in back, on the patio!" she shouted in response.

Seconds later, Vivian appeared carrying a foil-covered plate. "I baked this morning and thought you might enjoy some cookies."

Izzy popped up. "Always! Have a seat, and I'll bring you a cup of coffee."

Vivian set the cookies on the table and took one of the two empty chairs. "That would be lovely. Thank you, dear. Good morning, Sebastian."

The two were chatting companionably when Izzy returned with a third mug. Peeling back the foil on the plate, she exclaimed, "These look like cherry chocolate chip—I used to love them when I visited Carmel as a child!"

"I remembered and decided you deserved a treat after your morning's labor." When Izzy sent her a questioning look, the older woman smiled. "I saw you two unloading all those supplies yesterday."

"I'm working on the studio." Izzy took a bite of cookie and closed her eyes. "Mmm. These are even better than I remembered."

Vivian chuckled. "It's my favorite kind of recipe—idiot-proof." She nudged the plate toward Sebastian. "Try one. I can see you've been working hard, too."

"I shouldn't, but I will." He reached for a cookie.

Vivian took a sip of her coffee. "Consider the cookies an appetizer. I would like to invite you both over for dinner this evening, if you're not too tired."

Izzy brightened. She was tired, but not tired enough

to dampen the appeal of someone else's cooking. "Thank you. I'd love to come."

"Excellent. Sebastian?"

"I'm afraid I'll have to take a rain check. I have a conference call this evening."

Vivian sent him a skeptical frown. "I know I'm not the gourmet cook you are, but couldn't you come up with a better excuse? A conference call? On Sunday evening?"

He heaved a sigh and raised the back of one wrist to his forehead. "It's my lot in life. A tycoon's work is never done." But the twinkle in his eye belied the drama of his complaint.

Vivian shoved his upper arm and laughed. "Oh, you..."

He grinned before his expression sobered. "Seriously though, I do have a call at six, and I'm leaving at the crack of dawn tomorrow for a whirlwind trip to Singapore, so I'd better get home." He pushed to his feet.

"How long will you be gone?" Izzy asked. She'd grown accustomed to the comfort of knowing he was next door.

"Not long. I should be back late Thursday night. Ta-ta!"

As they watched him go, Izzy shook her head. "I can't figure him out. He's heir to one of the country's great fortunes, yet he lives in this tiny town which, while definitely upscale, is a long way from a major airport. He seems to relish spending at least half his time running a small-town newspaper that couldn't possibly turn a profit. But he's also actively involved in some other mysterious, apparently international, business that may, or may not, be related to the Larrabee banking empire."

Vivian chuckled. "Sebastian is a modern man of mystery. I've known him for years, but I have no idea what he's up to most of the time."

"I know I haven't lived here long, but I've never seen anyone come or go from his house. He's so supportive, helpful, and outgoing, but he doesn't seem to entertain friends or be involved in any kind of close relationship."

"Most weeks, he spends a day or two in San Francisco, and he travels abroad from time to time. I think Carmel is his personal retreat. He likes to maintain his privacy here. And I've never seen any sign, nor heard the slightest whisper, of him having a relationship. In fact, I have no idea of his sexual orientation, if he even has one. All I know is, he's a delightful person and an excellent neighbor."

"I can't argue with that. He's brought me food, given me my first work as a photographer, helped with my studio, and this morning, I found him trimming my shrubbery." Izzy shook her head in amazement. "I've never met anyone like him."

"And I doubt you will again. Sebastian Larrabee is one of a kind." Vivian finished her coffee in a single long swallow and rose. "Now I'd better go home and start putting the lasagna together for dinner."

"That sounds delicious. What time should I come?"

"Sunday is Lorna's day off, so we'll eat at six-thirty."

Izzy's brows knit in confusion. "Lorna? Lorna Ferris? The manager at Taste of Torino?"

"Yes. Didn't I mention it? She's my tenant. She's been renting my guesthouse since she moved to Carmel three months ago. We usually eat together a few nights a week. I get tired of cooking for one, and I think we both enjoy the company. Nice girl, even if she's a bit of a loner."

"She seemed very pleasant the few times I've met her. I'll see you at six-thirty."

Izzy spent the afternoon checking out camera equipment online and compiling a wish list. Two of the lenses she wanted were so expensive, she probably wouldn't be able to afford them for months — or even years — but committing her aspirations to writing provided concrete goals and made her new business feel more like a reality than a mere possibility.

At six-thirty, she walked across the street to Vivian's house, where she was greeted by the mouth-watering aroma of tomatoes, basil, and garlic the moment her hostess opened the door.

"That smells fantastic!"

Vivian beamed. "It's my own take on the familiar classic. Come on in. We'll be ready to eat in about ten minutes. Lorna is in the living room with the wine."

Vivian's house was somewhat larger than Aunt Dora's compact cottage and had a small entrance foyer with the living room off to the right.

When Izzy stepped inside, Lorna rose from the sofa. "Vivian put me in charge of the wine. Would you like a glass?"

Izzy smiled as she approached the open bottle sitting on the coffee table, along with a trio of glasses. "You don't have to wait on me. I'm sure you get enough of that at work."

Lorna reached for the bottle. "Oh, I don't mind." After pouring the dark, purplish-red liquid into a glass, she thrust it at Izzy. "Here."

"Thanks."

The woman seemed anxious, although Izzy couldn't understand why. Even if she was shy, as Vivian had suggested, they weren't complete strangers. Maybe she would relax if Izzy could draw her into conversation.

"I don't think I had a chance to tell you how sorry I am about Aldo's death. I'm sure it was a terrible shock to everyone at Taste of Torino, and his wife must be heartbroken."

"Serena is…Serena."

Interesting. "And what about you? How are you holding up?"

Lorna frowned into her glass. "I'm fine."

Izzy took a sip of her wine while an antique clock on the mantel ticked off the seconds in silence. She had no way of knowing if Lorna's reticence was due to her natural personality or the result of sorrow, but since grief counselors often recommended talking about the deceased as a way to come to grips with the loss, she tried again.

"I only met Aldo a few times, but he appeared to be quite a character."

Lorna didn't look up. "He had a big personality."

"And a way of turning heads everywhere he went. The times I saw him, he always looked so dapper, down to the coordinating pocket square in his jacket."

"Aldo was a stickler for details."

Izzy nodded, as if she were discussing a close personal acquaintance. "His taste was exquisite, at least most of the time."

Lorna's frown deepened, and she glanced up. "What makes you say that?"

"Have you ever been in his office?"

A wary look came into her eyes. "Several times. I'm the bakery manager. Why?"

Izzy suddenly realized where the conversation was going, and it was her own fault. However, since it was too late to change course, she had no choice but to follow through. With luck, maybe she would learn something useful.

"He took such pains with his appearance, and everything in his office was of exceptional quality except that awful brown sofa." She rolled her eyes and kept her tone familiar and confidential, as if they were two old friends sharing a bit of gossip.

Lorna refused to bite. "What were you doing in Aldo's office?"

How to make this sound insignificant and innocent. "I...uh...I've known the lead investigator assigned to Aldo's case for several years, and he asked me to take photographs while the cops searched the office because the regular CPD photographer was tied up elsewhere."

"You're working with the police?"

"Not officially, no—"

Before she was forced to explain further, Vivian called them to dinner, and Izzy followed Lorna into a small dining room that looked out onto the patio and garden.

After they were seated, Vivian gestured to the large baking dish in the center of the table and a basket of homemade garlic breadsticks. "Help yourselves." She glanced around the table. "Oops. Forgot the salad. I'll be right back."

Izzy and Lorna waited in awkward silence until she returned.

The mood around the table lightened as Vivian kept up an easy patter while they each served themselves. "Lorna, did you know Izzy's a photographer? She's had several pictures published in the *Acorn*."

"Interesting. Is that what you did before you moved here?"

"No. It was just a hobby, but I'm hoping to turn it into a full-time job."

"Good luck."

"Thank you." Relieved that Lorna seemed to have moved past the question of Aldo's office, Izzy steered the conversation in a new direction. "Vivian tells me you've lived in her guest house since you arrived in Carmel. Are you from out of the area?"

Lorna nodded, then downed a hefty slug of wine. "Southern California."

"L.A.?"

"Farther south."

"San Diego?"

"More or less."

Since Lorna didn't seem anxious to sing the praises of her hometown—wherever it was—Izzy switched gears again. "If Aldo hired you to manage Taste of Torino, you must have had experience working in a restaurant or bakery."

"I used to manage a coffee shop."

"It was obviously good preparation." Izzy poked her fork into her salad and came up with a plump black olive. "Whenever I stop in, business seems to be booming, even under such sad circumstances."

"The location is good, and Aldo wasn't involved in most of the day-to-day work, so his death hasn't affected the operation much. But I'm not sure how much longer I'll stay, now that he's gone."

Izzy couldn't help feeling sorry for her. Three months wasn't a long time, but some women seemed to be especially vulnerable to Aldo Pefferman's slick brand of charisma. Lorna might be one of them. Or maybe she was worried about her job, afraid Serena might sell the business to a new owner who would want to hire their own manager.

"Oh, dear, I hope you won't leave us so soon!" Vivian's voice rose in distress.

"I'll have to see how things go, but don't worry—I don't plan to skip out on my rent."

"That's not what I was concerned about. I'd hate to see you give up on the community so quickly. Carmel-by-the-Sea is such an interesting place."

"I can't argue with that, but..." Lorna's voice trailed off.

Their hostess changed the subject. "Izzy, is Bogart still living with you? I haven't seen him roaming the neighborhood as much lately." She smiled at Lorna. "Bogart is a handsome, and very independent, Burmese cat who used to live across the street with Izzy's Aunt Dora. She seems to have inherited him along with the house."

Lorna nodded but didn't look up.

In hopes of salvaging the dinner conversation, Izzy followed Vivian's lead. "He's tolerating me so far, although I'm not sure how long it will last."

"Why is that?"

"I installed a lock on his cat door yesterday to curtail his nocturnal socializing."

"I bet he doesn't like that. He's used to complete freedom."

"It's for his own good. We had a close encounter with a mountain lion in the park a couple of evenings ago. Then later that night, I spotted it in the front yard, staring into the bedroom window. I told Bogart he had to stay in at night unless he wanted to become cougar chow. I think he understood."

Vivian laughed. "If he didn't, I'm sure he'll find a way to let you know."

Izzy stabbed another forkful of salad. "Bogart and I weren't the only ones who saw the creature. Someone either very brave or very foolish was standing in the street in front of the house shining a flashlight on it. It was terrifying! I don't suppose either of you saw it."

Lorna appeared to have checked out of the conversation and was concentrating on her lasagna.

Vivian shook her head. "I'm one of those rare old ladies who's still able to sleep soundly, but I bet that lion is the same one Doris Ichida found lounging on the hood of her car one night last month when she was getting ready to leave for her overnight shift at the hospital."

Izzy's eyes rounded. "Yikes! I think Bogart and I will both be sticking close to home after dark from now on."

"I wouldn't recommend any midnight solo rambles, but you should be fine, especially if you carry a good, strong flashlight."

"Maybe the person I saw just happened to be out for a late-night stroll and spotted the cat in my yard." A shiver rippled up Izzy's spine.

Izzy and Vivian continued to visit, with Lorna adding a word or two from time to time. When the meal was over, she rose abruptly.

"Thanks for dinner. I'd better go. I need to do laundry."

"I enjoyed having you, as always, dear," Vivian replied.

After Lorna left, Izzy stood and began stacking the empty plates. "Did Lorna seem unusually edgy tonight?"

Vivian gathered the used silverware and glasses. "She can be moody sometimes, and she's upset about Aldo's death."

"I'm sure she is." Izzy followed her friend into the kitchen. "I wonder what brought her to Carmel-by-the-Sea. It's hard to imagine anyone would move to a tiny town far from home just to manage a bakery."

Vivian set her load in the sink and turned on the water. "I don't know. She's quiet and never talks about herself, but she's a nice girl and a good tenant. I hope she'll take my advice and give the town a little more time. As I've always said, Carmel is a good place to escape and reinvent yourself."

****

The next morning, Chantal jumped on Izzy the minute she walked through the door of the salon. "I've been thinking about you all weekend. Was your reconnaissance visit to Beauty by the Bay a success? I've never been there, but word on the street is it's very chi-chi. Did you learn anything interesting? Were Serena Pefferman and Dr. Holder hanging all over each other, like Dottie Cartwright insists?"

Izzy shrugged out of her jacket. "Hold on. One question at a time."

Chantal poured herself a cup of coffee. "If you give me a complete report, starting at the beginning, I promise not to ask another thing."

"Didn't your mother tell you not to make promises you can't keep?"

Chantal's laugh was unrepentant. "Point taken." She perched one hip on the edge of the desk. "So go ahead, spill."

"Well, the spa is lovely, with a Zen sort of feeling — neutral colors, blond wood, minimalist furnishings. Both Serena and her partner behaved professionally the whole time I was there. If they're involved in a passionate affair, they're good at hiding it."

Chantal's lips pursed in a moue of disappointment. "Dottie would be bummed out, but it makes sense. Aldo was a local bigwig. I doubt he would have tolerated his wife blatantly carrying on with another man in public."

Izzy had to agree. From what everyone said, Aldo was the kind of man who was concerned about his image and reputation.

"At least Serena doesn't have to worry about that anymore," Chantal continued. "And on top of everything else, now she can afford to do whatever she wants."

If there was one thing Izzy had learned investigating insurance claims, it was the validity of the old adage, *Follow the Money*. "I know that in addition to being a baker and chocolatier, Aldo was also a successful businessman, but do you think he was seriously wealthy?"

Chantal shrugged. "He had his fingers in a lot of pies and owned a lot of real estate. In fact, he owned this building. I wonder what Serena will do with it all?" A sudden look of consternation crossed her face. "What if she decides to sell the building or cancel my lease?"

"Relax. In this town, I'm sure commercial real estate holdings produce a hefty stream of income, and if she did decide to sell, the new owner would be buying that stream. They would have no reason to kick the current tenants out."

"But they might jack up the rent." Chantal's heavily-fringed eyes widened in alarm.

"That's possible," Izzy conceded, "but I don't think you should go looking for trouble before it exists."

Chantal slid off the desk. "Let's change the subject.

This whole conversation is making me queasy. There's another thing I wanted to talk to you about before the first customer comes in, something a lot more fun."

"I'm all for that."

"I've been thinking about redecorating the salon, adding more...I don't know...class."

Izzy glanced around the airy, high-ceilinged room, equipped with the requisite styling stations, a pair of shampoo basins, and separate area for the manicurist. "Did you have something particular in mind?"

"I was thinking of a series of oversized photographs — something dramatic, like black-and-white portraits of the staff or groupings of equipment." Chantal picked up a compact, tubular hair dryer with no obvious motor. "Like this. It has an interesting shape."

A profusion of ideas tumbled through Izzy's mind. She'd been wanting to expand her skills to portraiture, and the salon was full of tools of the trade that, with the right arrangements and lighting, would make striking still life compositions. Her pulse hummed with excitement. "That's a wonderful idea! If you're willing to work with an amateur, I'd love to give it a try. Once you approve the images, your only cost would be the printing."

Chantal tut-tutted. "Nonsense. You're a professional, and I'd expect to pay you." Her lips curved in an impish grin. "Although I wouldn't say no to a friends-and-family discount."

Izzy smiled in return. "It's a deal."

Fortunately, answering the phone and making appointments required only a fraction of her brain, because for the rest of the morning, the remainder was fully occupied with plans for her first installation. She could hardly believe her luck. A few short weeks ago, she'd lost her job, her fiancé, and her home, but now she had a new life, full of friends, hopes, and possibilities.

At one o'clock, she was gathering her things to leave when her phone buzzed with a text from Joe. As she read it, her excitement turned to apprehension.

We may have a problem. Call me ASAP.

CHAPTER TEN

Izzy's chest tightened as she stared at the text. Joe De Rossi wasn't a man given to unnecessary alarm or drama. If he thought they had a problem, they probably had a problem. Her fingers shook as she placed the call.

"Izzy."

"Yes. What's the matter? The situation sounded urgent."

"I hope not, but better safe than sorry." His voice had a gritty edge, like ground glass. "Where are you?"

"Just leaving Cece's. Where are you?"

"A few blocks away at police headquarters. We need to meet, but I'd rather go somewhere else. Carmel is a small town, filled with sharp-eyed residents who like to talk about other people's business. Sometimes that can work in law enforcement's favor, but right now I think it would be better if we weren't seen together or overheard by any of the locals."

"This sounds ominous."

"Consider it an abundance of caution. Do you have any ideas where we could go?"

She considered a minute. "We could try Fisherman's Wharf again. Since it's usually full of tourists, locals don't tend to hang out there."

"That works for me. I'll meet you at the entrance to the wharf in about fifteen minutes."

"Make it more like twenty-five. I still have to walk home and get my car."

"Oh...right...sorry. I'll see you then." And he hung up.

Joe sounded rattled and distracted, not his usual gruff, confident self. She wondered what had shaken him so.

When she got home, she didn't bother going into the house, just hopped in her car and took off. Mid-day November traffic was light, so she made it to the parking garage across from Fisherman's Wharf in twenty minutes. Joe was standing in front of the entrance checking his watch as she approached.

"I'm not late."

"I know. I'm just antsy. Have you had lunch?"

She was tempted to ask when he thought she could have squeezed that in, but seeing his troubled expression, she refrained. "Not yet. You?"

He shook his head. "I know a taco place about a block from here. The food's good, and no one will pay any attention to us."

"Sounds good."

Tico's Tacos was old, cramped, and smelled like hot grease—the kind of place where you could count on getting tacos like *Abuela* used to make. They placed their order at the counter, then chose one of the red vinyl-upholstered booths. Less than ten minutes later, a young man with a white towel marked with orange handprints wrapped around his waist appeared with their plates.

Izzy picked up a chicken street taco and took a bite. The meat was perfectly seasoned and cooked just right. She nodded as she finished chewing. "Mmm. Very good. How'd you find this place? You haven't been in the area long."

"One of the guys from work brought me here. It's good, quiet, and cheap. The perfect cop joint without being a cop joint."

"Speaking of cops, what did you want to talk to me about that was so urgent?"

Joe's gaze sharpened, and he set down his taco. "We executed a search warrant on Beauty by the Bay this morning."

"How did it go?"

"They had two clients at the time, so Dr. Holder and Mrs. Pefferman weren't exactly happy to see us."

Izzy grimaced. "I bet they weren't. They like to maintain a calm, upscale atmosphere. Being raided by the police is hardly in keeping with their desired image. Did you find any boxes like the one in the picture I showed you?"

"Two, right where you photographed them."

"Marcus was so angry when he found the first box, I'm surprised he didn't insist on searching the rest of their inventory after I left."

Joe nodded as he finished his bite. "I was surprised, too. I didn't expect the boxes to still be sitting on the shelf. I thought the most important take-away from the search would be their business financial records."

"How did they react to your discovery?"

"That was another surprise. You'd expect them to

be frightened, or at least apprehensive, but they were both furious. Their clients had left by that time, so they had no reason to restrain themselves. The doctor started waving his arms and yelling at Mrs. Pefferman that it was all her fault, how could she have been so careless, she was going to ruin the business, etc., etc. She, in turn, denied his accusations at the top of her lungs and claimed Christos Getz must have planted the stuff because of his animosity toward her late husband. Then she threw a jar of face cream at Holder. The jar missed its target, but it shattered a mirror and sent shards of glass and globs of goo all over the shop. It was a complete circus."

Izzy couldn't help herself — she chuckled at his description. "I'm sorry, but the image of those two... Did you arrest them?"

"Not for the fight. No one was hurt, and it isn't illegal to make a mess on your own property. As for the toxin, we need to check the boxes for prints and have the vials analyzed by the lab to confirm the contents before taking further action. We also need to try to figure out how it came to be in the spa. If either Dr. Holder or Mrs. Pefferman purchased it, even illegally, there might be some indication in their business financial records."

Izzy considered that unlikely. Who would be clueless enough to buy their murder weapon through their business account? But Joe was a thorough, by-the-book investigator. That's what had made him a successful detective.

She took another bite while she considered what he'd told her. "I'm glad you were able to secure potentially important evidence, but I still don't understand why you wanted to see me right away, and why it had to be in an out-of-the-way spot."

"Word gets around Carmel fast, and I didn't want us to be overheard. When you visited Beauty by the Bay, did you make the appointment in your own name?"

The hint of accusation in his tone put Izzy on the defensive. She lifted her chin and met his gaze head-on. "What would be the point of using an alias? I've only been in town a few weeks, but I already know a number of people. I couldn't expect to hide my identity for long."

Joe nodded. "True. That's one of the realities of living in a town of 3,200 people. However, the reason I'm concerned is that Serena Pefferman wasn't just screaming about Christos Getz. She was accusing you of being personally responsible for the search of their premises because of the timing of your visit and your apparent interest in the botulinum display. Something about being a sneaky rat..."

"Did she threaten me?"

"Not specifically, but—"

"Then I don't see the problem. No one heard her except Dr. Holder and your officers. She's hardly likely to spread the news of the search around town and risk damaging the spa's reputation. And even if she did, who else would care?"

Joe leaned forward, propping his elbows on the table. "I'm not worried about *who else*, I'm worried about you. Both Serena and the doctor were pretty worked up this morning. If one of them is a murderer, you might become the next target of their rage."

"I appreciate your concern, but I think you're overreacting. Serena accused Christos Getz of planting the counterfeit Botox. Are you going to warn him, too?"

Joe sat back. "Getz has been out of town, but I plan to talk to him as soon as he returns."

Izzy took another bite and nodded. Anticipating trouble was part of Joe's job, but at this point, she refused to believe she was in danger. Despite the mounting evidence, she couldn't shake her gut feeling that Serena Pefferman was not her husband's killer. The woman might be vain, and she might be greedy, but her concern for Aldo's well-being the day he died had felt genuine. Izzy would stake her life on it.

For a split second, it occurred to her she might be doing exactly that, but she dismissed the thought as foolishness brought on by Joe's warning.

"Izzy, I can tell from your stubborn expression that you think I'm being overly cautious, but you need to take this seriously. You've gotten yourself involved in a murder, and murderers are unpredictable."

She challenged his direct gaze. "I've been involved in murders before."

His frown deepened. "Those cases weren't the same, and you know it. You always joined the investigation safely after the fact. You never had the victim collapse in your arms, and you never knew the suspects personally. Besides, as far as the perpetrators were concerned, you weren't a threat. You were the one who was going to authorize their big payout."

He had a point. "Okay. I get it. This is different, but—"

"No 'buts.' What kind of security do you have at home?"

"The doors and windows have locks. What else would I need? I live in a modest cottage, and I'm home every night. The burglars around here are smart enough to target the fancy, unoccupied vacation homes."

"Which all have state-of-the-art security systems. Besides, I'm not worried about burglars." He paused a moment, as if weighing his decision. "I'll be over tomorrow evening after work to install a basic system."

A flash of panic grabbed her. "Wait a minute. How much will that cost? I'm making ends meet at the moment, but I'm still only working part time."

"Don't worry. It won't be anything elaborate, just a doorbell camera and alarm sensors for the doors and windows. Consider it an investment by the Department in the safety of our unpaid civilian consultant."

She shot him a skeptical look. "Somehow, I doubt there's a line item in the DA's budget for that."

Joe shrugged, but his eyes betrayed his amusement. "I can't let you do it."

"I'd like to see you try and stop me."

Izzy sighed. He was clearly prepared for a battle of wills, and the issue was not worth a fight. "All right. Fine."

He responded with a satisfied nod. "Good. I'll see you tomorrow around seven. In the meantime, keep your head down."

"What's that supposed to mean?"

"Just go about your business. Don't attract attention to yourself."

Since that pretty much summed up her life, she shouldn't have much trouble acceding to his request.

****

The next morning, Izzy went to work, as usual. Chatted with Chantal, as usual. Made small talk with the clients, as usual. All without calling attention to herself, as usual.

After lunch, to take her mind off Joe's impending visit and the reason behind it, she decided to take some pictures around town. Sebastian hadn't requested shots of any particular events, so she wanted to submit a few options to him for this week's *Acorn*. She had to admit that, in addition to the quick burst of satisfaction she got from seeing her name in print, his checks were helping to stretch her budget. She'd like to make it a regular occurrence.

Since she'd already photographed much of the busy commercial area of Ocean Avenue, she strolled up one of the residential side streets near her cottage, looking for any small detail that caught her eye. Initially, all details receded in the overwhelming sea of green. The town liked to describe itself as being located in an urban forest, and that wasn't far from the truth. Ancient pines towered over an understory of coastal oaks, whose gnarled limbs meandered up and out for thirty feet, or more, not to mention the row of iconic Monterey cypresses that framed the road above the beach.

Early in the twentieth century, Carmel-by-the-Sea had been conceived as a quaint, Bohemian, beachside artists' colony. The original village consisted mainly of Tudor and Spanish Colonial-styled commercial buildings, humble beach huts, and petite fairytale cottages. Over time, many of the old huts, especially those closest to the beach, had given way to grander, more modern structures. However, the small side streets were still dotted with original houses. Aunt Dora's cottage was one of them, and Izzy loved it for its quirky, unashamed authenticity.

Plenty of books had been published with photos of Carmel's picturesque buildings — there was no need to revisit that subject. Besides, at the moment, the trees, plants, and gardens held more interest. The temperate seaside climate allowed everything to grow year-round, and something was always blooming, even in November.

Because she'd grown up in a city with a mother who only had time for the latest rock bands, and Aunt Dora had been more interested in painting trees and flowers than growing them, Izzy knew nothing about plants. When she slowed her pace and examined each individual yard closely, she found herself fascinated by the variety. Behind every picket fence was an array of alluring and unfamiliar plants: dark green creepers with fuzzy purple flowers; tall, graceful bushes with bright red leaves; and succulents of every imaginable shape, size, and color.

She squatted down, focusing on eye-catching contrasts of color and texture—a late afternoon sunbeam falling on a single leaf, a cluster of red berries, the pattern of lichen and moss on a stone wall. She didn't want anything uniquely identifiable that would require the owner's permission to publish, but a collection of artistic close-ups that would give an interesting and original impression of Carmel gardens.

As she approached one house, she was distracted by voices coming from the front yard. A dense hedge surrounded the property and prevented her from seeing the speakers, but the tone of the argument caught her attention.

The woman's voice was sharp with annoyance. "Put that down. It's too heavy. You're going to hurt yourself."

An older man, possibly her husband, replied with equal rancor. "Will you stop fussing? I keep telling you, I'm fine."

"You certainly are not. That pot must weigh thirty pounds. Do I have to remind you it's only been four months since you got out of the hospital?"

"And I'm fully recovered. You said so yourself." His stubborn resistance was unmistakable.

"I said 'almost fully recovered.' Any injury now could set you back months, or even result in permanent disability. Besides, what if someone sees you walking around like this, lifting heavy pots?"

The man grunted. "What does it matter, as long as it's not Pefferman's lawyers."

Izzy had been edging away, not wanting to eavesdrop on the couple's domestic squabble, but she stopped at the word *Pefferman* and leaned closer to the hedge.

"This town has plenty of big ears with even bigger mouths," the woman pointed out. "Our lawsuit isn't common knowledge, but that could change in the blink of an eye with one careless remark. The last thing we want is to raise suspicion about your condition. As it stands now, Dr. Walker is willing to testify that you may never walk again on your own. We don't want him to change his mind."

"No one's going to find out, and I don't care what people say."

"You'll care plenty if we lose that ten million. We may not need the money, but after what he did, Aldo Pefferman owes us. I don't care if he is dead."

The longer Izzy listened, the more familiar the couple's voices sounded. Their hatred of the late city councilman was clear, as was the fact that they were discussing a lawsuit that could end up being extremely lucrative. Whether they'd had anything to do with Aldo's murder, she couldn't say, but based on their conversation, they were embroiled in a deception that involved a large sum of money. When her old insurance-investigator radar sent out alarm signals, she had to remind herself it was none of her concern—she was out of the business. However, she couldn't bring herself to let the matter go without confirming her hunch.

She pressed her nose against the hedge, trying to peer between the tightly-packed branches, but it was impossible. Slipping her hands into the tall shrub, she gently parted the foliage until she had a clear view of the front porch of the house and its inhabitants. As she'd suspected, they were Kurt and Dina Korman, the elderly couple she'd met in front of the library. Except that now Kurt was standing straight and tall, holding a sizeable potted plant, and looking quite fit, instead of sitting hunched on a park bench like a fragile invalid.

The wrongness of the situation burrowed into her gut.

I have to do something.

It's none of your business. Let it go.

But—

Ultimately, her inner moralist won out. She raised her camera and snapped a shot. Later, she could decide what—if anything—to do with it.

Suddenly, Kurt Korman stared straight at her, eyes narrowed in accusation. Izzy blinked and jerked her head back.

"Hey, you in the bushes—" He marched toward the hedge. "What do you think you're doing?"

She took off with her camera dangling from her neck, smacking against her chest with every step. Had Kurt opened the front gate and seen her running down the street? What if he recognized her? Looking into someone's yard might not be illegal, but the last thing she needed was to get a reputation as a peeper.

She was still running when she rounded the corner and nearly barreled into Dottie Cartwright, Chantal's gossip-loving client. Wrapped around Dottie's wrist was a sturdy leash, and at the end of that leash was a good-sized and enthusiastic Labradoodle.

When the dog jumped toward Izzy, Dottie gave the leash a firm jerk. "Down, Gunther!" After two or three final romps, the dog reluctantly obeyed. "I'm sorry." When Dottie glanced up, her eyes widened in recognition. "You're Izzy, the receptionist at Cece's, aren't you?"

She nodded. "It's nice to see you, Dottie."

"You look like you're out for a run, except for the camera." Dottie's brows pinched. "Is everything all right? Is someone chasing you?"

Izzy's pounding heart stuttered as her brain searched for a plausible response. "Uh...no. I'm fine. I was just out taking photos for the *Acorn* and realized I'm late for an appointment."

"Well, I won't keep you. I enjoyed your pictures of the Halloween festivities and can't wait to see the new ones. See you Monday morning, bright and early!"

Dottie had a standing weekly appointment at the salon for a wash and blow-out, during which she informed everyone within earshot of the latest and most noteworthy local news.

Already half-way to the corner, Izzy replied, "Yes, see you Monday!" as she waved backwards and hustled down the street.

Her mind was racing faster than her feet. Why did she have to run into Dottie Cartwright, of all people? Since Dottie was walking her dog, she probably lived in the neighborhood. And if she lived in the neighborhood, she undoubtedly knew the Kormans. And if she knew the Kormans, she would almost certainly mention meeting her stylist's receptionist running down the block, away from their house. What a mess.

Izzy had never been happier to see the little green cottage, and once inside, the safe haven of her childhood began working it's calming magic. Her sense of panic receded, her breathing slowed, and her rational brain took over.

So Kurt and Dina Korman were suing Aldo Pefferman's estate for damages incurred when he forced them to tear down their garbage can enclosure. That wasn't surprising. According to them, the stress of the incident had caused Kurt to suffer a serious stroke. Nothing the couple had said suggested they'd played a part in his murder. From their conversation, it sounded like they had filed the lawsuit weeks ago, before Aldo's death. After he died, all they had to do was change the defendant to his estate. Legally, his death shouldn't affect the outcome either way.

And did it matter if Kurt had recognized her, or Dottie mentioned meeting her? Even if Kurt was feigning his degree of disability to get a larger settlement, what was Izzy going to do—run tattling to Aldo's lawyers? She needed to get over herself. Any threat from the Kormans was all in her head.

To help put the unsettling incident out of her mind, she spent the rest of the afternoon editing the photos she'd taken, and was pleased when several of them turned out even better than she'd hoped. She sent the best three to Sebastian, along with a short proposal for a featured series on the gardens of Carmel. Satisfied with her afternoon's work, she fed Bogart and threw together a quick omelet and a salad for herself. By the time she finished her dinner, the vintage kitchen clock hanging on the wall above the stove read six forty-five. There was no point starting anything now — Joe would be arriving soon.

After cleaning up the dishes, she went into the living room to grab her shoes, which she'd abandoned inside the front door after her sprint home from the Kormans'. Halfway across the room, a sudden sharp pain stabbed the tender flesh of her right arch. Letting out a short squawk, she hopped on her left foot to the wall, where she switched on the lights and began scanning the floor for the culprit. Spotting an anomaly in the floral design of the dark blue oriental rug, she bent and picked it up.

It was the key she'd found in the park a few weeks ago. She'd tossed it on the coffee table and forgotten it. How had it ended up on the floor?

She shot a narrow-eyed glance at the cat, snoozing on the sofa. "This is your doing, isn't it?"

Bogart blinked at her in feigned innocence. As she straightened, the doorbell rang. She dropped the key on the table and went to answer it.

Joe stood on the porch with a plastic bag from a local electronics store. "All ready to go. This shouldn't take more than an hour."

She snatched the bag before he could protest and began pawing through the contents on the way to the kitchen.

He followed closely behind. "If you're looking for the receipt, you're out of luck. It's in my wallet."

She set the bag on the counter and turned to face him, making no attempt to hide her frustration. "This doesn't feel right. I wish you'd let me reimburse you."

"Don't worry about it. I got the law enforcement discount."

She pressed her lips together in skepticism. "I'm pretty sure that's not a thing."

He laughed. "I'll let you feed me, then. I grabbed a burger at a joint near the office, but it barely made a dent."

She almost laughed. As far as she could tell, the man was always hungry, regardless of when he'd last eaten. But what could she give him? With only herself to feed, she didn't keep much food in the house. She shot a searching glance around the kitchen until her gaze settled on a foil-wrapped paper plate at the far end of the counter, and she smiled. Cookies. Who didn't like cookies?

"How do you feel about homemade peanut butter cookies?"

His face lit with anticipation. "I love them! Haven't had one in years."

She retrieved the plate and offered it to him. "Vivian sent these home with me after dinner Sunday night."

He chose the biggest one off the top and took a bite. "Mmm. This is perfect. Thank Vivian for me, will you?"

"You should take a few home with you. She enjoys having an excuse to bake, but if I eat all these, I'll have to start wearing muumuus."

He cast a quick glance up and down her figure. "Not a chance. But if you're fishing for compliments, I'm not biting."

What was that supposed to mean? She decided to ignore it and pointed to the bag. "What's the first step?"

"We install the doorbell camera." He reached into the sack, then stopped and turned. "I wasn't thinking. I should have asked if you have basic tools."

"Basic and not-so-basic. Munro women believe in

getting the job done. I'll get Aunt Dora's toolbox." She retrieved a well-worn, red metal box from the garage and led the way to the front door.

When they returned to the living room, Bogart jumped down from the sofa and crouched on the floor at Izzy's feet, his tail flipping back and forth like an angry snake.

Joe opened the toolbox and pulled out an ancient screwdriver with a yellow plastic handle, then regarded the feline with a frown. "What's his problem?"

She bent down and rubbed the thick, velvety fur around the cat's face and neck. "He isn't sure about you yet."

Joe eyed Bogart warily. "The feeling's mutual."

Izzy laughed and continued petting the cat, who gave their visitor what could only be described as a smirk.

Returning his attention the project, Joe opened the door and switched on the porch light. He removed the existing doorbell with the screwdriver, and within fifteen minutes, the shiny new one had been installed. Personally, she felt its sleek design and glowing blue ring were at odds with the aesthetic of the 1920s cottage, but she kept that opinion to herself. If it made him feel better, she wouldn't complain. This murderer-on-the-loose situation wouldn't last forever, and she could always re-install the original vintage doorbell later if she wanted to.

"How does it work?" she asked.

"I'll show you. Where's your phone?"

She got her phone from the kitchen table, unlocked it, and handed it to him.

"There's an app—"

Of course, there is. There's always an app.

" — that allows you to monitor the system and see anyone within range of the camera, whether they ring the bell or not." He tapped the keys in rapid succession, then returned the phone. "I'll go outside, and you can see for yourself."

He opened the door, stepped onto the porch, and stared straight into the camera.

Izzy checked the image on her phone. "This is amazing. I can see clearly all the way across the street to Vivian's house."

"That's the idea. Nobody can approach from the front of the house without you seeing them."

"Then I should be perfectly safe. The wall between my property and Sebastian's is at least six feet high, and I'm sure he has the most up-to-date security system money can buy. The neighbors on the other side have a Newfoundland with a growl like an angry bear, and the people behind me have a thick hedge of some bushy plant with thorns."

Joe nodded. "That's good, but we're not done yet. Next come the window sensors that trigger an alarm when they're opened."

"Wait a minute. I'm not going to let you turn my house into a prison. I have to be able to open the windows."

His pointed look suggested she think a little harder. "You turn the system off when you're home and arm it when you go to bed or leave the house."

Duh. Then another thought occurred to her. "But what if I want to sleep with the windows open?"

He released an exasperated breath. "Izzy, are you trying to be difficult? You, of all people, should understand risk management. This is basically a safe town, and when the case is wrapped up and we've caught Aldo's killer, you can go back to living however you want. In the meantime, you need to practice reasonable caution. Now, I'm going to finish this job, take my cookies, and go home."

Izzy and Bogart followed him from room to room as he attached small white sensors to the windows.

When the work was complete, Joe held up a white keypad with numbers like an old-fashioned touch-tone phone. "Do you want the controls by the front door or the back?"

She thought about it for a minute, then replied, "Back, I think."

The three of them trooped into the kitchen, where Joe installed the keypad next to the door to the patio. After he finished, he showed her how to arm and disarm the system. "There, you're all set."

"Do you feel better now?"

"Yes, and so should you." He returned the screwdriver to the toolbox and flipped both latches shut.

"I do." She hated to admit it, but it was true. "I'm sorry if I've been difficult."

"Nobody likes to think they might be in danger."

She touched his sleeve. "I want you to know, I really do appreciate you doing this."

It might have been her imagination, but his smile seemed to carry a hint of extra warmth as he covered her hand with his and gave it a squeeze. "No problem."

As soon as he released her, she dropped her hand. "I'll put those cookies in a bag for you."

"Thanks."

After he left, Izzy tried to watch TV, but she was distracted and unsettled. Bogart climbed onto her lap and head-butted her hand until she scratched under his chin.

"You weren't exactly Mr. Hospitality tonight. I know you're just trying to protect me, but Joe's not such a bad guy, is he?"

Bogart narrowed his eyes. *Mrowr.*

She stroked his head and stared out the window into the darkness. "Yeah, you're probably right."

CHAPTER ELEVEN

Izzy was deep in a dream about leaping off a cliff and soaring out over the ocean when something pulled her out of it. As she tried to orient herself and open her eyes, she became aware of flashing blue lights outside her bedroom window and the sound of voices coming from the yard. She fumbled for her phone on the nightstand to check the time — it was one-fifteen.

Throwing off the covers, she stuffed her feet into an old pair of sneakers, and grabbed her fuzzy blue robe from the hook on the back of the bathroom door before dashing to the kitchen. Through the windows, she saw figures in heavy yellow suits flashing lights back and forth across the backyard.

Mrowr!

Bogart sat in front of the locked cat flap, quivering in a state of alarm.

Izzy scooped him up and stroked his back. "It's

going to be okay. You stay here while I find out what's going on."

She set him down and unlocked the door. When she started to open it, he made a mad dash for the opening before she stopped him with a sharp command and pointed finger. "I said stay, and I mean it."

He skidded to a halt in front of the door and shot her a golden-eyed glare, shimmering with resentment. With both eyes on the cat, Izzy slipped out the back door and shut it firmly before turning to face the chaotic scene in her small yard.

The acrid smell of smoke and petroleum burned in her nose, making her eyes water. Two firefighters stood near the entrance to her studio, spraying a smoking pile of something with hand-held extinguishers, while four others dragged a heavy hose around the side of the house. Incongruously, Sebastian stood to one side, dressed in his bathrobe and pajamas and holding a garden hose in one hand.

Izzy wrapped her arms around herself in an attempt to still the shivers that had overtaken her body. Whether from the cold night air or the shock, she wasn't sure. It didn't matter. She approached the firefighters in front of the studio. "What's going on?"

One shut off his extinguisher and turned. "Are you the homeowner?"

"Yes. Izzy Munro. What happened? Is there a fire?"

"Not anymore. I think we've about got it."

She dropped her gaze to a blackened, smoldering pile of what appeared to be the remains of clothing or rags.

"Someone dumped these in front of the door to your outbuilding, doused them with gasoline, and then lit them on fire. Fortunately, your neighbor here—" He

174

tipped his head toward Sebastian. " —spotted the blaze from his window. After calling us, he ran down to investigate. He was able to drag the combustibles away from the structure with a rake and douse the fire with your hose."

Izzy's heart contracted. Sebastian might not look like everyone's idea of a hero in his paisley silk robe and horn-rimmed glasses, but hero he was. He'd saved her studio — possibly even her house.

A firm voice interrupted her train of thought. "I need you to step back, ma'am, so we can finish mopping up. Then we'll be on our way."

She nodded and walked over to join Sebastian, who was regarding the proceedings with a rapt stare. Laying a hand on his sleeve, she reached for the hose in his hand. "I don't think we need this anymore. Why don't you come inside, and I'll fix us both a cup of tea."

He started, then glanced at the hose. "That would be nice. I'll coil this back up for you."

Izzy took the hose and dropped it. "Leave it. I'll put it away in the morning. Come on."

She led him into the kitchen, where Bogart stood on the counter. He meowed insistently as soon as he saw them, his defiant posture daring her to order him down.

With a frown, Izzy plucked him up and set him on the floor, eliciting another loud complaint. "You know you're not supposed to be up there. Sebastian will think we have no manners at all."

Sebastian chuckled and bent to rub the cat's head. "You can't expect to rein in a free spirit like Bogart with a bourgeois concept like manners."

"Don't encourage him. He's adjusting to domestication quite nicely, thank you."

"If you say so."

She opened the cupboard and reached for a pair of mugs. "What flavor tea would you like? I have lemon ginger, blackberry pomegranate, and hibiscus."

He gazed out the window at the firefighters, who were wrapping up their work, and released a heavy breath. "While those sound delicious, I think tonight I could use something more fortifying—something along the lines of a large brandy."

"After what you did tonight, you deserve one...maybe two. I'll check the pantry and see if I can find a bottle." She patted his shoulder. "It's not every day you put out a fire in your neighbor's yard in the middle of the night in your pajamas."

Izzy hadn't gotten around to cleaning out the motley collection of bottles and canned goods Aunt Dora had left on the shelves in the laundry room. If there was brandy anywhere in the house, this was the most likely place.

She finally found what she was looking for behind a dusty bottle of Spanish sherry and carried it into the kitchen. "You're in luck, but is a mug okay? I don't want to go scrounging through cupboards at this hour for an appropriate snifter."

"A mug is perfect." Sebastian took the bottle and poured a generous serving into one of the mugs, then turned to Izzy. "Are you sure you won't join me?"

"Actually, I'm sure I will. It's been quite a night."

He half-filled a second mug and handed it to her. "This should help you relax and get back to sleep. Just don't drink it too fast. My services do not extend to carrying unconscious persons to bed."

She raised her mug in a mock toast. "Message received. I'll keep that in mind. Shall we take these into the living room? The sofa's softer and there's a nice warm afghan."

"I'll leave the afghan to you. If I get too comfortable, I'll be the one to fall asleep."

After they settled onto the sofa, Izzy spread the cozy knit blanket across her legs. Bogart immediately hopped onto her lap, turning in circles until he created a satisfactory nest, then curled up and went to sleep.

At the first sip of the brandy, she choked, bringing tears to her eyes.

A look of alarm crossed Sebastian's face, and he started to rise. "Can I get you a glass of water?"

Izzy coughed again. "No, no. I'll be fine. I just wasn't prepared. I've never had brandy before."

He eased back. "I warned you not to drink it too fast. It's powerful stuff."

She took another tiny sip, and although it burned on the way down, she noticed a warm glow kindling in her stomach and glanced over at Sebastian. His face was pale, even in the golden lamplight, and behind his glasses, his eyelids drooped. "You must be exhausted. I don't know how to thank you for what you did tonight. It was above and beyond."

"Nonsense." What his smile lacked in energy, it made up in genuine concern. "I only did what anyone would do."

"I'm pretty sure that's not true, but can you tell me what happened? By the time I woke up, most of the excitement was over."

He took a hefty mouthful of brandy and swallowed slowly. "I was working at my desk when a bright flash went off in your backyard. At first I thought an electrical transformer had blown, but my lights were still on. Then I saw someone running away."

Izzy sat up straighter. "You saw the person who set

the fire?"

"Not clearly. It was just a dark figure, silhouetted for a split second by the flames."

"So you called 911."

He nodded. "Then I ran downstairs to see what I could do."

"You should have waited for the Fire Department. You could have been hurt."

He dipped his chin, regarding her over the top of his glasses. "Izzy, I wasn't going to let someone burn down your studio after all the work you've put into it. Besides, I could see the fire wasn't very big, and it hadn't spread to the structure yet."

She smiled. "Well, I'm grateful. As it is, there's just a pile of singed rags to clean up. I could have lost the whole studio."

"I bet you'll find that the fire department arson investigator has taken away the remnants for analysis, and you won't have any work to do in the morning except maybe scrub the smoke residue off the windows. I have a virtual meeting at ten o'clock, but I'll be happy to come over and help you after lunch."

"You'll do no such thing. If anything needs cleaning, I'll do it myself after work. If you find yourself with time on your hands, take a nap."

Sebastian ignored her directive and glanced at the clock on the mantel. "Speaking of work, we both have busy days ahead of us. We'd better try to get a few hours' sleep."

"True." Izzy lifted Bogart off her lap and deposited him on the sofa before pushing to her feet. She walked Sebastian to the door, then hesitated. "I know thanks are inadequate, but thank you again."

"I try to make myself useful."

"You're so much more than useful. Vivian described you as a delightful person and an excellent neighbor, and she was absolutely correct."

He responded with a wry smile. "I'm afraid the lack of sleep and shock from the fire have addled your brain." Then his voice softened. "Good night, Izzy. Go to bed." He stepped out onto the porch, turned with a brief wave, then headed down the stone path toward his home.

She closed and locked the door, then leaned back against it with a shiver. The living room might look cozy, with its warm lamplight and sleeping cat, but the house felt cold, empty, and dark—as if something, or someone, was lurking in the hidden places.

"Bogart, I'm going to bed. You want to come with me?" She'd never invited him before, but tonight the appeal of a warm body cuddled up next to hers was too strong to resist.

****

Izzy awoke with a groan when her alarm went off a few short hours later. She'd finally managed to get to sleep sometime after three, but had awakened several times during the night, convinced she smelled smoke.

The house was still and quiet. Bogart had wandered off—presumably to the kitchen. As she threw off the covers, the chilly morning air sent a wave of goose bumps rippling across her body. She needed coffee, but breakfast was a definite no-go. Her stomach lurched at the thought of food.

She shuffled into the bathroom and stood under the shower until the hot water began to wane, too numb to worry about the waste. While the water soaked her hair and ran down her face, one thought kept circling through her mind.

Who? Who would do this? And why?

Dried and dressed, she wandered into the kitchen, where she found Bogart sitting beside his dishes. He looked miffed but kept his complaints to himself.

After dumping the dregs of both bowls, she refilled one with fresh water and set it in front of him. "It was a rough night. I think you deserve turkey this morning, don't you?"

That elicited a hearty *mrowr* of approval, so she popped open a small can of the gourmet food she reserved for special treats and forked the contents into the second bowl. He immediately dove in, making wet munching sounds as he ate. Izzy started the coffee maker and gazed out at the studio while she waited.

As Sebastian had predicted, the arson investigator had taken the burned material away. This morning, the only sign of the fire was a darkened area on the ground near the door to the studio. A thin, gray film coated the windows, but she could wash that off when she got home from work.

Work.

She contemplated calling Chantal and begging off, knowing her friend and employer would understand, but the busy salon would be a distraction, and it felt important to stick to her schedule. At least she wouldn't have to face Dottie Cartwright until next week. By Monday, the world was bound to look different.

The morning was cool and foggy when she left the house. Tiny pinpricks of moisture dampened her cheeks before evaporating on contact. When she walked into CeCe's at five minutes before nine, Chantal rushed to her, enveloping her in the closest thing to a bear hug someone who barely topped five feet tall could manage.

"I'm so glad to see you! Why are you here? Do you need to go home? We can manage without you for one morning."

Izzy gently peeled her friend's arms from around her middle. "Don't worry about me. I'm tired, but certainly well enough to work for a few hours. I can always take a nap this afternoon if I need to."

"But your house…" Chantal's heavily-fringed dark eyes blinked away a sheen of moisture.

"Is fine. There was no damage at all. But the fire happened less than twelve hours ago. How did you hear about it?"

"Dottie Cartwright called me at home at eight-thirty this morning."

Izzy started to ask how Dottie knew about the fire, but stopped herself. Dottie wasn't a subject she wanted to get into with Chantal. She hung up her jacket and took her place at the reception desk. No sooner had she turned on the computer than Joe De Rossi strode through the door.

"Good. I hoped you'd be here." His voice was gruff and his jawline hard.

Her brows rose. "Good morning to you, too."

"You need to come with me."

Izzy frowned and crossed her arms. "Am I under arrest or something?"

"Don't be ridiculous." He turned to Chantal. "Can you do without her for an hour or two? We need to talk."

"Sure. In fact, you don't need to bring her back at all if you can persuade her to go home and get some rest."

Joe nodded. "Come on. Get your things."

Izzy eyed him mutinously and refused to budge. "What do you think you're doing, coming in here with your robocop face and voice?"

"Have you eaten?"

"Not this morning, but—"

"I'm taking you to breakfast. Let's go."

Izzy shot Chantal an unspoken question.

Her boss shrugged. "The man is offering to feed you. I say, go for it. We'll be fine here."

Izzy just had time to grab her purse and jacket before Joe hustled her out the door. Once they hit the sidewalk, she stopped long enough to slip on her coat, then gave her hair a defiant shake. "What is the matter with you?"

"I'm angry."

"Obviously, but why are you angry with me?"

"I'm not." He took her elbow and steered her toward the corner. "I'm angry with the lowlife who tried to burn your house down last night."

She pulled out of his grasp but continued to keep pace beside him. "I don't think anyone actually intended to burn down my house...and where are we going?"

"Taste of Torino should do the trick."

"What trick? And I thought you didn't want us to be seen together."

He stared straight ahead with a frown. "After last night, I've decided we need a change of strategy. If someone is brazen enough to attack your property, I want the whole town to know you're under police protection."

"And having breakfast with me at Taste of Torino is the next best thing to standing in the middle of Ocean Avenue, holding a sign."

He turned left at the next corner. "Exactly. Besides, this morning I could use a sfogliatella, maybe two."

"Wow, I'm impressed. I have to sound out the names of most Italian pastries. That rolled off your tongue as easily as a native's."

"I almost am. My grandmother was born in Naples, and she used to make a different type of pastry every Saturday morning. She was a fantastic baker."

He sounded so wistful and nostalgic, Izzy had a flash of jealousy. Her own grandmother had died before she was born. Aunt Dora had more than made up for the lack, but she hadn't had the time or interest for baking.

When they reached Taste of Torino, Joe held the door then followed her inside. As usual, the place was humming. They found themselves third in line to order, behind a family of tourists and two older ladies who were discussing an upcoming concert at the Sunset Cultural Center a few blocks away.

When they reached the counter, Lorna greeted them with a wan half-smile. "What can I get you?"

"We'll have three sfogliatelle, one black coffee, and one—" Joe shot Izzy a questioning glance.

"Cappuccino."

"To go?" Lorna asked.

Joe turned and spotted a single empty table in front of the windows. "No. We'll sit over there."

Lorna nodded. "I'll bring your order as soon as it's ready."

He handed her a couple of bills. "Thanks."

Joe reminded Izzy of an old-fashioned locomotive with a cow-catcher on the front as he plowed through the milling crowd and headed for the table. They'd barely taken their seats when Lorna appeared with two coffees, a plate of pastries, and two smaller plates. She didn't speak, just unloaded the tray and left.

Izzy placed one of the pastries on her plate, leaving the remaining two for Joe. "Lorna looks miserable today."

Joe added a splash of creamer to his coffee and stirred. "In spite of the crowds, the place probably feels a little empty after Aldo's death. As I recall, you told me word on the street was they'd been having an affair."

"I don't know how much reliance to place on that bit of salon gossip, but while I was having dinner with her and Vivian a few nights ago, she did say she might be leaving Carmel soon."

Joe grunted and attacked his pastry with a fork. "We need to talk about last night. Detective Nolan called me at seven this morning with the basics, but I want to know exactly what happened."

Izzy filled him in on what little she knew.

"So you were asleep, but your neighbor saw the perpetrator fleeing the scene around one o'clock in the morning."

"Sebastian was at his desk. Apparently, he has business interests around the world and often works late into the night."

"And his office overlooks your backyard?"

She nodded.

Joe raised one thick brow. "You'll have to make sure his shades are down before you go sunbathing on the patio in the buff then...unless you enjoy that kind of attention."

Izzy held out an arm and pushed up her sleeve, baring several inches of smooth, pale skin. "As you can see, I'm not a big sunbather, but even if I were, I doubt Sebastian would notice or care."

"Ahh...I see. Well, we can be glad he noticed the arsonist running away last night. Michelle Nolan is at Larrabee's house right now, taking his statement. With luck, maybe he'll remember some additional details that will help us identify the perpetrator."

Izzy considered the layout of her property. "Sebastian has an extensive security system, but I doubt his cameras cover my backyard."

A third voice interrupted their conversation. "Can I get you anything else?"

They looked up simultaneously to find Lorna hovering over them.

Joe frowned. "No, thanks. We're good."

She nodded and drifted away.

Izzy leaned forward and lowered her voice. "That was strange. They don't have table service here, and besides, Lorna's the manager, not a waitress. I wonder how long she was standing there."

"I don't know, but I think we've been here long enough to make our point." He pushed his chair back and stood.

Izzy followed him out onto the busy sidewalk.

"Your comment about Larrabee's security cameras gave me an idea. I've been kicking myself all morning for not installing a camera on the back of your house, but unless the perp climbed the fence from a neighboring yard, they must have approached the house from the front and left the same way. Your doorbell cam should have picked them up coming and going."

"We can check on my phone."

When she opened her purse to take it out, Joe stopped her with a hand. "Not here. Let's go to your house where we can review the feed from your phone in private. I'd also like to examine the scene for myself."

"Sure. Although, as I said, there's not much to see."

"Another set of eyes...you never know. Besides, I thought you were a big believer in picking up vibes from the scene of a crime."

Izzy recoiled at the idea of her sanctuary being a crime scene. The attack on her studio had been more than an invasion of her personal space — it was an assault on her peace of mind. She had to accept that someone had wanted to send her an ugly message, but the sooner she figured out who and why, the sooner she could rebuild the sense of security that was essential to her well-being.

CHAPTER TWELVE

When Izzy and Joe reached her house, she led him around the side to inspect what was left at the scene of the fire.

He poked the blackened area in front of the studio with the toe of his shoe. "You were right—there isn't much to see."

"The fire wasn't very large, and Sebastian said the arson investigator would probably take most of the debris away for analysis."

Joe squatted and sniffed the air, then straightened. "I can still smell the accelerant. I doubt they'll find much else, but I'll check with the lab tomorrow."

She pointed from the burn scar to the door of the studio. "The firefighters said Sebastian dragged the flaming mass away from the building with a rake, but I don't think it was set with the intention of destroying anything—especially not the house—and I don't think it was simple vandalism. This feels more like a message."

"What do your instincts tell you?"

"That it's a warning—like 'Go back where you came from' or 'Mind your own business.'"

He stared at the ground. "I think you're right. You've either made someone angry or nervous." Glancing up, he pushed to his feet. "Let's sit on the patio and take a look at the video on your phone."

They dragged two chairs next to each other so they could both see the screen, and Izzy pulled up the doorbell camera app on her phone. Since Joe had more experience with the system, she handed it to him, and he searched until he found the section of the recording before the Fire Department arrived. They leaned together until their heads almost touched and peered at the screen. Suddenly, a figure dressed in black dashed up from the street and across the front yard, carrying a large bag. Three minutes later, the same figure ran back across the screen, this time carrying only a can with a handle, and disappeared into the darkness.

Joe backed it up and ran it again. It was still impossible to make out any distinguishing details.

He handed the phone back in disgust. "I'd hoped this would give us something, but it looks like half the surveillance video I've seen—some kid in a black hoodie."

Izzy replayed the video, searching for any small detail she might have missed. "Here, take another look. If this is a teenage boy, he's not very big." She held the phone so he could see.

Joe peered at the figure as it streaked across her front yard. "Hmm. Based on the build and gait, I guess it could be a woman." He sat back and regarded her with one raised brow. "You've only been in town a few weeks. How many women have you ticked off enough to do something like this?"

"Oh, ten or twelve, at least."

"Izzy..."

She sighed. "I'm sorry, but it's easier to joke about than to accept that someone dislikes me enough to set fire to my property."

He reached out and covered her hand with his. "I know, but now I need you to think like a victim instead of an investigator. Have you had a conflict with anyone?"

"Other than Serena Pefferman, you mean?"

"Yes. After her accusations when we searched her spa, she's already at the top of the list."

Izzy pondered his question. She'd only met a few women and considered most of them friends, like Vivian and Chantal. There were also Dottie Cartwright and Lorna Ferris, but they were barely acquaintances, and she hadn't given either of them a reason to dislike her. Then she remembered Dina Korman. Both times she'd met the Kormans, they'd both been cordial, but what about Tuesday afternoon, when Kurt nearly caught her peering through their bushes? If either of them had recognized her, or if Dottie had mentioned running into her on the sidewalk, they might have feared she would expose their scheme to exaggerate Kurt's disability for their lawsuit. Would that be enough to motivate a woman like Dina to attempt arson?

Dina Korman was in her seventies and a respected neurologist. However, Izzy had the impression she was also a woman who fiercely loved her husband and would stop at little to take care of him and protect his best interests.

She glanced up and met Joe's dark, probing gaze. "There is someone else you should probably add to the list." She told him everything she knew about the Kormans, their history with Aldo Pefferman, and their pending lawsuit.

"Thanks. I'll talk to them."

She nodded. "The sooner, the better. Even if they had nothing to do with the fire, they might be in danger if Serena Pefferman is as unhinged as she seemed during your search of Beauty by the Bay."

"About that, the lab finished their analysis of the boxes we confiscated from the spa, and although the labels said botulinum toxin, the vials contained ordinary tap water."

"Not even a trace of the poison?"

"Nope."

She sat back with a frown and pondered the ramifications. "That's bizarre."

"Uh, huh. We've hit a wall, but we're going to keep digging."

"Did you tell Serena and Marcus?"

Joe nodded. "I stopped by with the news. I wanted to see how they'd react. As you'd expect, they were relieved. They also seemed as perplexed as we were about how the boxes came to be on their shelves."

"I suppose either of them could have swapped the contents."

"But why leave the boxes?"

Izzy cast her mind back to some of the claims she'd investigated in her prior life. "To cast suspicion on their partner? It would be helpful to see a copy of their partnership agreement. Does each partner get full ownership of the business in the event of the death or disability of the other?"

"It's worth checking into." He pulled a small notebook from his pocket and jotted down a few words.

"Speaking of legal documents, I assume you've spoken to Aldo's attorney about his will. Does Serena stand to inherit everything?"

"Every penny, and believe me, it's an impressive pile. The Peffermans kept their business interests separate during Aldo's lifetime, but now — in addition to her half-ownership of Beauty by the Bay — Serena has taken control of a very lucrative portfolio of Carmel real estate."

Izzy immediately thought of Cece's. "That's good for her, but Chantal's worried about the rent on her salon going up, or even losing her lease."

"I'm sure a lot of Aldo's tenants share her concern. However, it's also possible Mrs. Pefferman will decide to sell everything and move to the Riviera. You never know."

"True. But none of this gets us any closer to finding Aldo's killer, or my arsonist."

"It's been less than twelve hours since the fire, but as far as the murder goes, we're making progress." Joe cleared his throat. "At least we were, until *someone* added a pair of new suspects to the list."

Izzy ignored the jab. "What about Christos Getz?"

"He's still out of town, but I plan to interview him as soon as he returns."

"I hope you're able to rule him either in or out. I know it's been less than two weeks since Aldo's death, but it feels much longer."

"You've never been involved in a murder investigation from the beginning before. Sometimes we get lucky and have evidence to identify the perpetrator right away, but most cases require days or weeks of painstaking legwork."

"You said you were making progress, though. Have you learned anything new you can share?"

He leaned forward, resting his elbows on the table. "We've been through Pefferman's business finances and have found a number of questionable deals—sales to offshore shell corporations, borderline fraud, that sort of thing."

Izzy wasn't shocked. Aldo's manner had been polished to the point of slickness. "Do you think he was involved in money laundering?"

"There's no evidence of that yet, but let's just say everything wasn't always on the up-and-up."

"It's possible he could have been killed by someone he cheated in a business deal—money is a powerful motive—but his wife stood to gain the most financially from his death. Besides, he wasn't killed in a fit of anger. This was carefully planned and took some time to execute. You can't just walk into your local pharmacy and pick up a box of fake Botox."

"No." Joe's phone buzzed in his pocket, and he pulled it out to check the screen. "Forensics is finished with the debris from your fire, and it looks like they might have something. I've got to go." He pushed his chair back and stood, stuffing his phone back in his pocket.

"You'll let me know?" Izzy rose, too.

"As soon as I can." He disappeared around the side of the house.

She glanced at her watch. It was only ten-thirty, but she felt like she'd been up all night—which she had. Chantal had told her to stay home and rest, but after Joe's call, she was too antsy to sleep. And besides, she hated to leave her friend in the lurch. She shouldered her bag and headed back to Cece's.

Izzy managed to hang on at work until one o'clock, but as soon as she got home, she stretched out on the sofa and promptly fell asleep. She didn't wake up until Bogart nuzzled her nose at three-thirty. She dragged herself into a sitting position and rubbed her eyes.

Mrowr!

"Hello to you, too. And what do you want? It's too early for dinner."

Mrowr!

She scratched under his chin, eliciting a low, rumbling purr. "I think we both deserve a snack. Come on."

He hopped down and followed her into the kitchen, where she put the kettle on and opened a packet of kitty treats. After a cup of strong black tea and one of Vivian's peanut butter cookies, she was wide awake and ready to do something constructive.

She glanced down at the cat, who was finishing the last of the treats in his bowl. "Do you want to come outside with me? I'm going to wash the windows in the studio."

Bogart hung close as she gathered cleaning supplies in the laundry room — a bucket, rubber gloves, a sponge, squeegee, liquid soap, and paper towels. When she unlocked the back door and started to step outside, he shot between her feet, nearly tripping her.

"Hey, watch it! There won't be anyone to feed you if I break a leg," she called after him. He hesitated, turned, and gave her a disdainful look before scampering off. He scaled the back fence in a single bound and disappeared into the neighbors' jungle of a yard.

Izzy shook her head, then turned to the studio. Washing the windows would be good exercise, both physically and mentally. It would be easier to forget last night ever happened when all obvious traces of the fire were gone.

Halfway down the stone path, she stopped and frowned. The windows sparkled in the dappled afternoon sunlight. All remnants of oily smoke residue had disappeared. She dropped her gaze to the ground where the blaze had been set. The mulch was fresh and wet, with no sign of charring. There was only one way that could have happened. She set her bucket down, yanked her phone from her back pocket, and punched in a number.

Sebastian answered. "Hello, Izzy. I hoped you might still be napping. How are you feeling?"

"What do you think you're doing?"

"Um...working on the editorial for tomorrow's *Acorn*?"

"You've been doing a lot more than that this afternoon," she accused. "I told you I didn't need help washing the windows of my studio."

"Everyone needs help sometimes. The mature accept it graciously."

If not for the teasing note in his voice, she would have been insulted. As it was, her anger deflated like a balloon with a slow puncture. "But you already put the fire out single-handedly, in the middle of the night, in your pajamas. You've done so much for me since I moved in—I feel guilty."

"Izzy," his voice was gentle, "friendship isn't a scale to be kept in balance."

"But I don't do anything for you," she protested.

"You elevate the quality of my newspaper with your photos. By the way, the first installment of your 'Gardens of Carmel' feature will appear this week. I

194

loved the article you came up with to accompany your pictures, and I'm sure our readers will, too."

"I hope so. I don't know anything about plants, but I enjoyed doing the research."

It was only after hanging up that she realized Sebastian had successfully eluded the issue of their lopsided relationship, yet again.

The next morning, she left for work a few minutes early, allowing time to stop by the market near the salon to pick up a copy of this week's *Acorn*. She carried it into Cece's and dropped it on the desk while she hung up her jacket.

Chantal glanced over from her station, where she was organizing her combs, brushes, curling iron, and various styling products for the day. "Ooh, is that the new *Acorn*?" She hurried over and began flipping through the pages. "I placed an ad for the salon this week, and I want to see how it looks." She found the ad on page three and handed the paper to Izzy. "Here. What do you think?"

The full-color ad showed a chic young woman with a shaggy blond pixie cut and bright red lipstick, winking at the camera. The text read: *Start Your Next Adventure at Cece's.*

"I love it. It makes the salon experience look fun."

"That's the whole idea. Visiting the salon should be fun. I want every customer to walk out that door feeling confident and ready to take on the world." Chantal spread her arms in triumph.

"That's a lot to ask of a simple haircut."

Chantal crossed her arms. "There's no such thing as a *simple* haircut. Think back. How did you feel when you left here the day we met?"

"Lighter. Relieved. Maybe a little in awe."

"Transformed."

Izzy grinned. "If you say so."

"Don't try to argue, and don't minimize the feeling. I know transformation when I see it. Knowing you look your best is one of the most important building blocks of self-confidence."

Izzy raised a hand in defense. "I wouldn't dream of arguing with an expert. If you ever get tired of running the salon, you should take up motivational speaking. You're a natural."

Chantal gave her long, dark mane a toss and batted her lashes. "I'm all about self-confidence." Then her expression sobered as she pointed at the *Acorn* in Izzy's hands. "Now, we'll just have to see if this ad strikes a chord with customers who want to feel better about themselves."

"Are you kidding? Everyone wants to feel better about themselves."

"I hope you're right. I adore Sebastian Larrabee, but advertising in the *Acorn* isn't cheap." She returned her attention to the page. "But before I get back to work, shall we see what oddities the police log has for us today?"

"Absolutely. It's my favorite part of the paper."

Chantal laughed. "It's everyone's favorite part of the paper." She began to scan the column, then pointed to an item. "Oh. My. Goodness. Look at this."

Two inebriated subjects at Carmelo and Ninth were in a verbal argument at 0039 hours over an injury the male sustained. The male was bitten by accident in his private area during amorous activity. There were several other issues the couple was arguing about. Parties had to be separated for the night due to not getting along. The female was picked up by a sober family member, and the male agreed to go to sleep for the night. They will revisit the ongoing issues when sober in the morning.

Izzy shook her head. "Tourists."

"I hope so. How would you like your neighbors to know you're up to that kind of shenanigans in the middle of the night?"

Izzy laughed. "I'm not worried." She took the paper from Chantal and spread it on the desk. After running her gaze from one side to the other, she turned the page.

Chantal bent over to get a closer look. "What are you hunting for?"

"I gave Sebastian a proposal for a new series about Carmel gardens, along with several photos. He said the first installment would be in this issue." She flipped another page. "Ah, here it is."

The pictures weren't of the best quality — newspaper photos never were — but they were eye-catching, and the article she'd written to accompany them was short, but informative.

"Those are pretty," Chantal said.

"They don't look half-bad, although the originals are better — sharper and crisper — and the play of light is more distinct."

"You should print large copies and sell them as a series."

An image of dramatic, oversized versions of her photos flashed into Izzy's head. "That's a great idea! I'd also thought about turning them into a book."

"Ooh, I bet the local bookstore and giftshops would carry it. A book on Carmel gardens would make a great memento for visitors."

"Speaking of large prints, we should set up a time to

start on the series you wanted for the salon."

"Absolutely." Chantal pulled out her phone to check her calendar. "How about Sunday afternoon? I'm having brunch with my parents, but I should be available by two o'clock."

Since work was her only regular activity, Izzy didn't have a schedule to check. "That will be perfect. I'll be around, so come over whenever you're ready." She smiled in anticipation of her first photoshoot in her new studio. Which reminded her of the fire. Which reminded her how lucky she was to have a friend and neighbor like Sebastian.

Chantal interrupted her train of thought. "I've been meaning to ask you, what are you doing this evening around five-thirty?"

Once again, Izzy didn't have to check her schedule. "Nothing special. Why?"

"The Merchants' Association is sponsoring a wine tasting in the courtyard of the Sunrise Vineyards Tasting Room, and I wondered if you'd like to come with me. I'm meeting my cousin, Felipe — forty-two, tall, dark, handsome, *and* divorced. I think you two would really hit it off."

"The wine tasting sounds fun, but no matchmaking, please. It's been less than a month since my split from Bryce. Getting involved with another man is the last thing on my mind right now."

"Oh, all right," Chantal groused. "No matchmaking. But Felipe is a great guy and — "

"Chantal!"

"Okay, okay. If you stop by around five-thirty, we can walk to the tasting room together."

"It's a date."

Izzy spent the afternoon looking at furniture on a big

build-it-yourself website and choosing the basic pieces she needed to furnish her studio. Chantal was coming the day after tomorrow for her first photo shoot, and Izzy didn't want her to think the place was a barn. She chose a white slab desk and a desk chair for her work space, and two red upholstered chairs with a low, white, kidney bean-shaped coffee table for client meetings. It was all very Scandinavian Minimalist. When she checked the website for the address of the nearest store, she found one in a Bay Area suburb about an hour's drive north that had everything on her list in stock and made a plan to head out first thing in the morning.

At four o'clock, it was time to start pulling herself together. There wasn't much she could do to perk up her tired eyes, but she could at least try to dress decently. She opened the tiny closet and flipped through her limited choices. She had a pretty blue-patterned chiffon cocktail dress she'd worn to a few parties with Bryce, but it felt wrong—too dressy and feminine. There was nothing fussy about Carmel. The town had a casual, restrained vibe of understated wealth. And while Izzy might not have wealth, she was a master of understated.

She selected slim black slacks—you could never go wrong with black—and a black-and-brown patterned jacket cut in simple, straight lines. After fifteen minutes in the bathroom with the products and implements she'd gotten from Chantal, she'd revived her curls and looked reasonably fashionable. A hint of blush, a swipe of mascara, and warm mocha lipstick completed the subtle, don't-notice-me look.

She fed Bogart, locked him in for the night, and set off for Cece's.

The air was crisp, and the sunset lit the sky across the bay in soft horizontal streaks of orange, pink, and peach.

There was a bounce in Izzy's step as she contemplated her first social event as a single woman in five years, and her first since moving to Carmel. The Halloween parade didn't count. It had been a mob scene, and besides, a man had nearly died in her lap. Dinner at Vivian's didn't count, either, because it had only included three people. According to her self-styled definition, a social event required a minimum of four guests.

Chantal was saying goodbye to her final customer of the day when Izzy arrived. The stylist scanned her from head to toe with a nod of satisfaction. "Very nice. And your hair looks great."

She couldn't resist fluffing her curls with one hand. "All the credit belongs to you."

"Naturally." Chantal grinned and reached for her purse. "Now, let's go before the horde drinks all the good stuff."

Izzy hesitated. "Horde? You didn't tell me there would be a horde. I'm not very good with hordes." She allowed herself to be herded outside and waited on the sidewalk while Chantal locked the door.

"You'll be fine. The crowd won't be that large. There's plenty of open space in the plaza, and these things usually draw around a hundred people. Although I have to admit, they can get a little horde-like around the bar."

"I'll tuck myself into an inconspicuous corner."

"You'll do no such thing. Now, come on."

Chantal half-dragged her down the block to the intersection with Ocean Avenue, where they turned right and started up the street, away from the beach and toward the Sunrise Vineyards tasting room. They had nearly reached the next intersection when screams erupted from the crowd of shoppers on the sidewalk several blocks ahead. Izzy rose on her tiptoes and craned her neck, trying to identify the cause of the commotion.

"Look! Over there!" Chantal pointed to the opposite side of the landscaped, divided parkway, the downhill side.

Izzy spotted a small white car barreling down the steep hill. It appeared to be out of control, blowing through stop signs and intersections, rapidly picking up speed on its breakneck race to the ocean. People waved and shouted but were helpless to stop the speeding vehicle.

By the time the car careened past, Izzy could see it was a vintage Mercedes convertible. The driver's long, blond hair whipped across her face, enough to partially obscure her features but not the mouth opened wide in a terrified scream. Most of the onlookers stayed where they were, frozen in shock, but a few ran down the hill, following the car. Without hesitation, Izzy and Chantal joined the chase.

The road narrowed from four lanes to two as it neared the beach parking lot, and the median disappeared. As usual, the lot was full, making the path of the runaway car even more treacherous. It was impossible to tell if the Mercedes still had steering, but the driver's hands remained welded to the wheel as the vehicle bounced off one car after another before crashing headfirst into a massive SUV parked across the end of the lot.

By the time Izzy and Chantal reached the wreck, someone had called 911, and a middle-aged woman with the practiced movements and medical vocabulary of a seasoned professional had taken charge of the scene.

When Izzy managed to catch a glimpse of the interior

of the car through the milling crowd, her stomach clenched. Whether the driver was dead or merely unconscious, she wasn't moving. She was wearing a lap belt, but the car had been built long before the introduction of air bags, so the force of the collision had smashed her head into the steering wheel. Blood had sprayed across the broken glass of the windshield and dripped onto the dashboard. Droplets of red dotted the pristine white leather upholstery.

The woman tending to the driver checked for a pulse, first at the wrist, then at the neck. When she gently lifted the driver's head and leaned it back against the headrest, Chantal gasped and clutched Izzy's hand.

The driver of the wayward Mercedes was Serena Pefferman.

CHAPTER THIRTEEN

Izzy turned away from the sight of Serena's blood-streaked face. She didn't know if Aldo's widow was dead, or merely unconscious, but the impact of the steering wheel had caused serious injury. If Serena survived, she would require extensive plastic surgery to repair the damage.

When a siren pulsed in the distance, Izzy glanced up the hill and spotted the same red Fire Department ambulance that had attended Aldo descending the avenue, followed by two Carmel PD squad cars. Moments later, the crowd that had gathered around the wrecked Mercedes moved back to make way for the EMTs and their stretcher.

She couldn't hear the conversation between the lead EMT and the woman attending Serena, but Izzy saw no signs of movement when they removed the victim from her car and placed her on the stretcher. The emergency personnel were professional and efficient, but their movements were methodical, lacking the speed and urgency one would expect if they were trying to save a life.

Chantal tugged on her sleeve. "Let's go. There's nothing we can do here."

Izzy nodded, and they turned to make their way back through the remaining onlookers. Her mouth tasted like dust, dry and faintly metallic. "I need to go home. I don't think I can go to the wine tasting with you."

"Don't worry about it. I'll stop by and make our excuses so Felipe doesn't think I stood him up. After what's happened, the organizers will probably shut the event down, anyway." Chantal turned her head and glanced back at the somber scene. "I can't believe two prominent citizens—husband and wife—both died violent deaths within two weeks of each other. That kind of thing doesn't happen in a town this size."

Izzy sighed. "Maybe it's me. Maybe I brought bad juju with me from the big city."

"Don't be ridiculous. Tragedies happen everywhere. We just aren't used to it in Carmel."

As they trudged up the steep sidewalk toward downtown, the ambulance passed them, moving with the flow of traffic without its lights or siren.

****

After a restless night punctuated by dreams of getting lost on the way to high school, then forgetting her locker number and missing a test because she was late, Izzy dragged herself out of bed and padded barefoot into the kitchen. Bogart was waiting beside his empty bowls with a look of judgy disappointment.

Izzy stroked his head as she bent to pick up the bowls. "I'm sorry if the level of service doesn't meet your standards, but thanks for not waking me earlier. It was a rough night."

Mrowr.

"I knew you'd understand."

After feeding him, she scrambled two eggs with cheese while waiting for her coffee. Yesterday, she'd decided to drive up to the Bay Area furniture barn this morning to pick up the pieces she wanted for her studio. She didn't want to abandon her plan just because another Pefferman had had the misfortune to die in front of her.

The images of Serena's broken body being extracted from her mangled sports car lingered in Izzy's mind — sharp, crisp, and eerily surreal. She still struggled to accept that it was anything other than a bad dream.

She felt better with a hefty dose of caffeine and a few calories in her, so she took a quick shower, hopped into the Subaru, and headed north.

Three hours later, she pulled into her driveway, the back of her car laden with heavy, flat-pack boxes. She climbed out, opened the hatchback, and surveyed the contents, trying to figure out the best way to get the boxes back to her studio. A pair of dock workers at the store had loaded the car for her, and she could probably slide the boxes out and to the ground by herself. However, she would need a dolly to wheel them to the backyard. Maybe Sebastian had one he could lend her. He seemed to have everything.

Before she could act on that thought, though, another car pulled up and parked behind her.

Joe De Rossi climbed out carrying a white paper bag. "I called, but you didn't answer, so I thought I'd swing by and hope to catch you."

Izzy pulled her phone from her purse and saw she had a missed call. "I was probably on the loading dock when you called. I must not have heard the phone over all the noise. What can I do for you?"

Joe surveyed the back of the Subaru. "It's more what I can do for you." He raised his bag. "I brought lunch. Let me set this on the porch, and I'll help you unload all that. Do the boxes go into the house?"

She shook her head. "Around in back. It's a few basic pieces for the studio. Chantal's coming over tomorrow afternoon for a photoshoot, and I'd like the place to look as professional as possible."

"That sounds like fun. Hang on a second."

After depositing the food on the front porch, he returned and lifted the top box a few inches, testing its weight. "Let's slide this out. We should be able to carry it around to the studio, no problem."

He was right, and twenty minutes later the car was empty, and the boxes lay on the studio's concrete floor.

Joe brushed his hands off on his pants. "I'll help you put all this together after lunch. Right now, I'm hungry. Let's eat."

She led the way to the front porch, where he'd left the bag. "You don't have to keep bringing me food every time you want to talk, you know."

His expression sobered. "I do know, and that's the point. I know what it's like to make the adjustment from being part of a couple to living on your own. Food can be low on your list of priorities."

He was right. Because of work, she'd never had time for elaborate cooking, but she and Bryce had made joint decisions about where to eat or what to bring home. Now, she had to force herself to prepare regular meals, and sometimes it didn't feel worth the effort. "Thank you. I appreciate it."

This time, Joe had brought barbecue from a place in Salinas she'd never heard of. He lifted a pair of impressively thick, pulled pork sandwiches from the bag, along with two small containers of coleslaw and two large dill pickle spears, and arranged them on the plates she'd taken from the cupboard. "I found this place shortly after moving here. I think you'll like it. If not," he shrugged, "there's that much more for me."

She leaned over and sniffed. "It smells good. I think I'll give mine a few seconds in the microwave to warm it up."

"That sounds good. I'll zap mine after you finish."

The air was cool, but the sun was shining, so they decided to eat outside on the patio.

Izzy took a drink from her glass of water. "Now, do you want to tell me what brings you here on a sunny Saturday?"

"It might not be anything, but I thought you'd want to know about the evidence the forensics tech found in the residue of your fire."

"Definitely. You said it might be important."

His lips thinned in a grimace. "I don't know how helpful it will be, but at least it's something. First, the fuel was a bundle of rags doused with an accelerant, in this case gasoline. No surprises there. The only potentially interesting piece of evidence was found on a scrap of fabric that remained unburned." He pulled out his phone and searched for a photo, then held it out to her. "Take a look."

Izzy took the phone and enlarged the image with her fingers. "It looks like a laundry marker. When Bryce used to take his work shirts to the cleaners, before I convinced him of the magic of wrinkle-free fabric, they wrote his name and the name of the cleaners on the inside of the lower portion of the button placket in indelible ink." She enlarged the picture further and squinted. "The edges are scorched, but the writing looks like AN AND. It could be part of a name."

Joe took his phone back. "That's what I thought. Unfortunately, it doesn't help much. Detective Nolan doesn't know of anyone in town with those initials, and it's unlikely someone would use their own clothing to start a malicious fire. It's more likely the arsonist picked up a bunch of old clothes at a thrift shop for a few bucks." He shook his head and took a big bite of his sandwich.

"That's true. So we don't know any more than we did when the firefighters left Tuesday night."

His frown deepened until his brows nearly met. "It's frustrating. We can't seem to catch a break on either the murder case or the arson at the moment. And now, on top of that, we have Serena Pefferman's death to investigate."

Izzy's appetite faded. She'd managed to put Serena out of her mind for most of the morning. "So she is dead. A small part of me hoped she'd just been knocked unconscious."

"What do you mean? Did you witness the accident?"

She nodded. "Chantal and I were walking up Ocean Avenue on the way to a wine tasting when Serena came barreling down the hill. She was screaming and looked terrified—the car was completely out of control. Then the crash at the bottom..." She shook her head, remembering the shattered glass, the blood, and Serena's blond head slumped over the steering wheel. "It was horrible."

"I didn't know you were there."

She managed a weak smile. "Lately, I seem to have a knack for being in the wrong place at the wrong time."

Joe reached over and gave her hand a brief squeeze. "I'm sorry. I've seen the accident photos. Nobody gets used to a sight like that."

"Chantal kept saying what a shocking coincidence it was. First Aldo is murdered, and then his wife dies in an accident a short time later."

He took a drink then looked her straight in the eye. "I don't believe Mrs. Pefferman's death was either a coincidence or an accident. Her car was severely damaged, but the evidence tech who examined the wreckage thinks the brakes were tampered with."

Izzy sat back, trying to digest the news. "You're telling me both Aldo and his wife were murdered? Do you think the same person is responsible for both deaths?"

"Without more evidence, it's impossible to say. There are three possibilities. Either the same person killed them both. Or Serena murdered her husband, and someone else killed her. Or they were killed by separate individuals, and the deaths are unrelated."

"That's about as wide open as it could be. Do the police have anything at all to go on?"

"Not much, but it's been less than twenty-four hours. When Michelle Nolan called me last night, she'd just finished talking to Dr. Holder. He said Serena received a phone call just as they were closing the office. He didn't know the identity of the caller, but she became very agitated and was screaming into the phone by the time the call ended. Then she said she had to meet someone and stormed out."

Izzy pursed her lips. "Hmm. The call might—or

might not—be related. Did the police find her phone?"

"Yes. It was badly damaged in the crash, but the techs are working on it now. Even if they can't retrieve any data from it, her service provider should be able to identify the caller. Unfortunately, that can take some time."

"If Serena had accidentally hit the gas instead of the brakes and plowed into a building, it might have been because she was upset, but if her brakes were disabled…"

He finished her thought. "The caller might have been luring her into her car, knowing it would crash if she built up enough speed."

"What a tangled mess. You may not have definitive evidence yet, but what does your experience tell you?"

"That the least complicated answer is usually the best." He took another bite of his sandwich.

"Which would rule out the third option. The chances of there being two separate killers with different motives seems too remote to be worth pursuing, unless the evidence points you in that direction."

"I agree. Unfortunately, the DA's office doesn't have unlimited resources."

The train of the conversation sparked a thought in Izzy's mind. "Speaking of evidence, were you ever able to find out anything about that locket we found in Aldo's office."

"Actually, yes, although I don't know how much help it will be. We sent inquiries to jewelry stores around the state and learned the locket was custom-made about ten years ago by a jeweler in Oceanside for a customer named Ian Anderson."

"The I. A. in the inscription," she mused, half under her breath.

"Presumably. I've put a junior investigator to work tracing the man, but it's a slow grind. I wish he had a name like Mortimer or Hieronymus. You can't imagine how many Ians there are in California."

"And since I doubt Mr. Anderson dropped the locket himself, you'll also want to try to identify K. I don't envy your investigators. Ten years is a long time. Anything could have happened by now. The Andersons could have gotten a divorce or moved out of state."

"On top of that, it didn't escape my notice that the AN AND laundry mark on that charred scrap of fabric could originally have read Ian Anderson." His lips tightened in frustration. "Of course, it could also belong to a Susan Andrews or Dylan Andretti or any of a thousand other names."

She gave him a wry smile. "This doesn't get any easier, does it?"

"Never."

Without thinking, Izzy scooped up a forkful of coleslaw. She popped it into her mouth and was surprised to discover she was hungry again. The mental gymnastics of trying to untangle the web of intertwined evidence in the Pefferman cases seemed to have spurred her appetite. She glanced at Joe, who was wolfing down the remainder of his sandwich with the iron stomach of a veteran homicide detective.

She finished half her sandwich, then dabbed her lips with her napkin to take care of any traces of barbecue sauce. "That was good, but I think I'll save the rest for dinner."

"I'll help you carry this stuff inside, then we can attack the boxes in your studio." He rose and picked up his dirty dishes. "We'll have that furniture assembled in no time. I'm a whiz with a Scandinavian multi-tool." He demonstrated by flipping his fork around in his fingers until it shot out and clattered to the table.

Izzy laughed. "Maybe I'd better tackle this project alone."

Joe proved to be more adept with a mini-wrench than a fork and had one of the chairs assembled before she finished attaching the legs to the coffee table.

She tested the chair by sitting and trying to wiggle from side to side. The joints remained solid and tight. "Good job."

Brandishing the tool, he smiled. "Be sure to keep this somewhere you won't forget. The chair's good for now, but the wood is soft, and the screws tend to loosen. You'll need to tighten them from time to time."

"That sounds like the voice of experience."

"Hey, it isn't easy to furnish a house on a cop's salary."

"I understand, believe me. Insurance companies don't have the deepest pockets, either."

Joe began work on the second chair while Izzy finished the coffee table. When it was done, she sat back on her heels and regarded the finished product with a critical eye. For the money, it didn't look half-bad. One leg didn't quite touch the floor, giving it a bit of a wobble, but the old concrete surface wasn't perfectly level, either. A small rug under the seating area should solve the problem.

After setting the second chair on its feet, he came to inspect her handiwork. "Simple, but stylish. I like it. Do you want to work on the desk together?"

"That would probably be easiest. The top is pretty heavy."

They sliced open the box and arranged the pieces on the floor. She tried out one of the new chairs, resting her back and allowing her mind to wander, while he studied the wordless instructions.

"I was just thinking about Christos Getz," she mused. "He was involved in a major feud with Aldo, and Serena accused him of planting the boxes of illegal toxin at Beauty by the Bay. Based on what I've seen, he's a real hothead. Do you think that might have given him sufficient motive for both murders?"

"It's hard to say. I haven't talked to the man yet. But that reminds me, he got back in town Thursday afternoon, and I have an appointment to interview him at the Carmel PD station first thing Monday morning."

"That should be interesting." Figuring out what role, if any, Christos Getz might have played in the killings was an intriguing puzzle. Then she had an idea. "Would it be possible for me to sit in?"

"Izzy—" Joe's tone contained a hint of warning.

"I know it's irregular, but as soon as these murders are solved, Sebastian is going to need an in-depth article for the *Acorn*. With my inside knowledge of the cases, I would be better positioned to write the story than any of his regular reporters, and observing a witness interview might give me some unique perspective. Of course, I wouldn't write anything without your okay."

He hesitated, his dark gaze boring into her, weighing the risk. "I guess that would be all right. You wouldn't be in the room with us—you could watch on a monitor in the squad room—and since you've observed Getz interacting with Pefferman, your insight might be helpful."

Suddenly she remembered. "But I have to work Monday morning."

"You start at nine, right? Getz has agreed to meet me at the station at eight o'clock so the interview doesn't interfere with him opening his shop."

She would have to get up a little earlier than usual, but observing a police interview would be an interesting experience. "I'll be there at eight."

"Better come a few minutes early so we can get you settled before Getz arrives. I'd rather he didn't know you were sitting in."

She would prefer that, too. She didn't want to stir up suspicion in town, so the less obvious her connection to the police, the better.

"That's settled, then." Joe laid the instruction sheet aside and picked up the mini-wrench. "Let's get this desk put together. I've got three loads of laundry at home calling my name."

Izzy's eyebrows shot up. "You're spending Saturday night doing laundry? I thought I was the only one with such an exciting social life."

He shrugged. "You've got to do what you've got to do, when you've got time to do it."

Fifteen minutes later, the desk was in one piece instead of ten and set in position, with her new office chair tucked beneath.

He handed her the all-important tool. "Now —"

"I know. Keep it someplace I won't forget." She stuffed it into the pocket of her jeans. "Thanks so much for your help, and for lunch. I could have assembled these pieces alone, and I probably would have eaten something eventually, but this was much better." She tamped down an unexpected twinge of shyness and gave him a confident smile.

"I'm happy to help. I'll see you Monday morning, assuming no one else is murdered between now and then."

"Don't even joke about it."

After Joe left, she cleaned up the dishes and returned to her studio, carrying her laptop, along with its associated cables, so she wouldn't be constantly draining the battery. Editing her photos on the kitchen table didn't feel professional, especially since she now had a dedicated space. She set the computer on the desk and reattached the cords, hoping she remembered where they belonged, before plugging everything into a surge protector on the floor. After flipping the *ON* switch, she scooted out from under the desk, perched on the edge of her new chair, and pushed the power button. The device took a minute or two to pull itself together, but soon it was back up and running normally.

She swiveled in her chair and surveyed the space with a surge of satisfaction. A colorful rug would help, and she needed some moveable lights, but otherwise, the studio was ready to go.

As she locked the door to return to the house, her gaze dropped to the spot where the unknown hooded figure had set the pile of rags ablaze. Even though no visible trace remained, a chill rippled through her. She realized the police didn't have much to go on, but not knowing who had set the fire, or why, ate away at her sense of security.

Two hours later, she was stretched out on the sofa, reading a book with Bogart asleep on her chest, when the doorbell rang. He objected when she lifted him to answer it, then immediately settled into the warm spot she'd vacated.

When she opened the door, she found Vivian standing on the porch.

"Grab your coat and camera, and let's go to the beach. The sunset is breathtaking."

Izzy raised her gaze above the roofs across the street

to a sight unlike any she'd ever seen. It looked like a magical artist had dipped a brush into glowing pots of crimson, pink, orange, and gold, and smeared it back and forth across the sky, from north to south, horizon to horizon. "Wow."

Vivian made a shooing motion. "Like I said, hurry."

Izzy complied, and they set out on the short walk to the beach. As soon as the shoreline came into view, it was obvious they weren't the only ones with the same idea. Clusters of people dotted the smooth white sand, *ooh*ing and *aah*ing and pointing at the sky. Children and dogs chased each other, splashing in the bubble-fringed edges of the gentle waves that lapped the shore. Izzy snapped shot after shot as she and Vivian strolled the length of the beach.

When they reached the southern end of the sandy crescent, she checked her camera. "My battery's getting low — I'll have to re-charge it — but some of these are going to be beautiful. Sebastian might want one or two for the *Acorn*."

Vivian raised a hand to shade her eyes as she gazed out to sea. "I'm sure he would, but you should consider printing and framing the best ones. Before you know it, you'll have enough to mount a show in your new studio."

Butterflies danced in Izzy's chest. Her own show. It was a dream she barely dared acknowledge. She didn't have enough experience. She couldn't possibly be ready for such a step.

"Oh yes, you are," Vivian stated, as if she'd read her younger friend's mind. "Making art is scary. Putting your skills and your soul on public display is scary. There will always be critics. But it's the only way, believe me. I spent my career helping artists overcome their fears. Even your Aunt Dora occasionally suffered a lapse of confidence, in spite of her success."

"Aunt Dora?"

Vivian nodded.

"But she was the most self-assured person I ever met."

Vivian shrugged. "It's the price of creativity."

Before Izzy could respond, a cacophony of voices rose above the rhythmic slap of waves. Up ahead, a crowd had gathered in a wide circle on the sand at the base of the parking lot. She and Vivian hurried forward to see what all the excitement was about.

In the center of the circle of onlookers, well past the barricades, sat a bright red sports car, up to its wheel wells in soft sand. A dark-haired young man, who appeared to be in his late teens, sat in the driver's seat, gunning the engine in angry frustration as the wheels spun uselessly.

A young woman wearing a short blue dress and high-heeled boots swung the passenger door open and clambered out, shouting the whole time. "I can't believe you did this! You are such an idiot! How am I supposed to get home now?" She pulled her phone from her purse and began a loud conversation with someone as she plowed awkwardly through the deep sand toward the parking lot.

The young man climbed out and started after her. "Crissy, come back," he wailed in a plaintive, but-baby-you-know-I-love-you voice.

"You are such a loser, Ryan. *Watch me do donuts on the beach*," she mocked. "I just called my dad to come get me."

Ryan's shoulders sagged. Before he could soothe his irate girlfriend, a police car rolled into the lot, and a middle-aged officer stepped out. He approached the young man, who produced his driver's license and some excuse Izzy couldn't hear.

A few minutes later, a black pick-up truck pulled up in front of Crissy, who was sitting on the curb with her arms wrapped around herself to ward off the evening chill. She jumped up, climbed into the cab without a backward glance at her possibly-now-ex-boyfriend, and the truck rolled off up the hill.

The truck had barely left when a bright yellow and blue tow truck from Carmel Towing arrived. The driver got out and spoke to the officer, who gestured toward the stranded sports car. The tow driver nodded, climbed back into his truck, and drove to the edge of the sand. After hooking a winch to the frame of the compact red car, he slowly dragged it backwards until it rested on solid pavement. Ryan approached the tow truck and handed the driver a credit card. His expression and body language screamed *misery*,

Izzy leaned toward Vivian. "Poor Ryan. In addition to his girlfriend, I hate to think how much this escapade will end up costing him."

The older woman shook her head. "The things we do for love."

CHAPTER FOURTEEN

The next morning, Izzy had time for a leisurely breakfast, so she allowed herself a special treat, a plate of French toast. A slice or two of bacon would have been a nice accompaniment, but that wasn't a reasonable option now that she was single. Without Bryce, it would take her at least a month to go through a whole pound. However, the crispy, eggy toast, swimming in melted butter and maple syrup, more than made up for the lack.

Chantal wouldn't be arriving for her photoshoot until after two o'clock, and thanks to Joe's help, the studio was ready for its debut. Since her model had promised to bring an assortment of equipment from the salon to use as props, there wasn't much for Izzy to do. She could devote as much time as she wanted to working on the sunset photos she'd taken at the beach last night.

After breakfast, she showered, dressed, and took her

camera out to the studio. As she sat in her new desk chair, removed the camera's memory card, slipped it into the port in the side of her laptop, and pulled up her editing software, her nerves tingled with excitement. This was her first action in her new, dedicated, professional work space, and it felt like a major step.

The photos turned out even better than she'd hoped. With some judicious editing, several might even be good enough to print, as Vivian had suggested. Izzy swiveled her chair around and regarded the large, open room. Was there enough space to set up a small sales gallery in one corner? She wouldn't open it to the public, but if someone expressed interest in seeing more of her work, she'd like to have a nice display area.

Editing the sunset photographs reminded her of the drama she and Vivian had witnessed on the beach. She wondered if, after their embarrassing public spectacle, Ryan and Crissy had made up. Had he persuaded her to take him back? Had she forgiven him for the failure of his grand gesture? Her own romantic life might be a disaster, but Izzy wouldn't want to be a teenager again for anything.

What was it Vivian had said? *The things we do for love.* The emotion seemed to bring out the best and the worst in people.

Which made her wonder about the Pefferman murders. She didn't know enough yet about Serena's death to speculate, but when she and Joe had discussed possible motives for Aldo's poisoning, they probably should have paid more attention to the power of love, as well as it's corollary, hate. Unless you were dealing with a sociopath, murder tended to be an emotional business. Money, anger, and revenge were strong motives, but only because of the emotions wrapped up in them. From an investigative perspective, cold, hard evidence was essential to catching a killer, but so was understanding what drove them to commit such a violent—and permanent—act. A change of focus might be the key to solving both cases and allowing life to get back to normal in the quirky seaside hamlet of Carmel-by-the-Sea.

Izzy had just put the kettle on to make tea when the doorbell rang at two-fifteen. When she opened the door, Chantal grinned and hoisted a shopping bag filled with the tools of her trade—hair dryer, curling iron, wave wand, brushes, and assorted bottles and jars.

"All ready!" She bustled into the house on her stiletto-heeled boots. "This is so exciting. I've been looking forward to it all week."

Izzy led the way to the kitchen. "I'm making tea. Would you like a cup before we start?"

"No thanks. After brunch with my family, I'm so full of my mom's *bacalhau à Brás*, I'm afraid I'll explode."

Izzy plopped a teabag in a mug and poured hot water over it. "That's a new one to me. What is it?"

"Practically the national dish of Portugal—salted cod, shredded with scrambled eggs, onions, and fried potatoes."

"It sounds...interesting."

"It's fabulous. I'll bring you with me to my parents' house one Sunday, and you can taste it for yourself."

Izzy was used to spending Sundays lounging around the house or catching up on chores. A meal surrounded by Chantal's large, boisterous family might feel overwhelming at first, but if she hoped to make a place for herself in her new community, she would have to push the limits of her comfort zone. "I'd love to. Thanks."

221

Mug in hand, she shepherded Chantal out the back door to the studio.

As they crossed the yard, her friend glanced around. "I thought you had a fire back here. Everything looks perfect."

Izzy fitted the key into the lock and turned the knob. "I have Sebastian to thank for that. He spotted the fire and immediately called the Fire Department. Then he ran over in his pajamas and put it out with a garden hose."

"Oh, my goodness! The man deserves a medal. If it were anyone else, the story of his heroism would have appeared on the front page of the *Acorn*. As it is, no one but you, me, and the firefighters will probably ever know."

Izzy stepped inside and flipped on the lights. "That's not all. He also removed all traces of the fire AND washed the soot off the windows. You know that ad on TV, *It's like it never even happened*? I have to keep reminding myself there was ever a fire."

Chantal set her bag of accessories on the floor. "We should do something special for him."

"I've been trying to think of something, but he's impossible. As far as I can tell, he's good at everything and is completely self-sufficient. On top of that, he takes his own helpfulness for granted."

"You'll have to get creative."

"Let me know if you have any brilliant ideas. For now, let's get started on your photos. You look fabulous, by the way."

She did. Since they had decided to do the shoot in black and white, Chantal had dressed the part. Her tight black leggings emphasized her petite figure, and her leather jacket, tall boots, and lace-trimmed blouse formed the perfect contrast. She looked like a sexy female pirate or highwayman with a hairdryer in place of a sword.

For the first shot, Izzy posed her seated on a tall stool in front of the solid white wall, with one foot on the floor and the other on the rung of the stool. Chantal's smooth, thick hair flowed over one shoulder and down the front of her jacket. She needed no coaching to exude confidence and sophistication.

Izzy took several more shots of her subject wielding various styling implements before deciding she had enough. "That's good. We've got some photos I think you're going to love. Now let's try setting up a few still lifes."

Chantal helped arrange the jars and bottles in various combinations with the dryers and irons, and watched with interest when Izzy adjusted the positioning of the objects to create dramatic shadows. "These pictures are going to be a wonderful addition to the salon, assuming I still have a place to hang them by the time they're ready."

"You haven't heard anything about your lease?"

"No, and now that Serena's gone, I don't even know who my landlord is."

"At the moment, I suppose it's Serena's estate. I wouldn't worry too much about your lease. It will probably take the Peffermans' lawyers years to unravel all their business holdings. In the meantime, just keep paying your rent, and I doubt anyone will bother you."

Chantal flipped her hair back over her shoulders and studied the arrangement on the table. "I hope you're right. I still can't get over the tragic coincidence of Serena dying in that horrible accident such a short time after her husband's death. I keep seeing her slumped over the steering wheel with blood all over the car. It gives me nightmares." She shuddered.

"According to the police, her accident might not have been an accident."

Chantal's eyes widened. "What are you saying?"

Izzy moved two small jars of styling cream in front of the crimping iron and stacked one on top of the other. "It sounds like someone tampered with her brakes."

"Is that what your detective friend said? Do they think it was the same person who killed Aldo?"

"They don't know, but they're considering all possibilities."

Chantal pursed her lips. "I wonder if it was Dr. Holder. He's gorgeous, and you know how violent love triangles can be."

"Actually, I don't."

Chantal continued as if she hadn't heard. "Or maybe Christos Getz. He's slimy — reminds me of the dead eels on ice in my dad's fish market."

Izzy wrinkled her nose. "That's quite a comparison."

"I've never been a big fan of eels."

Izzy had to admit she wasn't either. She snapped several more shots, wishing again that she had more flexible lighting. Portable lights were the next item on her wish list, as soon as she could afford them. "I think we'd better call it a day. The angle of the light is getting too low."

Chantal began reloading her gear into the empty shopping bag. "This was a lot of fun. I can't wait to see the pictures." She looked over at Izzy, who had set her camera on the desk next to her computer. "Hey, I've got an idea. Let's walk downtown. I can get my mom a box of her favorite chocolates from Taste of Torino, then we can stop in next door and check out Christos Getz."

A tiny muscle at the corner of Izzy's right eye twitched. "What do you mean *check out*?"

"You know, ask him innocent-sounding questions and see if he looks guilty."

This sounded like a recipe for disaster. "What kind of questions? And what, exactly, do guilty people look like?"

Chantal rolled her eyes. "You know...edgy, nervous...guilty. Come on. You got to go undercover at Beauty by the Bay. Now, it's my turn. Besides, we might learn something useful. What's the worst that could happen?"

"An unknown arsonist has already tried to burn down my studio. I don't need everyone in town to hate me."

"I'll do the talking. You don't even have to come inside, if you don't want to."

Chantal was clearly getting more and more excited about the idea, and Izzy hated to disappoint her. Besides, if she didn't go, her friend might try to interrogate Getz on her own, and that idea was even scarier. "Okay. We'll do it."

Chantal grinned and picked up her bag. "This is so exciting. I wonder if we should wear disguises."

Now, it was Izzy's turn to roll her eyes. "Have you ever met Getz before?"

"No."

"Neither have I. If we don't tell him our names, he'll have no idea who we are."

"True, but maybe we could make up aliases. I could be Lola—I always wanted to be named Lola—and you could be...hmm, let's see..." She studied Izzy's face. "You look like a Margo."

"We are not using aliases. We're casual visitors to his

shop—that's all. It would be weird if we introduced ourselves by name."

"Weird, but fun." Chantal's eyes twinkled.

"No."

"Oh, all right."

They locked the studio, stowed Chantal's bag in her car, and set off on the short walk downtown. They chugged their way up Ocean Avenue, winding through throngs of window-shopping tourists until they passed Taste of Torino. When they reached the door to the stairs that led up to Aldo's office, they paused a moment outside Christos Getz's skin care shop. A white sign with red letters filled the window.

BIG SALE! STORE CLOSING.

They looked at each other with raised brows, then Chantal opened the door and sauntered inside.

The owner himself was behind the counter, removing small glass jars from the shelf and packing them away in a cardboard box. When the bell over the door jingled, he turned with a broad smile. "Good afternoon, ladies. You're just in time for the bargain of the century."

Chantal turned and pointed to the window. "Your sign says the store is closing."

Getz's smile never faltered as he stepped out from behind the counter with one of the jars in his hand. "And that's why today is your lucky day." He held out the little blue jar. "This cream is miraculous. It's exactly what you need to brighten your skin, even the tone, and smooth those pesky wrinkles at the corners of your eyes. And today, I can offer it to you for half price—only one hundred eighty-seven dollars and ninety-nine cents!"

Chantal instinctively pulled back. "Oh, I don't — "

"Combined with this under-eye tightening gel," he plucked a tube from a basket on the counter, "you'll look sixteen again. I promise."

Chantal met Izzy's gaze with a silent *help me.*

Izzy thought, *you got yourself into this,* but she replied with a barely perceptible nod and turned to Christos Getz. "Maybe it would be better to come back another time, when you aren't so busy packing. Are you moving to another location in town?"

Getz's brows met in a frown. "No. I will be leaving Carmel-by-the-Sea in a few days. Today is the best day to take advantage of these spectacular price reductions on our most effective and luxurious treatments." He scanned her face, his gaze lingering near her eyes. "I believe you would benefit even more than your friend."

From behind his right shoulder, where only Izzy could see her, Chantal grinned and stuck out her tongue.

Izzy ignored her. "Maybe we can come back before you close for good, but I'm afraid I don't have time today. I don't know about you, *Lola,* but I need to be going."

Chantal stepped forward and tucked her arm through Izzy's. "I'm with you, *Margo.*" She gave Getz a breezy wave as they headed for the door. "Goodbye for now."

As soon as they were outside, Chantal dissolved into a fit of giggles. When she'd composed herself, she wiped her eyes. "That was so much fun! I told you it would be."

"I don't know about fun, but at least we learned something interesting."

"We did?" Chantal opened the door to Taste of

Torino, and they stepped inside. Due to the hour, the place wasn't too crowded, but several customers stood in line, waiting to place their orders at the counter. Izzy and Chantal wandered up behind them.

In deference to the other customers, Izzy lowered her voice as she continued their conversation. "We learned that Christos Getz is pulling up stakes and leaving town in a few days. I need to let Joe know before he interviews Getz tomorrow morning." She pulled her phone from her purse to send him a text. "I'll be sitting in."

Chantal stopped dead. "You're going to interrogate a suspect with the police?"

"I won't actually be in the interview room. I'll just be observing on a monitor in a different room."

"That still sounds exciting. Do you think your detective friend would let me observe, too?"

"I'd be surprised. He doesn't know you, and you have no official interest in the case."

"Neither do you. Ask him," Chantal urged.

She had a point. Izzy shrugged and pulled up Joe's number. She texted him the information about Christos Getz, as well as Chantal's request to be present at his questioning. Joe's answer was predictable.

She closed the app and looked at Chantal. "No."

"No?"

"Unauthorized persons are not allowed beyond the lobby at the police station." Izzy took a step forward. "Pay attention. We're next."

Without looking, Chantal mirrored Izzy's movement and almost ran into the broad back of a young man wearing a USC football jersey. She flashed him an embarrassed smile. "Oops. Sorry." A frown drew her brows together. "If your friend authorized you, he could authorize me, too."

"I asked, but he said no."

Chantal's lips pursed in a pout. "Oh, all right, but be sure to tell me what Getz says."

"I will. As much as I can, anyway."

They finally reached the front of the line when the couple ahead of them took their bag of pastries and departed. Lorna Ferris was working alone. Her face was pink, and a sheen of perspiration dampened her forehead.

Izzy gave her a sympathetic smile. "It looks like you could use more help."

Lorna didn't return her smile, but simply brushed back a loose tress that had fallen out of the barrette she used to restrain it. "What can I get you?"

"I'll take a dozen of those." Chantal pointed to a display of beautiful dark chocolates molded in the shape of flowers.

"In a box?"

Chantal responded with a perplexed frown. "Yes. They're for my mother."

"Oh."

She packed a box with twelve of the delicate confections, rang it up at the register, then handed it across the counter. "Thanks. Come again." The words sounded mechanical.

Chantal thanked her, but as they left the shop, she whispered, "That was strange. Of course, I need a box. Did she think I was going to stuff my face with a dozen chocolates on the spot?"

Izzy suppressed a grin. "Probably. Everything about you screams *ravenous chocoholic*."

Chantal ignored the comment. "I get that she's busy and overworked, but when she first started here, she was outgoing and friendly. Now, she seems crabbier and more withdrawn every time I see her."

"I only met her a few weeks ago, but I think she's taken Aldo's death pretty hard. Last week she said she might be leaving Carmel soon. Vivian's been trying to talk her out of it because she's a good tenant, but I think she might be better off with a change of scenery."

They were waiting for traffic to clear at the next corner when a voice behind them called out. "Ms. Munro, is that you?"

Izzy turned to see Dina Korman pushing her husband's wheelchair down the sidewalk toward her. She stepped aside to allow the other pedestrians to cross the street and waited until the Kormans caught up. Her nerves fluttered, but she mustered a smile. "Hello, Mrs. Korman, Mr. Korman. How are you?"

A hint of tempered steel ran through Dina's answering smile. "We're doing as well as can be expected, dear. And how are you?"

Izzy didn't miss the slight emphasis on the word *you*. "I'm...um...fine."

"I'm glad to hear it. Dottie Cartwright said she ran into you just down the street from our house a few days ago. You had your camera and were quite out of breath."

Izzy's gut tightened. She should have known better than to hope Dottie would keep their meeting to herself. The woman had an insatiable appetite for meddling. "I'd been photographing Carmel gardens for a new series in the *Acorn* and was running late for a meeting."

Dina's smile remained fixed, but her eyes narrowed slightly. "If you're interested in gardens, you must come and see ours. Kurt used to spend hours working on it. That was before his stroke, when everything changed."

Her husband remained slumped in his chair, staring

silently at his hands resting on his bony thighs.

Izzy was growing progressively more uncomfortable with the couple's charade and was anxious to move on. "I'm sure your garden is lovely, but I don't know how many installments Mr. Larrabee will want for the series."

Dina reached out, curling her fingers around Izzy's forearm. "Even if he isn't interested, you should stop by and see our garden for yourself. You could stay for tea."

Something in the woman's tone reminded Izzy of the wicked witch in the forest attempting to lure Hansel and Gretel into her gingerbread house. "Thank you. Maybe I will...when I have time." Izzy turned to Chantal. "We need to be going. You've got that thing tonight."

Chantal's brow wrinkled in puzzlement. "That *thing*?"

"Yes. Remember?" Izzy nodded for emphasis.

"Oh, yes. Of course. We'd better hurry."

"Goodbye, Mrs. Korman, Mr. Korman." Grabbing her friend's elbow, they started across the street.

"Don't forget, dear," Dina called after her. "We'll be looking for you."

When they safely reached the other side, Chantal glanced back over her shoulder. "That was bizarre. Dina acted like we'd never met, but she used to be one of my regular clients before Kurt's stroke. And she kept pestering you about visiting their garden. What was that about?"

Izzy debated whether to tell Chantal what she'd seen, but knew her inquisitive friend would keep pushing until she had the full story. "What I told her was the truth—as far as it went. Last Tuesday, I was near the Kormans' house, taking garden photos for the *Acorn*, when I heard raised voices coming from their yard. I peeked through the hedge and saw them arguing about Kurt lifting a heavy pot."

"How could he lift anything heavy? The man can't even walk."

"That's what they want everyone to believe, but he was standing perfectly straight, holding a pot full of succulents that must have weighed at least thirty pounds. I think he spotted me through the bushes, because he started walking toward me. I took off but had the bad luck to run into Dottie Cartwright, who was walking her dog." The memory grated, and she picked up her pace.

Chantal wobbled as she tried to keep up. "Hey, slow down, will you? I've got short legs and tall shoes."

Slowing immediately, Izzy glanced at the offending boots. "I don't know how you wear such high heels all the time, especially when you're on your feet all day. I wouldn't last an hour."

"You're so tall, you'll never have to worry about it. You have no idea what it's like to have to climb up into the cooler in the grocery store to get a quart of milk off the top shelf."

Izzy laughed at her friend's disgruntled expression. "No, but you'll never have your knees hit your chin when you ride in the back seat of a compact car."

"True. I guess we all can find something to complain about. But I don't know what to think about the Kormans. I wonder why they're pretending Kurt is more disabled than he is. Maybe to gain public sympathy. Although I don't see how that would benefit them, now that Aldo's gone."

Izzy turned left off Ocean Avenue onto Lincoln. "Based on their conversation, they're in the process of suing his estate, blaming Kurt's stroke on the conflict with Aldo over a trash container."

Chantal gave a knowing nod. "Ah. The more serious the injury, the bigger the settlement."

"That's about the size of it."

"And they think you're onto their scheme. So that weird invitation to visit their garden might have been a thinly veiled warning."

"It sounded like that to me."

Remaining uncharacteristically quiet until they reached the next corner, Chantal paused to check for cross traffic. "Do you think there's a chance Dina was the one who set the fire in your yard? Her behavior this afternoon seemed so out of character."

"I've considered it. There's no evidence to connect her to the arson but — like her insistent invitation to visit — I think the fire was a warning, rather than an attempt to cause real damage."

"It's hard to believe a respected doctor in her seventies would do something like that."

Izzy had seen enough people do unlikely things not to dismiss any possibility outright. "I'm sure Kurt's stroke was very stressful for her, and stress can do strange things to people."

"I know, but..."

"If she's responsible — and that's a pretty big *if* — I need to find a way to convince her I'm not a threat."

"Have you told your investigator friend about Dina? He needs to know."

"He knows."

Chantal persisted. "Has he interrogated them yet?"

"Joe doesn't interrogate people — he interviews."

"Potayto, potahto."

Izzy grabbed her friend's arm to prevent her from walking straight into a car that was turning the corner in front of them. "He hasn't spoken to them yet, but I'm not convinced they had anything to do with the murder or the fire. The Kormans are exaggerating Kurt's condition for greater financial compensation from Aldo's estate. That doesn't mean they had anything to do with his death. Greed and revenge are separate motives."

"Why settle for one when you can have both?"

She had a point.

When they reached Chantal's car, parked at the curb, she unlocked the driver's door then paused. "I've been thinking—if the Kormans poisoned Aldo, does that mean they killed Serena, too? It's hard to imagine either of them climbing under a car to fiddle with the brakes." She tossed her purse on the passenger's seat. "I guess they could have hired somebody."

"Go home and relax. We need to stop speculating. We don't have enough information to reach an informed conclusion. Besides, catching murderers is the job of the police, not a hair stylist and a photographer."

"But it's a puzzle, and puzzles are fun." Chantal climbed into her car. "Thanks for taking the photographs. I can't wait to see how they turn out."

"I'm sure they'll be great. The camera loves you. I'll show you the digital proofs as soon as they're ready."

After Chantal closed the car door, Izzy stepped back and waved to her friend as she drove off. As she pawed through her purse for her keys on the way to the front door, her mind replayed their conversation, along with the events of the afternoon.

Something was very off about Christos Getz closing his business and leaving town immediately after Serena's death. Izzy couldn't figure out how killing her might benefit him, unless they were secretly connected in some way, and Joe's investigation, thus far, had turned up no signs of that.

And what about the Kormans? Could they have killed Aldo for revenge and Serena because she stood between them and ten million dollars? If the widow had been pushing her lawyers to play hardball on the lawsuit, her death would effectively remove that impediment. Still, Izzy had a hard time accepting that a couple in their seventies had planned and executed two murders.

Then there was the possibility that the Pefferman's deaths were separate and distinct events.

Throw in the arson, and Chantal was right — it was a puzzle.

CHAPTER FIFTEEN

Monday morning, Izzy awoke to her alarm at six-thirty, something she hadn't done since that fateful final day at Pacific Western Life. Joe was meeting Christos Getz at the Carmel police station at eight o'clock, and she wanted to be there before he arrived. After showering, she dressed as inconspicuously as possible in camel slacks and a black blazer from her former work wardrobe. Despite the earlier hour, when she walked into the kitchen, Bogart was already in place beside his bowls, doing his best impression of an ancient Egyptian cat statue.

She gave his head an affectionate scratch. "You look divine this morning. All you need is a gold earring."

She filled his bowls, then set them in front of him before starting the coffee maker and fixing herself a bowl of yogurt sprinkled with granola. After breakfast, she unlocked the cat flap so he could go about his kitty business for the day and checked her watch. She had time to walk to the police station, but she was feeling edgy. Joe had assured her she'd be in another room, watching the proceedings on a monitor, and that Getz wouldn't be able to see her, but the knowledge didn't banish her unease. She didn't want to arrive windblown, sweaty, and out of breath from the hike all the way to the top of Ocean Avenue, so she decided to drive.

She arrived at the station a few minutes early and found Joe waiting in the lobby.

He signed her in at the front desk, then escorted her to a desk in the corner of a room filled with officers talking on the phone and tapping away at computers. When he turned on the oversized monitor, a small, empty room appeared on the screen. "You'll be able to watch the interview on this screen." He handed her a pair of headphones and plugged them in. "These will help tune out the noise so you can hear what's being said."

Beneath the smell of Dial soap and some kind of minty toothpaste, Izzy picked up the faint odor of burned toast clinging to his shirt. Something about the combination of scents triggered a sudden flashback to the brief kisses she and Bryce had exchanged every morning at the apartment door as they parted ways and headed off to work.

When Joe straightened, he took his morning-male aroma with him. "By the way, thanks for the call yesterday. I appreciate the heads-up about Getz leaving town. It's important to go into an interview knowing more than the subject thinks I do."

"It might not mean anything, but I thought you should know."

"At the very least, it's an interesting coincidence worth checking out. Wait here, and I'll come get you when I finish with Getz." He glanced at his watch. "He should be here any minute...assuming he shows."

Just then, a uniformed officer stuck his head through the door. "Christos Getz is here. He's waiting at the desk."

"Thanks, I'll be right there." Joe turned back to her. "Can I get you anything? Police station coffee is notoriously bad, but I think they've got water and juice."

She smiled. "No, thanks. I'm fine. I'll see you when you're done."

A few minutes later, she watched the screen as Joe and Christos Getz entered the interview room and took seats on opposite sides of the small table.

Joe pulled a notepad and pen from his jacket pocket. "Thank you for coming in, Mr. Getz. I appreciate your cooperation."

"Of course. Aldo's death was a shock to everyone, and now Serena..." He threw his hands in the air.

"I understand you run a skin care business."

"Yes. We provide the most luxurious and exclusive products to the most discriminating clients."

Joe glanced up from his notepad and pinned Getz with a direct gaze. "Do you offer Botox treatments to your customers?"

"No. I am not licensed for that."

"Would a business like yours be able to purchase botulinum toxin directly from the manufacturer or distributor?"

Getz tapped his fingers against the table in a rapid staccato. "As I told you, I'm not licensed."

Joe nodded. "How long have you owned the

business next to Mr. Pefferman's bakery?"

"Nearly five years."

"And how would you describe your relationship with him?"

Getz gave a soft snort. "I'm sure you've already heard plenty on that subject from the good citizens of Carmel."

"I want to hear it from you."

"Put simply, Pefferman and I did not get along." Getz crossed his arms with finality.

"Why not?"

He dropped his arms and leaned forward, his dark eyes snapping with emotion. "Because the man was an interfering, overbearing ass. He thought he could tell everyone in town what they could and couldn't do."

Joe hesitated then glanced at his phone, which was lying on the table near his elbow. Izzy didn't hear a chime or buzz, but the face of the phone lit up, so he must have received a call or text. He picked it up, scanned the screen with a scowl, then slapped it back down on the table with more force than necessary.

He was still frowning when he returned his attention to Getz. "Excuse the interruption. Now, can you be more specific about the nature of your disagreement with Aldo Pefferman?"

"He didn't like my sales methods. I think he was jealous because I've been so successful."

Izzy was glad neither man could see or hear her. Otherwise, she would have struggled to contain her response. Taste of Torino was packed with customers throughout the day, while Christos Getz had to drag people in off the street.

Joe merely nodded and scribbled something in his pad. "Did Mr. Pefferman ever threaten any action against you?"

"He tried to get the city to ban me!" Red-faced, Getz quivered in outrage.

Joe leaned back in his chair, his expression bland and his voice calm. "I'm sure that made you angry."

"Of course, it did!"

"Angry enough to kill?"

Getz sputtered. "You can't think I had anything to do with his death!"

"I'm just asking. You admit you were angry because Mr. Pefferman was trying to ruin your business."

Getz straightened in his chair and lifted his chin. "My business does not rely on a single shop. I own a string of high-end skin care establishments in the Los Angeles area, including two on Rodeo Drive in Beverly Hills."

Joe jotted something in his notebook. "I see. So the Carmel shop represented an expansion for you."

"A minor one, yes."

"Yet now that Aldo Pefferman is dead, you're closing it."

"Again, yes. And I assure you, there is no connection between the two. I had no motive to kill the man."

Joe tilted his head and tapped his pen against the notepad. "Would you care to elaborate on that?"

Getz leaned forward, resting his elbows on the table, an earnest expression on his face. "I understand how it might look, but Aldo and I were on good terms the day he died."

"I have witnesses who say otherwise."

"Then they're wrong. The morning after our…uh…minor altercation at the City Council meeting, Aldo came to see me with a very generous offer to buy out the lease on my business and pay me a handsome relocation fee."

"Basically a bribe to get you to leave town."

Getz shrugged. "One might look at it that way. However, I was getting tired of dealing with his harassment and spending half my time traveling back and forth between L.A. and Carmel. This way, I can simplify my life and make a tidy profit in the process."

"I would have expected Pefferman's death to nullify the contract," Joe observed.

"Apparently not. He must have given his attorneys instructions, because a few days after he died, they contacted me to let me know his estate intended to honor the contract. The deal is scheduled to close next Wednesday, and afterwards I'll be leaving Carmel for good. So, you can see, I had nothing to gain from Pefferman's death."

Joe closed his notebook. "I agree, it looks that way at this point." He pushed to his feet. "Thank you for coming in, Mr. Getz. We'll need your contact details in Los Angeles in case any further questions arise, but I think that's all for now."

As Getz rose, he pulled out his wallet and handed Joe a business card. "Here's my number. I'm always happy to assist the police."

A few minutes later, Joe rejoined Izzy. "Ready to go?"

"Yes. It was interesting, although I'm not sure how much help my observations will be."

He rested a hand against the small of her back while he held the door open for her. "I want to hear your overall take on Getz. But I'd rather discuss it in a less formal setting. I'll walk you to work, and we can talk on the way."

"I'm afraid I drove. I wasn't sure how long the interview would take, and I didn't want to be late."

They emerged from the narrow hallway into the main reception area, and Joe nodded to the desk sergeant as he steered her toward the door. "We can talk in your car. Do you mind?"

"No…that's fine, I guess."

"Where are you parked?"

She pointed to her car in the second row of the station lot.

"I'll ride to the salon with you. I can walk back."

They drove the five blocks to the salon in silence. Since most of the shops wouldn't open for at least another hour, Izzy had no trouble finding an empty spot in front of the yoga studio next door. With a few deft flicks of the wheel, she slipped the Subaru into the space next to the curb with an ease born of years of city driving. Then she shut off the engine and faced Joe.

"Now, what's with all the sneaking around? I feel like I'm in a *Mission Impossible* movie."

"It's nothing like that. I just wanted to have a casual, off-the-record conversation, something that's hard to accomplish in a police station."

She peered at his solid features, noting a subtle tightness in the lines that bracketed his mouth. "That's not the only reason. There's more to it, isn't there? You're worried about something."

He stared out the window and ran a hand through his hair with sigh. "I should never have involved you in this investigation."

"Aldo collapsed on top of me. I don't know how you could have kept me out of it."

"But I've made things worse by allowing you to stay involved."

She laid a hand on his arm. "What things are worse? Joe, tell me what's wrong."

"I received a text during the interview with Getz."

Izzy nodded. "I could see that on the monitor. I could also see you weren't pleased. Who sent it?"

"It came from an anonymous number."

"I assume the message related to the Peffermans' murders."

"It did. And it threatened you."

She pulled back and stiffened. "Me? In what way? Let me see it." She stuck out her hand, palm up.

Joe slid his hand into his pocket, but hesitated. "I shouldn't—technically, it's evidence."

"So what?" She didn't care if she sounded agitated. She *was* agitated, and growing more so with every passing second. "I've seen plenty of evidence on this case already. I'm even responsible for locating some of it. Remember the locket and the counterfeit Botox?" She flexed her hand, motioning him to hand it over.

"All right. All right." He pulled out his phone, opened it to the text, and gave it to her.

Close your investigation. You know the truth. Serena Pefferman killed her husband, and her death was an accident. Leave Izzy Munro out of it, unless you want something worse to happen to her. The fire was just a warning.

Izzy re-read the message three times, then handed the phone back to Joe. "Well, at least this tells us something."

"What, exactly?"

"That the arsonist wasn't some random teenage prankster. Not a single word is misspelled or replaced by adolescent text-speak."

Joe's lips tightened, and his brow furrowed. "This isn't funny, Izzy."

She sobered. "No, it isn't. But it definitely ties the fire to the murders, which means I've made someone nervous. What I can't figure out is how? I've only been involved in the investigation peripherally. It would help if we knew who sent the text. Who has your number?"

He replied with a dismissive huff. "Hundreds of people. I'm a cop. I give my business card to everyone I interview, in case they think of something pertinent later. Besides, if one were persuasive enough, it wouldn't be hard to get my number from the District Attorney's office."

Izzy pondered the possibilities. "The timing of the text feels suspicious."

"It sure does — right in the middle of my interview with Getz. Who else knew you were coming to the station this morning?"

"Only Chantal. I was with her when I texted you yesterday afternoon. Remember? She asked if she could join us."

Joe sighed. "I like Chantal, but she's not exactly tight-lipped, and her salon is the biggest gossip mill in town."

Izzy felt driven to defend her friend. "But she wasn't working yesterday, and her first client today isn't due for —" she glanced at her watch " — another fifteen minutes. She wouldn't have had a chance to mention it to anyone, except possibly her mother."

"Who happens to run the busiest market in Carmel and could have told anyone."

Izzy sank back against the seat, deflated. "I guess it's possible. I'll ask Chantal if she's said anything to anyone."

"That would help. I'm sick of stumbling around in the dark, and I don't want to put you at any further risk."

Izzy ignored his comment about risk. She wasn't afraid of the unknown texter—they were clearly reluctant to harm her—and she wanted the Pefferman's murders solved as much as Joe did. "What did you think about Christos Getz's answers this morning?"

"We'll check out his business holdings in L.A. and his travel schedule, and confirm the purchase agreement with Pefferman's lawyers, but right now I don't think Getz is our man. What was your impression?"

"The same as yours. His only motive would have been anger, and it sounds like Aldo defused that with the offer to buy him out. Besides, neither the poisoning nor Serena's car crash was a crime of impulse or passion. Both required considerable planning."

"So, we're still nowhere." His mouth turned down in disgust.

Izzy ran through everyone she could think of with an interest in the case. "Have you had a chance to talk to Kurt and Dina Korman?"

"Not yet. When I called, they were up in Palo Alto, seeing a specialist at Stanford Medical Center about Mr. Korman's condition. I'm afraid I put them on the back burner and forgot about them. Why?"

"Well, they're back in town. Chantal and I ran into them Sunday evening, and Dina was acting...I don't know...strange."

"Strange? How?"

"It's hard to describe, but it wouldn't hurt to talk to them."

"Okay. I'll call them again this morning to set up a time." He jotted a note in his pad.

"I'm not convinced they had anything to do with Aldo's death, since apparently they're continuing their lawsuit against his estate, but it would be good to rule them out."

"At this point, I'm happy to be able to rule anyone out." Joe scrubbed his hand across his jaw. "We also have to consider Serena's murder. I can't think of any reason for the Kormans to kill her."

"Unless she controlled the purse strings of Aldo's estate."

Joe scribbled another note in his pad. "Another thing to clarify with his attorneys." He looked up at Izzy. "Is there anything else you haven't told me?"

Irritation poked her like a prickly weed. Did he think she was holding out on him? "Not that I can think of, but I have a few questions for you."

"Shoot."

"Have you learned anything more about the locket?"

He shook his head. "We're still working to identify the right Ian Anderson."

"What about the sabotage to Serena's car?"

"So far, that's another dead end. We've determined that the brake lines were cut and the fluid drained. Residue on the concrete floor indicates it was done in the parking garage of the Plaza shopping center, probably while Mrs. Pefferman was at work on the day she died. Unfortunately, the only cameras are at the entrance and exit, so it's impossible to connect anyone with the damage."

"Would it have required someone with automotive knowledge or skills?"

"Probably not. These days, you can learn to do just about anything on YouTube."

"What about her phone?"

"Our techs made some progress there, but it doesn't help much. Serena did receive a call Friday afternoon at the time Dr. Holder indicated, but it was from a burner, so we still don't know who called her."

Izzy sighed. "I'm glad I never wanted to be a homicide detective. I don't know how you do it. This is so frustrating."

"Some cases are easy—other's, not so much. It's like anything else. You keep your head in the game, focus on the details, and persevere until it all comes together."

Izzy had a sudden thought and checked her watch. "Uh, oh. I lost track of the time. I was supposed to be at work ten minutes ago."

Joe reached for the door handle. "If you tell Chantal it was all my fault, I'm sure she'll forgive you." He climbed out of the car, then leaned down and stuck his head back in. "Remember, the arsonist is still at large. Keep your guard up and be sure to let me know if you see or hear anything unusual. I'll talk to you soon." With a firm *thud*, he closed the door and headed down the sidewalk in the direction of the police station.

Izzy grabbed her purse and hopped out of the car. Hopefully, things were quiet enough at the salon that Chantal hadn't missed her. When she pushed open the door, she immediately spotted Dottie Cartwright seated at Chantal's station, draped in a brown plastic cape.

Chantal was dabbing Dottie's gray roots with a small squirt bottle of chestnut brown dye when Izzy entered. "There you are! I was beginning to worry your detective friend had decided to lock you up."

Dottie squirmed around until she was facing Izzy. "Lock you up? Where were you this morning?"

Izzy wasn't anxious to share her early morning activities with the Carmel town crier. "Just visiting with an old friend I used to know in San Francisco who lives in this area now."

Chantal's perfect brows rose in question. Izzy gave

her head a tiny shake, to which her friend replied with a barely perceptible nod.

Chantal dripped more dye onto Dottie's part and rubbed it with gloved fingers. "He's quite good looking. Do I sense a *thing* brewing?"

With an inward groan, Izzy set her purse on the reception desk and unbuttoned her jacket. While she appreciated Chantal's effort to divert Dottie's attention from her connection with law enforcement, she wished her friend had come up with something other than a possible romantic liaison.

As she feared, Dottie latched onto the inuendo with enthusiasm. "Ooh, who is this mystery man? Tell me all about him."

The last thing Izzy wanted to encourage was speculation about her relationship with Joe. At this point, she wasn't even sure she could define it. She enjoyed their working partnership, but could it develop into more? Did she want it to? "Just a friend I knew when I worked in insurance."

In her experience, the mere mention of the word *insurance* was enough to make most people's eyes glaze over, and it seemed to work with Dottie.

The woman twisted back to face the mirror. "Oh, well, be sure to share the news if anything interesting develops."

"You'll be the first to know." *Right.*

By the time Chantal finished with Dottie, her next client was waiting, so she and Izzy didn't have a chance to talk until nearly one o'clock. When the final pre-lunch customer left, she pounced. "So spill. How did the interview go? Was it just like on TV?"

"Fine and pretty much."

Chantal's expectant expression melted into

disappointment.

Izzy plucked her jacket from the hook on the wall and picked up her purse. "You didn't miss anything exciting...except that we were able to rule Christos Getz out as a suspect."

"What do you mean? I'd call that exciting! What did he say?"

"Apparently, the morning after their dust-up at the City Council meeting, Aldo made Getz a very attractive offer to buy out his lease, and Getz accepted. Despite the Peffermans' deaths, the estate is going through with the deal, which explains the Going-Out-of-Business sale. Getz wouldn't have had any motive to kill Aldo or Serena."

Chantal sank into her stylist's chair, dejected. "I guess not." Then she perked up. "Did you tell Joe about the Kormans and how weird they were when we ran into them yesterday?"

Izzy slipped one arm into the sleeve of her jacket. "I did, and he plans to talk to them. He also said he'd confirm the status of their lawsuit with Aldo's lawyers."

"So two people are dead. If Getz is out, and we all agree the Kormans are unlikely suspects, who does that leave? Marcus Holder? I suppose he might have had issues with Serena—business partners often do—but I don't know why he'd want to kill Aldo."

Izzy couldn't think of a reason, either. Unless Joe was withholding important information—and she didn't think he was—the investigation had stalled out. There had to be something, or someone, they were missing.

CHAPTER SIXTEEN

The next morning, Izzy received an email from Sebastian asking if she had any photos for this week's *Acorn*. With everything else that had been happening, she hadn't been out with her camera for several days. If she wanted her pictures to continue to be a regular feature in the paper, she'd better get busy and come up with something engaging.

Thanksgiving was only ten days away. Maybe she should drive out to Carmel Valley and look for wild turkeys. They were striking and colorful when they fanned their tails. Unfortunately, they were also elusive, and she didn't have enough time before the Thursday evening deadline to go turkey hunting. Beach sunsets might be a better bet. She'd taken some breathtaking shots the other night with Vivian, but she was saving those to print herself.

At nine-thirty, Chantal's eleven o'clock appointment

called to cancel because her husband had fallen off a ladder while cleaning the gutters and she was taking him to the ER to get checked.

When Izzy gave her the news, Chantal shook her head with a tight-lipped frown. "Ralph is so stubborn. He's nearly eighty and refuses to admit his balance isn't what it used to be. He did the same thing last year. Marge keeps threatening to throw the ladder away. One of these days, he's going to break his neck."

"Since you'll have some free time before your next client, maybe you can help me decide where to hang the photos we took Sunday and how large they should be. I plan to edit them this afternoon, then I'll start calling shops in the area to see who can make canvas prints the size we need."

"Ooh, that sounds exciting. I can't wait to see them."

"I took a quick look last night, and I think you'll be pleased. You look very glamorous."

Chantal struck a pose and batted her lashes. "Glamour. That's me all over."

"Absolutely."

They both laughed and went back to work.

After Chantal's ten-fifteen client left, she swept the floor under her stylist's chair and joined Izzy at the front desk. "I think I've got a tape measure in here somewhere." She pulled open a drawer and began pawing through the contents. "Aha. I knew it!"

They spent the next half-hour pondering and measuring and came up with a plan for four photos, three to four feet high and four to five feet wide.

Izzy returned the tape measure to its drawer. "The pictures are going to look great—very dramatic in black and white."

"How soon do you think they'll be ready?" Chantal

asked. "I want to host an evening reception here at the salon to show them off. Not that I'm anxious to lose you as an employee when you become a famous photographer, but it's the perfect opportunity to introduce your work to the community."

Izzy had never considered herself a hugger, but she was so grateful, she embraced Chantal before she had a chance to talk herself out of it. "Thank you. This means a lot to me."

"I'm delighted to be able to help. Photography is your business, and we women in business have to support each other."

****

Later that afternoon, as the sun sank toward the thin cloud bank that hung suspended above the horizon, Izzy grabbed her camera and set out on the short stroll to the beach. Tourists were in short supply this time of year, and most locals were either still at work or at home starting dinner, so the curved swath of perfect white sand was nearly deserted. A few hungry sanderlings ran along the verge of the water, poking their long, curved beaks into the froth left in the wake of the receding tide, searching for tasty morsels. The orange-striped sky and soft swish of waves filled her with an overwhelming sense of peace.

She slipped off her shoes, rolled up the legs of her jeans, and clambered through the deep, soft sand until she reached firm footing at the ocean's edge. Taking her time, she strolled south toward the jutting rocks of Carmel Point, stopping every few feet to snap another shot of the glowing neon clouds, the reflection of the setting sun on the water, or the birds enjoying their supper. The aura of the evening was magical, whether Sebastian chose to use any of the photos in the *Acorn*, or not.

The light was fading as she reached the rugged outcropping at the end of the beach. She was about to turn around and head back when she noticed something bobbing in a pool of shallow water, trapped behind a cluster of rocks. She couldn't tell what it was, but the shape was too smooth and regular to be a piece of driftwood. Intrigued, she rolled her pants up farther and waded out to pick it up.

Back on the beach, she examined the object more closely. It was a narrow wooden box, about a foot in length and perhaps eight inches wide and high. It looked like an antique, with an arched lid of richly-stained birds-eye maple and a mother-of-pearl inset around the keyhole. One long scratch from where it had banged against the rocks marred the hinged side, but the rest of the finish was intact, so it couldn't have been in the water long. It was such a pretty thing, Izzy couldn't imagine how it had ended up in the ocean. Someone must have lost it. She glanced up and scanned the beach and the walking path along the low cliff, but no one else was in sight.

She decided to take the box home and clean it up. If she asked Sebastian to run a small ad in the *Acorn*, the owner might see it and reclaim their treasure. If no one responded, the box would make an interesting photographic accessory.

When she arrived home, she carried the box inside and set it on the kitchen counter. She gently blotted the outside with a towel, but in the spots where the finish was thin — the edges and corners where the pieces joined, especially the lid — the wood was saturated. She could only hope anything inside was waterproof, or it was likely to be ruined.

She had no idea of the best way to dry old wood without ruining it. One of the antique dealers in town might have a suggestion, but all the shops were closed until tomorrow morning. She decided to leave the box on the counter overnight to air dry with the help of a small portable fan she found on the top shelf of the linen closet. In the morning, she could make a few calls to investigate proper preservation and/or restoration techniques.

****

When she stepped into the kitchen the following morning, she spotted Bogart on the counter, sniffing the box and rubbing the side of his face against it. He seemed to be ignoring the fan so far, but Izzy had a vision of his tail having a close encounter with the spinning blades.

"Get down from there!" She turned off the fan before snatching the cat up and setting him on the floor. "You know you're not allowed on the counter."

He stared at her and blinked, clearly unimpressed.

"Don't give me that attitude, or you won't get your breakfast until I'm done."

She turned away from him and picked up the box, holding it up to the morning light that poured through the window over the sink. Fortunately, it didn't look much different from the night before. With luck, the owner would be able to have it restored without too much trouble or expense, assuming she was able to locate them.

Bogart sat at her feet, straight and tall, flipping the tip

of his tail, while she scrambled two eggs. She shot him a quick glance as she slid the eggs onto a plate.

"Are you sorry? You don't look particularly penitent."

He narrowed his eyes then flipped his whole tail like Indiana Jones cracking a bullwhip.

Izzy eyed him sternly. "I'm disappointed in your attitude. I thought we had developed a better relationship than that."

Mrowr.

"I guess I shouldn't be surprised. Sebastian warned me you were your own cat and tolerated humans mainly as servants."

Mrowr.

"Oh, all right. You win."

She set her plate on the table and picked up his bowls. When she returned them to the floor, clean and refilled, Bogart twined around her ankles in a figure eight pattern, purring loudly and caressing her calves with his tail. When she stroked the thick, soft fur on his head and neck, his purr increased to motorboat volume.

Izzy chuckled. "You're welcome. I'm glad to see you're not completely without manners."

After breakfast, she took the box outside to photograph in better light, then drafted a brief ad and emailed it, along with the photo, to Sebastian for placement in Friday's *Acorn.*

Chantal had a dental appointment that morning, so Izzy had a quiet hour to herself between nine and ten. The phone rang several times, but between calls she researched photo studios and print shops and found three that said they could reproduce her photos for the salon on large-scale canvases. One was too expensive, and one couldn't take the project for three weeks, but the third shop had reasonable rates and would be able to do the work next week. When Chantal bustled through the door, Izzy shared the update.

"That's great!" Chantal pulled off her cream-colored cashmere beret and smoothed her hair. "I want to start planning the reception. How long do they think the job will take?"

"I don't know. I'll find out when I take them the memory stick Monday afternoon."

Chantal hung her coat on the peg next to Izzy's, then returned to her station and began organizing her combs, brushes, and scissors for her first appointment. "I'll look at my calendar. The first weekend in December might be good. My mom and I always go overboard decorating the salon for the holidays, but it's super festive."

"I'm sure it will be beautiful, but I don't want you to go to a lot of trouble or expense on my account."

Chantal turned, one hand perched on her hip. "Izzy, you've got a lot to learn about running a business. Yes, the reception will be to celebrate your photographs, but every event I host here means additional publicity for the salon. I'm sure Sebastian will send a reporter to cover it for the *Acorn*." Her dark eyes sparkled. "You might even have time to snap a few shots to go with the story."

Izzy had to smile at the petite woman's unsinkable confidence. Vivian had been right when she'd described Chantal as a firecracker. "If I spend enough time around you, I'm bound to become a success, in spite of myself."

"You're darned right."

****

When Izzy got home, the first thing she did was check the condition of the wooden box. It felt dry to the touch, but now the lid sat slightly askew, suggesting the wood had warped as it dried. While she was examining the joints for additional signs of damage, the doorbell rang. Carrying the box with her, she went into the living room to answer it.

Vivian stood on the porch holding a small mixing bowl covered with plastic wrap. She smiled when Izzy opened the door. "I made a big batch of chicken salad with raisins and walnuts this morning—too much for just me. I thought you might like some."

Fancy chicken salad was one of the things Izzy occasionally picked up from the deli but never went to the trouble to make for herself. "That would be great. And your timing is perfect—I was just about to start fixing lunch. Come on in."

Vivian stepped into the living room. "What's that?" She gestured to the box.

"Isn't it pretty? I found it in the surf near Carmel Point last night. It doesn't seem to be badly damaged. I've been trying to dry it out."

"May I see it?"

"Sure. I'll trade you."

Izzy handed her the box and took the chicken salad to the kitchen, where she popped it into the fridge. When she returned, Vivian was studying the box closely.

"This looks English to me, from around 1820, or so. I think it might have been a document box or perhaps a large tea caddy."

"If I'd known you were an antiques expert, I would have called you last night when I brought it home. I wasn't sure of the safest way to dry it to minimize the damage."

"I'm not an expert, by any means, but I was an art dealer for more than fifty years. I've seen my share of antiques." Vivian turned the box to view the hinge side. "Whatever method you used to dry it appears to have been the right thing. The finish doesn't look too bad."

"I wasn't sure what to do, so I left it on the kitchen counter with a fan running on low."

Vivian nodded. "Air drying is safest." She raised the box to her ear and gave it a slight shake. "I wonder if there's anything inside."

"I wondered the same thing. I'd like to try to preserve the contents in case I'm able to locate the owner."

"I expect it's locked." Vivian applied light pressure to the lid. "As predicted. And I'm sure we'd damage it if we tried to pry it open."

Izzy took the box and peered into the keyhole. "It's too bad nobody uses hairpins anymore. If I had one, maybe I could pick the lock."

Mrowr.

Both women swiveled to face the sofa, where Bogart was regarding them with an intense feline stare.

"What's up with you?" Izzy asked. "I know you're not hungry."

Mrowr!

Vivian raised her brows. "He's quite insistent, isn't he?"

"It might be the box. For some reason, he's taken a liking to it. I found him up on the counter this morning, nuzzling and sniffing it."

"It was in the ocean—maybe it smells fishy. Or maybe something inside is producing an odor."

Izzy wrinkled her nose. "I hope not." She sniffed the box. "I don't smell anything yet, but if something is rotting inside, I want to get it out. Yet another reason I wish I had a key."

Mrowr!!!

Bogart bounded from the sofa to the coffee table. He looked Izzy straight in the eye and deliberately brushed the key she'd found in the park onto the floor.

Vivian chuckled. "A key...like that one?"

The cat watched in approval as she walked over and picked up the key. He purred loudly, bumped her arm with his head, then hopped back to the sofa and settled in his favorite corner.

Vivian turned the key over in her hand. "What does this open?"

"I don't know. I found it in a flower bed in the park a few weeks ago. It has an interesting shape, so I brought it home, thinking I might use it as an accessory in a photo."

"It's pretty. It also looks like the kind of key that would open a box like that."

Izzy eyed the box in her hands. "You don't think there's a chance..."

"A lot of those old boxes had simple locks with keys that were basically interchangeable, like skeleton keys. There's only one way to find out." Vivian handed Izzy the key.

She took the key and guided it into the keyhole. It fit. "So far, so good."

"See if it turns."

She applied just enough pressure to turn the key, ready to stop at the first sign of resistance. It was sturdy, but she didn't want to risk breaking it off in the lock.

Click.

Her pulse jumped at the soft sound. What were the chances? She glanced at Vivian with raised brows, then slowly raised the lid.

"What's inside?" Vivian crowded in for a closer look.

Izzy poked at the contents with a single finger. "It looks like some papers and a couple of photographs. Everything's still damp, so it's hard to tell."

"We'll have a better idea what we're dealing with if we take it into the kitchen and spread the pages out on the table."

They trooped into the kitchen, where Izzy set the box on the table and gazed at the contents. "I'm afraid to touch anything. I wonder if we should be wearing gloves."

"I think it will be fine if we pick each sheet up by the corners and lay it on a dry towel. It's not like we're dealing with the Declaration of Independence or something."

Izzy retrieved several clean tea towels from Aunt Dora's collection in the pantry and spread them on the table. Then she carefully lifted the first item — a birthday card featuring a pair of amorous chipmunks — from the box. She followed Vivian's direction and laid it on a towel, touching only the top corners.

"Open it," Vivian urged. "There might be a signature that would give us a clue to the owner.

Izzy gingerly unfolded the card. Beneath a mushy poem was the inscription, *All my love, Ian*.

Her senses tingled. "Ian. According to Joe, that's the name of the man who commissioned the locket we found in Aldo's office."

Vivian's dark eyes twinkled. "Ooh, a clue! This is so exciting! What else is in there?" She peered into the box.

The next piece Izzy removed was a photograph of a couple embracing on a beach. From the contours of their bodies, they appeared to be young, but the salt water had damaged the surface, making it impossible to identify their faces. Izzy set it beside the card. Next up was another photo, a professional head shot of the same young man whose picture was inside the locket. It bore the embossed signature of the photographer in one corner and looked like a graduation photo.

"This must be Ian," Izzy mused, gazing at his longish blond hair and earnest expression.

Vivian nodded. "It's sweet and sad at the same time. This is probably some woman's memory box. I hope we can locate her and return her treasures."

"So do I."

Next, Izzy removed another birthday card, this one floral and romantic. Its inscription read, *From Ian to Kate. You are my everything.*

"So her name is Kate. We're making progress. Is there anything else?"

"Just this." Izzy lifted the final item from the box.

It was a folded sheet of paper, lighter in weight than the greeting cards but heavier than ordinary notebook or printer paper—more like a formal document of some kind. She set it on a towel and carefully peeled the halves of the page apart. Thanks to its seawater bath, the ink was fuzzy, but she was still able to make out most of the words.

It was a certificate of marriage, dated fifteen years earlier and signed by the Reverend Susan Campbell of the First Methodist Church of Encinitas, commemorating the union of Ian Stuart Anderson and Katelyn Lorna Ferris.

Vivian's brows shot up. "So Kate is...Lorna? She never mentioned being married. I wonder what happened to Ian?"

Izzy's thoughts turned to Bryce. She'd pitched

everything that reminded her of her ex-fiancé and their years together. "If they're like half the couples in this country, they probably split up."

"You could be right. My first impulse was to return the box to Lorna as soon as possible, but it might stir up painful memories."

"I don't think we should mention it to her right now. As far as we know, she threw the box into the ocean in a symbolic gesture to rid herself of reminders of Ian."

Vivian nodded. "She's seemed so unhappy lately. I don't want to upset her unnecessarily. I wonder if she threw the locket away, too."

Izzy considered the question. "I don't know. She could have accidentally dropped the locket in Aldo's office at any point during the past three months. I doubt she hid it under the sofa on purpose."

"No. I'll grant you, she can be a bit odd at times, but that would be just plain weird." Vivian frowned and shook her head. "These murders have me rattled. I think I need a cup of tea."

"Good idea. I'll make tea for us both and a chicken salad sandwich for myself. Can I get you anything?"

"No, dear. I've already eaten. Thank you." Vivian peered out the window over the kitchen sink toward the studio. "I don't suppose the police have any idea who set the fire in your yard."

Izzy took a plate and two mugs from the adjacent cupboard. "Not yet. My new doorbell camera caught the perpetrator running across the front yard, but you couldn't tell who it was."

"Two murders and an arson." Vivian shook her head with a frown. "This kind of crime wave is unheard of in Carmel. It's got everyone in town on edge. Have you heard if the authorities are making any progress finding the Peffermans' killer or killers?"

Izzy took the bowl of chicken salad from the refrigerator and scooped a healthy spoonful onto a slice of bread. "Not that I know of. They've been able to rule out a few potential suspects, but I don't think they have anyone in their sights at the moment." She finished making her sandwich, then filled the mugs with boiling water. "The sun's out. Would you like to sit on the patio?"

"That sounds lovely."

They carried their dishes outside and settled at the table.

Vivian took a tentative sip of her tea, testing the temperature. "I've been thinking...I know you've been working with the police on their investigation, but I want to help, too. We'll all breathe easier once this whole mess is cleared up."

Inside, Izzy cringed, though she tried not to show it. Vivian might be eighty-five, but she was an energetic and determined eighty-five, and Aunt Dora would haunt her forever if she allowed any harm to befall her best friend. "Did you have something in mind?"

Vivian set her mug down with enough force to send a few drops sloshing over the rim. "We need to help the police focus on their most promising leads."

Izzy swallowed a lump of chicken salad sandwich a few chews too soon and half-choked. "How do you propose we do that?"

"Well, you haven't mentioned Serena's business partner, Dr. Holder, and I think he deserves more attention. Besides, if we can rule him out, the authorities won't have to waste valuable time investigating him."

Vivian had a point. Joe hadn't mentioned Marcus Holder in a while, but as far as Izzy knew, he was still on the list of suspects. However, she foresaw a potential snag. "I guess we could sniff around town, asking questions about the doctor, but I'm not sure I dare set foot in Beauty by the Bay again. My first visit was a disaster and ended with Serena chasing me out the door waving a jar of over-priced face cream."

"Don't worry, I have a plan." Vivian leaned forward in her chair, her gaze razor sharp. "Since you've met Dr. Holder, you could introduce me. A woman my age is the perfect patsy...er, customer...for those fountain-of-youth concoctions. While he's trying to sell me treatments, you and I can double-team him with questions. Between the two of us, the man won't stand a chance."

Vivian's excitement was endearing, and Izzy found herself warming to the idea. They had nothing to lose, and it was always possible they might learn something useful. Besides, if their questions irritated the doctor, so what? What was the worst that could happen?

CHAPTER SEVENTEEN

Vivian was so excited, she insisted they visit Beauty by the Bay that very afternoon and raced home to change into something "more glamourous," leaving Izzy to gulp down the remainder of her sandwich. When Vivian returned, she was dressed in black slacks with a sparkly gold sweater and half a dozen gold bangle bracelets on each arm.

When Izzy opened the door, Vivian struck a pose with one leg bent and an arm raised high in the air. "What do you think?"

"You look very…um…very."

"That's the idea, dear. I call it my 'aging movie star' look."

Izzy laughed. "Then I'd say you nailed it."

"I need to convince the good doctor that not only do I want all his miracle products, but also that I can afford them."

Izzy stepped out onto the front porch then turned to lock the door. "You could always drop phrases like 'when I was in Cannes last month' and 'I can't stay too long, I'm interviewing staff for my new yacht.'"

"I'm glad you're getting into the spirit of our little adventure," Vivian said as they headed down the walk. "This is going to be so much fun."

"I thought the purpose was to help the investigation, not have a good time."

Vivian gave a breezy flip of the hand. "There's no reason we can't combine the two."

"Have you thought of questions we should ask?"

"Of course." Vivian opened her purse and pulled out a folded sheet of notebook paper. "Here's a list. You can study it on the way."

Twenty minutes later, they stood in front of Beauty by the Bay.

Izzy glanced at her co-conspirator. "Are you ready?"

Vivian drew a deep breath, then released it slowly. "Absolutely." She grasped the brass knob on the sea-blue door and pushed.

The main room of the wellness spa was deserted.

"They must be open for business," Vivian whispered. "The door was unlocked."

Izzy glanced around. The lights were on, and soft music played in the background. A sudden gruesome thought grabbed her. What if Serena's killer had returned to take care of her business partner? What if Dr. Holder was lying injured or dead in one of the back rooms?

Before her morbid imagination ran any further amok, the man himself appeared in the doorway, hale and hearty, wearing a broad smile.

"Ladies, welcome! Please come in. I am Dr. Marcus

Holder. How can I help you?"

Vivian shot Izzy a questioning glance, which she returned with a subtle shake of her head. Since Marcus showed no sign of recognizing her from her previous visit, she didn't want say anything that might remind him.

Vivian responded with a tiny nod, then turned to the doctor with a smile. "I have an important event coming up, and I want to look my best. I'm hoping you can help me. I've heard such wonderful things about your treatments."

Marcus approached with sympathetic concern oozing from every pore. "Of course, Mrs....?"

"Just Vivian. Vivian Silver."

"Well, Vivian, I can recommend a treatment regimen that will lift and brighten your skin so that the years literally melt away."

"Just what I'm looking for," Vivian chirped with a cheerful smile.

"If you'll take a seat over here, so I can examine you..."

He led the way to the desk where Izzy had sat with Serena. She stood back a few feet while Vivian made herself comfortable in the consultation chair.

Marcus sat on a stool opposite Vivian and turned on the over-sized, lighted magnifier. "Now, please lean forward." He adjusted the glass and pursed his lips as he peered at her face close up. After a few minutes, he turned off the light and sat back. "You have very nice skin for a woman of your age. It's thin, but with good texture. However, I believe we can make significant improvements."

He spun around and chose a jar from one of the shelves on the wall behind him. "This firming serum is like a face lift in a jar. It will tighten the sagging skin along your jawline and around your eyes. An injectable filler will plump your lips nicely and draw attention away from the lines around your mouth."

When a vision of Vivian with bright red, over-inflated lips popped into Izzy's mind, she almost choked.

Dr. Holder sent her a sharp look. "Can I get you some water?"

"N-no, thanks." She coughed again. "I'll be fine."

He returned his attention to Vivian. "I believe we can take thirty years off your appearance without surgical intervention. How does that sound?"

"Astonishing."

"I guarantee you'll be thrilled with the results. Would you like to begin today? I have time to perform the first treatment this afternoon."

Vivian shot Izzy a quick glance before replying. "How fortunate, although I must say I'm surprised. We weren't sure you'd even be open so soon after poor Serena's death."

"Oh, did you know her?"

Vivian lifted her glittering gold shoulders in a casual shrug. "Only the way one knows anyone in a town this size. Her accident was such a shock. You must be bereft."

"It was tragic but I'm coping. Now about those treatments—"

Vivian glanced around the sleek, modern room. "You have a lovely facility. Your overhead must be quite high. I expect it will be difficult, from a financial perspective, to carry on alone, unless you had plenty of insurance. I understand business partners often insure one another, don't they?"

Vivian's skill as an actress and her guileless smile almost sent Izzy into a fit of giggles.

However, her question seemed to have hit a sore spot with Marcus. His lips tightened, though the frown didn't extend to his unnaturally smooth forehead. "I raised the issue of insurance with Serena several times, but she always dismissed my concerns. I can't deny her death put me in a real bind." Then he glanced over Izzy's shoulder and his expression brightened. "Fortunately, a savior on a white steed arrived just in the nick of time."

Vivian twisted in her chair, and Izzy turned to face the hall leading to the treatment rooms. In the doorway stood a man who appeared to be in his mid-thirties, wearing a short white coat with something — possibly his name — embroidered in red above the pocket. His hair was smooth and black, his skin a warm olive tone, and his teeth were so white Izzy almost reached for her sunglasses.

Marcus rose and strode across the room. With a broad smile, he wrapped one arm around the man's shoulders and squeezed. "Ladies, allow me to introduce my new partner in Beauty by the Bay, Dr. Fernando Rojas. Fernando and I have been close friends for many years, although we haven't been able to see each other as often as we would have liked." His smile warmed as he gazed into the younger man's dark eyes. "After Serena's unfortunate demise, I was lucky enough to persuade him to purchase her share of the business and join me here on a full-time basis."

Vivian shot Izzy a quick glance with a single raised brow, then smiled at the pair. "Congratulations to you both. It's wonderful that you were able to turn such a sad situation into something positive."

"Yes, indeed." Marcus released his new partner and motioned for him to follow him back to the consultation table. "And you are very lucky as well, Ms. Silver. Dr. Rojas is brilliant with injectable fillers and is also a top-notch lip man. You can be the first patient in Carmel to benefit from his skills. Let's take a look at the appointment schedule and see how soon we can work you in."

Vivian's bracelets jangled as she rose from the chair. "I believe I'll need to give that a little more thought, Dr. Holder. Do you have some literature on the procedure I might study?"

A wave of disappointment crossed Marcus's face, but he nodded. "Of course. Let me get it for you."

He went to the main reception desk, then returned with a brochure, which he handed to Vivian.

She tucked it into her purse. "Thank you. In the meantime, I'll take a jar of the firming serum."

His smile returned. "Excellent. I know you'll be happy with the results. And as soon as you're ready to proceed with the additional treatments, Fernando and I will be here, ready and waiting."

Izzy waited while Vivian paid for the jar, then flashed the doctors a smile and a quick wave before hustling her friend out the door. As soon as they were outside, she lowered her head and said in a loud whisper, "You didn't have to buy that stuff. Did you see how much it cost?"

"Of course I did, and the experience was well worth the price. I can't remember when I've had more fun. You should have joined in."

Izzy shook her head. "You didn't need my help, and it was a pleasure to watch you work. You're a natural-born actress...or con artist."

Vivian laughed hard enough to draw stares from a couple sitting outside a wine bar. "It's a fine line between the two."

Izzy slid a supporting hand under her friend's elbow as they climbed the few steps from the tiled plaza to the street level sidewalk and headed for home. "I'm glad you suggested this expedition. Not only did it give you an opportunity to exercise your inner thespian, but we learned two important things that should help the police rule out Marcus Holder as a suspect, at least in Serena's murder."

After deftly dodging a teenage boy on a skateboard, Vivian picked up her pace so they could cross the next intersection with the waiting crowd. "It doesn't sound like he had anything to gain financially from her death."

"According to him, he was at risk of losing the business entirely."

"Fortunately, he had that handsome young Dr. Rojas waiting in the wings." Vivian's brows flashed knowingly.

"Uh, huh. And from what he said, their relationship pre-dates their business partnership. Did you see the way he treated Fernando? He certainly didn't look at Serena like that during my previous visit."

"Apparently, all that talk of an affair between the two was merely idle gossip." Vivian caught the toe of one shoe on an uneven section of sidewalk and grabbed Izzy's arm for stability. "Oops. That was a close one. The city had better get busy and repair these sidewalks, or the tourists are going find themselves knee-deep in a sea of fallen old people."

"Who's old? You're just a kid by Carmel standards."

"True. Here, ninety is just hitting your stride." Vivian raised her bag from Beauty by the Bay. "And wait until

I've slathered this magic potion on my face for a few weeks. The doctor said it would make me look thirty years younger!"

"You'd better be careful with that stuff or you'll get picked up for skipping school."

Vivian chortled and squeezed Izzy's arm. "I'm sorry what's-his-name was dumb enough to let you go, but I'm so glad you moved to town. I wish Dora was here to enjoy your company, but I'm doing my best to fill her shoes."

Izzy felt a fleeting pang at the mention of her great-aunt. "I miss her, but you're doing a wonderful job."

She walked Vivian to her house, then crossed the street and found Bogart waiting when she opened the door.

Mrowr.

"Hello to you, too." Izzy closed the door and locked it.

Mrowr!

"Don't try to convince me you're starving. It isn't even five o'clock."

Mrowr!!

"Oh, all right."

The feline followed her to the kitchen, complaining all the way, and watched her prepare his dinner.

"You know, you're mighty demanding for a non-paying guest."

As expected, His Highness ignored her. She left him to his meal and wandered into the living room, trying to decide what to do with herself. Despite Bogart's histrionics, it wasn't actually dinnertime yet. Besides, after her lunch of Vivian's delectable chicken salad, she wasn't hungry.

What she wanted was to talk to Joe, to tell him about

the visit to Beauty by the Bay. He was probably still at work, but she preferred to avoid the receptionist in the DA's office, so she tried his cell. When the call went straight to voice mail, she tamped down her disappointment and left a message saying it wasn't urgent and asking him to return her call at his convenience.

Feeling both deflated and fidgety, she decided creative work was the best thing to take her mind off murders, suspects, and all things grim. She changed into a pair of soft, well-worn jeans and her old Cal Bears sweatshirt and headed to the studio to edit the sunset photos she'd taken the previous evening.

Unfortunately, the distraction failed. The pictures reminded her of finding Lorna's box, which led to more questions about the woman herself. Fruitless speculation led Izzy in frustrating circles, and after an hour she headed back to the house. Finally hungry, she devoured the remainder of the chicken salad straight from the bowl while standing at the sink, gazing through the window into the dark backyard.

After washing the bowl, she joined Bogart on the living room sofa, hoping to find something on television that would hold her attention until bedtime. But before she turned on the set, she noticed her phone, lying on the coffee table. She'd meant to take it with her in case Joe returned her call, but had forgotten. When she picked it up, she saw he'd sent her a text.

Sorry I missed your call. I'll be tied up all evening. Call you in the a.m.

Her earlier disappointment returned, and she sighed. Her news would keep — it wasn't earth-shattering — but it would have been nice to hear his voice.

With determination, she picked up the remote and began pushing buttons until settling on a sci-fi alien movie she'd seen several times. It might not captivate her imagination, but in contrast to real life, at least she could be sure the good guys would conquer the monsters in the end.

****

The next morning, Izzy was eating a piece of toast with raspberry jam and checking the news on her phone when it buzzed, startling her so she nearly dropped it. When she saw Joe's name, she relaxed. "Good morning."

"Hi, Izzy. Sorry I missed your call yesterday. What can I do for you?" He sounded rushed and out of sorts.

"Actually, it's what I can do for you...possibly."

"Yes?"

"I've learned a few things you might find interesting."

"If it helps with these Pefferman cases, you'll have my undying gratitude. I'm about ready to pull my hair out." His frustration was palpable through the phone.

"I don't know how helpful it will be, but I've got some additional information about that locket we found in Aldo's office. Also, Vivian and I visited Beauty by the Bay yesterday and talked to Marcus Holder."

"Hold on a second." His voice was muffled as he spoke to someone in the room. "Izzy? Sorry for the interruption. I'm at the office in Salinas now, but I'll be in Carmel around the time you get off work. Can you meet me at Luigi's? We can grab some lunch while you tell me what you've learned."

"That works for me. If you're not there, I'll get us a booth."

"Great. Thanks. See you then." He hung up before she could say goodbye.

She tried not to be annoyed. After all, the man was tasked with solving two murders. All she had to do was answer the phone at a hair salon.

Cece's was busy, and the morning passed quickly. When Izzy arrived at Luigi's around one-fifteen, she scanned the quaint, Mediterranean-themed restaurant for Joe, but didn't see him. She gave the hostess her name, stated that a gentleman would be joining her, and requested a booth in the back. Once seated, she settled down to wait, perusing the menu and list of daily specials. She was trying to decide between penne with mushrooms and artichoke hearts, and spaghetti carbonara when Joe slid into the seat opposite her.

He was frowning and out of breath. "Sorry I'm late. A truck full of turkeys overturned on 68, blocking the highway, and when I finally got here, I had to circle the block three times to find a parking place."

The server appeared with two glasses of water, a basket of sliced bread, hot from the oven, and an additional menu. "I'll give you a few minutes, then I'll be back to take your order."

Joe accepted the menu with a nod. "Thanks."

Izzy eyed his rumpled shirt, crooked tie, and uneven shave. "Rough morning?"

He took a long drink from his water glass. "Rough night. Rough morning. You name it. There was a gang-related triple homicide in King City last night, and the DA's investigators have been called in to help the local PD and the Sheriff's Department. I need something to break on the Pefferman murders so I can devote more time to these new cases."

"I may be able to help you, at least in a small way."

He ran one hand across his rough jaw. "That would be great. What have you got?"

Before she could launch into her recent discoveries, the server returned to take their orders. She decided on the penne, and Joe chose chicken parmesan.

As soon as the young man collected their menus and left, Izzy leaned forward and lowered her voice. "First, as I mentioned, Vivian and I went to Beauty by the Bay yesterday afternoon."

Joe looked skeptical. "Are you sure it was wise to involve Ms. Silver? She's got to be eighty."

"She's eighty-five, and it was her idea. She played the part of a prospective client and had a fantastic time."

"Wasn't Holder suspicious when he saw you again?"

"He didn't appear to recognize me, so I stayed in the background and let Vivian have full rein."

Joe selected a thick slice of bread from the basket and dipped it in the shallow bowl of olive oil between them. "I assume you learned something interesting or you wouldn't have called me."

She nodded. "First, Marcus didn't have any insurance on Serena, and her death put him in such a bind, he was afraid he might lose the business."

Joe's brows rose. "You're right—that is interesting. So he had no financial motive to kill her."

"No obvious one, anyway. Then there's the second part. He introduced us to his new partner, a Dr. Fernando Rojas—very young, very handsome, and clearly besotted."

Joe's brows rose higher. "With Holder?"

She nodded. "And vice versa. I think the rumors of an affair with Serena were nothing but salacious gossip."

"Hmm." He tore off another chunk of bread and popped it into his mouth while he pondered the new information. "That would seem to leave Dr. Holder without a clear motive, personal or financial, to kill either of the Peffermans."

"You should be able to move him to the bottom of the suspect list, or take him off altogether."

"He wasn't at the top, but I think we can safely focus our attention elsewhere. Thanks."

At that point, the server arrived with their plates, and the conversation stalled for several minutes. Joe must not have had time for breakfast, because he dove into his meal like a hungry bear. Izzy could barely remember the single piece of toast she'd eaten nearly six hours earlier, and Luigi's penne was beyond delicious. She made a mental note to check out their delivery options.

She'd eaten nearly half her meal before she remembered the rest of her news. "There was something else I wanted to tell you."

He glanced up from his plate, his mouth full.

"I found a small wooden box in the ocean Tuesday evening."

He swallowed, then took a drink. "Okay. And how does that affect our cases?"

"I'm not sure it does, but there were several interesting items inside."

"Such as?" He sliced off another piece of cheesy, tomato-y chicken breast.

"Old letters, cards, and a photograph of a young couple on the beach, along with a certificate of marriage, dated fifteen years ago, between Ian Stuart Anderson and Katelyn Lorna Ferris."

Joe set his fork down. "So *K* from the locket in Aldo

Pefferman's office is Lorna Ferris."

Izzy nodded. "It feels significant. I'm just not sure how."

"I might have an idea. I spent an hour this morning with the forensic accountant who's been working her way through Pefferman's business papers and accounts. I had asked her to pay special attention to his past business deals, in case we're dealing with a disgruntled investor or partner."

At the mention of finances, Izzy perked up. Finally, a possible motive that made sense. During her work for the insurance company, money had been at the root of every murder she'd uncovered. "The accountant found something?"

"Last year, Aldo was involved in a project with a group of real estate investors from the San Diego area. They planned to tear down a block of structurally unsound buildings just north of Ocean Avenue and replace them with new shops with apartments on the second floor. Due to a series of snags with the city Architectural and Planning Commissions, the project never progressed past the demolition phase."

She remembered a recent article in the *Acorn*. "Is that the area people are calling 'The Great Abyss?' It's nothing but a big hole."

"That's the place. Apparently, when the deal went bust, Pefferman managed to protect himself, but the outside investors lost everything. One of those investors was named Ian Anderson."

"So Aldo ruined Lorna's husband." As a motive, it was a double whammy—both financial and personal.

"It looks like it."

The pieces were falling into place, but a few still didn't quite fit. "From all appearances, Lorna came to

Carmel alone. I wonder what happened to Ian."

Joe's serious expression became grim. "He committed suicide last February."

She remained quiet as the weight of his words sank in. "Then I think we know who killed Aldo Pefferman, and why. That only leaves—"

An insistent buzz from Joe's phone interrupted her. He glanced at the screen and held up one hand. "Hold that thought. I'm sorry, but I've got to take this."

Izzy nodded and scooped up another forkful of penne. It was starting to get cold, and she hated to waste a bite. As she chewed, she watched a succession of emotions cross Joe's face. He didn't say much, but his brows rose, then knit into an intense frown. Finally, he thanked the caller for the information and ended the call.

He stared at his phone on the table for a moment, then raised his gaze to meet hers. "You were saying, we know who killed Pefferman and why. Well, now I know how. We just need the evidence to connect the dots."

CHAPTER EIGHTEEN

Izzy immediately lost interest in the remaining pasta on her plate. "What happened? Who was that? What did they say?"

Joe's expression remained serious, but his eyes held a glint of satisfaction. "It was Michelle...Detective Nolan. They've just identified the murder weapon."

"Murder weapon? But Aldo was poisoned."

He nodded. "And we haven't been able to connect a specific person to the act because we didn't know when or how the botulinum toxin was administered. Now, it looks like we finally have our link."

"But it's been nearly three weeks. I'm surprised new evidence turned up at this point."

"It actually turned up before Pefferman's death. City trash collectors found a used syringe in the alley behind Taste of Torino when they emptied the dumpster the day before Halloween. They were concerned about possible illicit drug use in the alley, so they turned it in to the police. Because nearly everyone in the department was involved with security for the parade and associated activities, the syringe was set aside and forgotten. A few days ago, an officer came across it in the evidence locker while looking for something else and sent it to the lab as a matter of routine. They just got the results back."

"And...?"

"The residue in the syringe tested positive for highly concentrated botulinum toxin, and there was chocolate on the needle."

Bingo!

More pieces of the puzzle were falling into place. "Then the poison wasn't in Aldo's insulin. Someone injected it into candy at the shop."

Joe nodded. "Likely someone who knew about Pefferman's weakness for his own product."

Izzy remembered Serena's behavior during the parade. "His wife was well aware of his love of chocolate. She was giving him a hard time about it just before he collapsed. But I'm sure everyone who worked at Taste of Torino was also used to seeing him munching on the merchandise."

"Including Lorna Ferris."

Izzy met his knowing gaze. "Including Lorna Ferris."

"The lab isn't sure they'll be able to pull any usable prints from the syringe, but they're working on it. If they're successful, I've asked the technician to compare them to the exclusion prints we took from Serena and Lorna." Joe's eyes crinkled in the corners as he flashed a smile of relief. "We're close, so close."

But Izzy still saw hurdles. "What if the prints belong to Serena? Knowing she murdered her husband won't get us any closer to figuring out who killed her."

"It could lead to additional lines of inquiry. At this point, I'd settle for solving one murder. It would free up time and resources to devote to the second." He leaned back into the corner of the booth, reached for his water glass, and took a long drink.

She was pleased to see him looking more relaxed than he had in weeks. He'd sat down at the table tired and frustrated, but the latest developments had breathed new life into the investigator, as well as the investigation. "The DA is lucky to have you. I doubt I'd have the focus or persistence to keep pursuing a case after it bogged down the way these have."

"You say persistence, my mother would say stubbornness."

"Whatever it is, I hope it pays off, and you're able to wrap both cases up soon. Vivian says catching the killer, or killers, will lift a weight off the entire community, and I agree."

Joe glanced down at his half-eaten plate and picked up his fork. "I don't know about you, but all this talk of case-solving has made me hungry."

She diplomatically refrained from mentioning the vigor with which he'd attacked his food the moment it appeared. "I'm afraid we talked so long, it's gotten cold."

"You know what that means, don't you? Dessert!" He motioned to the server, who stood near the front desk.

"Yes, sir. What can I get you?"

Joe looked across the table at Izzy. "Do you like tiramisu?"

"Who doesn't?"

"We'll take two, and I'll have a coffee." When he

raised a brow in an unspoken question, Izzy nodded. "Make that two."

"Right away. Are you finished with these?" The young man gestured to their plates.

Izzy pushed hers toward him. "Yes, thank you."

Joe watched the server disappear into the kitchen. "The food here is good. We'll have to come back when we have fewer distractions."

"I'm not complaining, but it seems like you're always feeding me. You don't have to, you know. I doubt it's included in your job description or departmental budget."

He chuckled. "Don't worry — this meal isn't on the taxpayers' dime." Then his smile disappeared, and his expression became unreadable. "I'm Italian, and like my mama always says, we express our feelings through food."

Izzy's breath stilled in her chest. What was that supposed to mean?

Fortunately, their tiramisu and coffee arrived before she had time to make herself crazy trying to analyze his words. They finished their meal in comfortable companionship, almost as if he'd never made the strange comment. Almost. When Joe pulled out his wallet, she considered insisting on paying for her own meal but decided to let the matter rest, for now.

They parted on the sidewalk outside the restaurant, and he headed for Carmel Police headquarters, while she made her way home.

****

The next morning, Izzy was waiting at the door of the salon when her employer arrived, out of breath, juggling her purse and a large tote, with the latest edition of the *Acorn* tucked under one elbow.

Chantal fished out her key and stuck it in the lock. "Sorry I'm late. I had a meeting this morning with the caterer about the reception for your photographs. How does two weeks from tomorrow sound? That will be the weekend after Thanksgiving — the perfect kick-off to the holiday season."

"It sounds great, although I feel bad that you're going to so much trouble and expense."

Chantal shoved the door open with one hip, then pinned Izzy with a level gaze, which wasn't easy, given the difference in their heights. "We've been over this before. We're friends. You deserve the exposure for your work. And it's valuable publicity for the salon. Now, no more fussing. Got it?"

Izzy snapped to attention with a crisp salute. "Got it."

Chantal laughed as she unloaded her bags at her station and began preparing for her first customer.

The morning moved along at a steady pace until Izzy got a call from Susan Sandborne, cancelling her eleven-thirty appointment. She'd been shopping in Monterey, but now her car wouldn't start, and she was stuck waiting for AAA.

Chantal came to the phone and offered to fit Susan in at the end of the day. When she finished, she handed the phone back to Izzy. "Crisis averted. Susan is sweet, but she tends to get excited if her schedule is disrupted. I keep telling her, it's only hair."

With time to kill, Chantal began thumbing through the copy of the *Acorn* lying on the desk. "I see the Historical Commission is worked up about someone's remodeling plans again. Those people need to lighten up before they all have strokes. I love the charm of Carmel as much as the next person, but it isn't possible to remain frozen in 1923." She flipped the page, then another. "I have to check the police log cartoon of the week."

When she found what she was looking for, she burst into laughter and turned the paper so Izzy could see.

Person on San Antonio reported a pit bull had jumped into their car and was eating their lunch. Officers had to use a long catch pole to remove the dog.

An illustration of a satisfied-looking pit bull with a hot dog in its mouth accompanied the post.

Izzy smiled and shook her head. "Only in Carmel."

Chantal reclaimed the paper and continued her perusal. "Here's something interesting." She glanced up at Izzy with a quizzical expression. "It's from you."

Izzy frowned and reached for the paper. There was her advertisement, searching for the owner of the box she'd found in the surf. In all the excitement, she'd forgotten to cancel it. She didn't want to drag Chantal into the situation by admitting she had already discovered the identity of the owner of the box, but had failed to return it. "It's a nice piece. Vivian thinks it's an antique. I'd like to return it, if possible."

Chantal nodded and turned another page, apparently not interested enough to pursue the matter. "Well, everybody reads the *Acorn*, so if the owner is in town, they're bound to see your ad."

An hour later, Izzy was relieved when Chantal's friend's daughter showed up to take over the reception desk for the afternoon. Seeing her ad in the *Acorn* had left her agitated, with a sense of rising tension.

She had just turned the corner onto her street when her phone buzzed. As soon as she pulled it from her purse, she saw the call was from Joe. "Hi, what's up?"

"The prints matched."

His statement caused a momentary confusion. "What prints matched who?"

"The lab tech was able to isolate two partials from the syringe—one on the cylinder and one on the plunger. They belong to Lorna Ferris. Michelle Nolan is typing up the arrest warrant now. As soon as it's ready, we'll head to Taste of Torino to pick her up."

Movement and voices in a driveway up ahead caught Izzy's attention. She halted, her fingers tightening around the phone. "You won't find Lorna at work."

"How do you know?"

"Because I'm looking right at her, talking to Vivian in her driveway. They appear to be having some kind of argument, and Lorna keeps reaching for Vivian. I've got to go." She ended the call and rushed forward without a plan in mind beyond keeping her friend safe.

Hoping to distract Lorna, Izzy waved and called out, "Hi, what's going on?"

Lorna spun. "Izzy! What are you doing here? I warned the detective there would be trouble if you didn't stop interfering."

Ah. Another question answered. "So you're the one who sent the text while he was interviewing Christos Getz."

The wild-eyed woman ignored her question. "I needed him to see that he had all the necessary information to wrap up both cases. Serena killed Aldo. Christos killed Serena. All done, neat and tidy. But no, he had to keep dragging you in. Why couldn't you just mind your own business?" Her voice was almost pleading.

Izzy's nerves were jumping, but she forced herself to remain calm. "I don't know what you mean."

Angry tears leaked from the corners of Lorna's eyes. "You refused to leave Aldo's death alone. The man was nothing to you. I thought luring a mountain lion into your yard with a package of chicken would send you scurrying back to the big city, but no. When that didn't work, I had to be more direct and set your shed on fire. But you still didn't get the message. This is all your fault!" Without warning, she grabbed Vivian and wrapped one arm around her neck in a chokehold.

Sucking in a quick breath, Izzy froze. The woman had clearly snapped. The only thing that mattered now was Vivian's safety.

"This has nothing to do with Vivian. Let her go." Keeping her voice low and even, Izzy started inching toward the pair at a slow, steady pace. "What's my fault? What's the problem?"

"She knows about the box, "Vivian croaked. "She saw the ad in the *Acorn*."

Izzy swore under her breath, but forced her expression to remain calm and non-threatening. "I can get the box for you. Fortunately, the water didn't do much damage."

Lorna edged toward a beat-up gold Toyota Corolla parked nearby on the driveway, its interior piled high with boxes and clothes. "I don't want it back. Throwing it into the ocean was my final farewell to Ian." She choked off the last word in a sob. "I never want to see this hellhole — or anyone in it — ever again. And nobody better try to stop me." She squeezed the arm around Vivian's throat for emphasis.

Izzy's chest tightened, but she raised her hand in a

calming gesture. "Everything's going to be all right. Let Vivian go."

"I don't want to hurt her, but she's my insurance. I'll release her as soon as I'm safely out of town." Lorna cast a glance down the street. "But since you're here, I have to assume the police will show up any minute. If they do, they aren't likely to risk shooting an old lady."

"Nobody's going to shoot anybody."

Lorna looked at Izzy as if she were simple. "Of course they will. I killed them. I killed them both."

Both. That answered the question of Serena's murder. "But why?"

"You found the box. You know why."

"I know you were married."

Tears appeared again in Lorna's eyes, but she dashed them away with the back of her free hand. "And Aldo Pefferman killed my husband as surely as if he'd shot him in the middle of Ocean Avenue."

"So you came to Carmel looking for revenge."

Lorna's features hardened. "I came to Carmel looking for money. That might sound shallow or mercenary, but I wanted Aldo to pay for what he'd done, to pay for what he'd stolen. I wanted him to return the money to honor Ian's memory and balance the cosmic scales."

Out of the corner of one eye, Izzy noticed movement behind Vivian's neighbor's hedge. When she glanced closely, she spotted Joe, crouching behind the bushes. He moved one hand in a wide circle, which she took to mean there were other officers in the surrounding area, then motioned that she should keep talking. She gave a tiny nod before returning her attention to Lorna.

"What did Mr. Pefferman say when you asked for the money?"

"He refused to take me seriously. It made me so mad, I took off my locket to show him the wonderful man he'd ruined." Lorna's cheeks reddened, and her voice shook. "When I asked for the locket back, he snapped it shut and tossed it across the room like he was throwing away a piece of garbage. Then he laughed and told me to be a good girl and get back to work, and patted my behind. He loved letting everyone in town think I was having an affair with him." She snorted and tossed her head. "As if I would ever have let that pig touch me. If I'd had a knife, I would have cut his hand off."

"Was that when you decided to poison him?" Izzy didn't want to turn her head and risk drawing attention to Joe's hiding place, but she hoped he was getting all this, loud and clear.

"He had to pay, one way or another."

"So you injected the poison into his chocolate."

Lorna's smile was ice-cold. "It was so easy. We were making candy to hand out at the parade, and I knew he'd never be able to resist if I offered him a few pieces 'just to taste.'"

"I have to ask, since that form of the toxin is illegal in this country, how did you get it?"

"A friend in San Diego drove down to Mexico and picked up a few boxes for me."

"And after the poisoning, you filled the empty vials with water and somehow slipped them into the display on the shelves at Beauty by the Bay."

Lorna's lips parted in a self-satisfied smile. "That was a stroke of genius, if I do say so myself. The Monday morning after Aldo died, I stopped by with coffee and pastries to offer my condolences. As I expected, Serena was at home wallowing in her grief, and Marcus was so busy dealing with the local looky-loos, he never noticed me add my boxes to the display. I figured if the cops found the bottles, they would point straight to Serena, the arrogant cow."

While Lorna was distracted recounting her story, Izzy had noticed a couple strolling up the street from the opposite direction. As they drew closer, she recognized Detective Nolan and Officer Lopez, both dressed in street clothes. It was a relief to know the cops were tightening the net. Although Lorna didn't appear to be armed, the stand-off had to end soon. Vivian's face was ashen, and her balance was starting to waver.

Izzy returned her attention to the woman holding her friend by the neck, and forced her expression and voice to remain as sympathetic as possible. "I understand why you wanted to make Aldo pay, but why Serena?"

Hot color flooded Lorna's face. "The woman was a monster. She thought she was so beautiful, with her perfect skin, perfect features, and perfect figure. Everything about her was fake, and she treated everyone else like they weren't fit to kiss her Brazilian butt-lifted backside."

In an attempt to maintain the pretense that she was on the woman's side, Izzy wrinkled her nose. "She sounds awful, but since she spent most of her time at Beauty by the Bay, couldn't you just avoid her? I don't understand why she had to die."

"Serena was as bad as her husband. She deserved to die because she laughed at me, too."

"After Aldo's death?"

Lorna nodded. "I went to see her a few days later and told her about the money her husband owed me. When I told her I wanted it back, she burst out laughing, called Ian a naïve fool, and said I was ridiculous." A small muscle beside her mouth twitched. "That was it — I was done."

"Sabotaging her car was very clever. How did you know what to do?"

"You'd be amazed what you can learn with a simple internet search. Once I'd watched the instructional video a few times and was sure I knew what to do, I waited in the Plaza parking garage until no one was around, then slipped under Serena's car, and snip, snip." She imitated the motion of scissors with her free hand.

Izzy nodded, anxious to keep the woman distracted and talking until Joe, Michelle Nolan, and Officer Lopez were in position to move in and make the arrest. "But how could you be sure it would kill her? Malfunctioning brakes might just have caused a minor fender-bender."

"Oh, I thought of that. To make sure she'd be driving fast down the steepest hill in town, I called her at the spa and told her I had evidence she'd ordered the toxin that killed her husband. I threatened to turn the evidence over to the police unless she met me at the beach parking lot in fifteen minutes with ten thousand dollars. It wasn't nearly what she owed me, but I just wanted the whole thing to be over. If Serena paid me off, I promised to leave town, and she'd never hear from me again."

"That was smart."

Lorna ignored Izzy's attempt at a compliment. "She got hysterically angry—screaming into the phone, calling me names, and making all kinds of wild threats. That's when I got my real revenge—I laughed at her." Her lips curved upward at the memory. "After that, her death was just the icing on the cake. Although, I have to admit, it was satisfying to see the look on her face as she flew past me down Ocean Avenue."

Izzy glanced past Lorna and saw that Detective

Nolan and Officer Lopez had stopped in front of the house next to Sebastian's and Michelle was on her phone. She needed to come up with something to stall for time. "Would you like your locket back? The police found it in Aldo's office, and I'm sure I can arrange to have it released to you."

Lorna shook her head. "I don't want it, not now. I would never be able to look at it again without seeing Aldo's ugly face. Besides, that part of my life is over. I'm leaving here with a clean slate, and I'm taking Vivian with me."

Vivian tried to resist, but her kidnapper was several inches taller and several decades younger. When Lorna tightened her grip around her hostage's neck, Vivian's hands clawed at the restraining arm, and a gurgling sound issued from her throat.

Izzy instinctively lunged forward, but Lorna squeezed tighter and shouted, "Get back!"

Suddenly, a sleek brown bullet shot out of the bushes and twined itself around Lorna's ankles. Izzy barely had time to recognize her feline roommate before Bogart opened his jaws and clamped his needle-sharp teeth into his target's Achilles tendon.

Lorna shrieked and fell to the ground, taking Vivian with her. The next two minutes passed in a blur as Izzy rushed forward, Joe crashed through the hedge, and the two Carmel PD officers raced across the street.

Izzy was closest, so she reached Vivian first and pulled her to her feet as the cops converged on Lorna. "Are you okay?"

Vivian rubbed her throat. "I think so. I'm glad you and the rest of the cavalry arrived when you did, although I'm sure I would have figured a way out on my own, if necessary. I might not look it, but I'm a tough old bird."

"You are, indeed." Izzy slipped a protective arm around her friend's shoulders, then glanced at the handsome Burmese sitting a few feet away, regarding the proceedings with smug self-satisfaction. "However, I think Bogart is the real hero here."

"Oh, absolutely," Vivian agreed.

Never one to shun the limelight, he closed his eyes, lifted his furry chin, and basked in their admiration.

Joe stood to one side while his colleagues conducted their arrest. Lorna struggled briefly, then collapsed to the ground, keening softly, as Officer Lopez slapped handcuffs on her and read her her rights.

Michelle Nolan hauled the captive to her feet, then nodded to Lopez. "I'll keep an eye on her while you get the car."

He nodded and trotted off down the street.

"Hey, what's going on here?" a male voice called out.

The assembled group turned to see Sebastian crossing from his front yard.

"This is such a quiet street — I had to come see what all the excitement was about." His gaze darted from Vivian to Lorna and back. "I sense a major story here."

Vivian shrugged loose from Izzy's embrace. "This is one for the front page of the *Acorn*, believe me." She pointed to Bogart. "That cat just saved me from being kidnapped by a murderess."

"What?" Sebastian's eyes rounded behind his horn-rimmed glasses. "I can't wait to hear this!"

Before Vivian could launch into her tale, Officer Lopez arrived in the squad car, and he and Michelle loaded Lorna into the back and drove away.

After they left, Joe turned to Vivian. "I know you've been through a traumatic ordeal this afternoon, but I'd like to take a preliminary statement from you while the details are still fresh in your mind. We could go to the station, but it's likely to be pretty chaotic when they bring Lorna in."

"Let's go inside. I baked brownies this morning, and I don't know about you, but I could use a cup of good strong coffee." Vivian hesitated on the front steps and turned. "You too, Bogart. I've got a can of tuna with your name on it."

At the sound of the word *tuna*, the cat trotted up the steps and followed her into the house.

Joe lowered his voice and glanced from Izzy to Sebastian. "No matter how tough Vivian says she is, she's been through a lot today and isn't used to being questioned by the police. It might be against protocol, but I think she could use the support of friends right now."

Before Izzy could reply, Sebastian answered for them both. "Whatever we can do to help."

Worry gnawed at her as she followed the men up the steps and into the house. Each time she remembered the look on Vivian's face when Lorna squeezed her neck, the same potent mix of fear and anger rose in her throat. Joe was right. Vivian was putting on a brave face, but she must have been terrified.

Vivian directed the men to the dining room, then headed into the kitchen with Izzy in tow. "I need to fix a plate of tuna for my hero here." She bent to pat Bogart's head. "Then I'll start the coffee, if you'll get the cups and plates down."

Izzy opened the cupboard to retrieve the dishes. "Are you sure you're up to this?"

"Don't worry about me, dear. I'm pretty resilient. At my age, you have to be."

"I can't help but feel guilty. If only I'd remembered that ad in the paper..."

"Don't be silly." Vivian set a saucer of choice tuna on the floor and was rewarded with a purr that could be heard down the block.

After starting the coffeemaker, she reached for the pan of brownies on the counter. "Hand me a knife, will you?" She pointed to a shallow drawer.

Izzy complied but still couldn't shake the feeling that she was at least partially responsible for the assault on Vivian. "Based on the contents of the box alone, we suspected Lorna was connected to Aldo's death. I should have realized she might be violent."

Vivian stopped cutting brownies and pointed the knife at Izzy. "Now stop that. Nothing that happened is your fault. The only person to blame is Lorna, and even she's a victim, in some respects."

Izzy sighed. "It's all a big mess, isn't it?"

"It is, but I've seen a lot of messes in my time, and we'll get through this. At least we no longer have to worry about a murderer roaming the village. Everyone can relax, and things can get back to normal...or what passes for normal in Carmel-by-the-Sea."

When Vivian winked, Izzy couldn't help but laugh. Instantly she felt lighter, brighter—as if an ominous cloud had dissipated. The coffee was ready, so she filled the cups while Vivian finished putting brownies on the plates, and together, they carried everything into the dining room.

The interview turned out to be relatively brief. Vivian explained that she'd found Lorna packing her car, and when she questioned her about it, the woman had flown into a rage. Izzy had arrived while they were arguing, and Joe had witnessed the rest.

When they finished, he tucked his notebook back into his pocket and downed what was left of his coffee. "I think that's all for now, Ms. Silver. If we need anything more, I'll give you a call. Are you sure you don't need medical attention?"

Vivian pursed her lips in a stubborn frown. "I wish you would all quit fussing about me. I'm fine, and I'm sure you have more important things to do."

Joe rose from his chair. "In that case, I need to get over to the station." He glanced at Izzy. "I'll call you later."

She nodded. "Vivian, are you sure you don't want me to stay with you for a while?"

Vivian rolled her eyes. "What do I have to do, a tap dance?"

Sebastian chuckled and pushed to his feet. "I guess I'll be going, too. Take care, Vivian, and call me if you need anything."

She led the way to the door and opened it. "Go on, now. I'm going to lie down for a bit and rest my eyes." After shooing them outside, she closed the door.

After parting with Joe and Sebastian, Izzy made her way up the driveway of her own home, accompanied by Bogart. The arched, trellised gate welcomed them into the sanctuary of the front courtyard, where she paused on the porch and drew a deep breath of the fresh, ocean-scented air. She reminded herself that, surreal as it seemed, the nightmare of the past few weeks was over. As Vivian had said, they could all relax, and life would return to normal.

When she unlocked the door and stepped inside, her gaze caught on Aunt Dora's old mantel clock. Although her body insisted it must be after midnight, the clock read three-twelve.

She glanced down at her feline companion. "You must be worn out from all your heroics. How about a nap?"

Mrowrr.

"Yeah, me too."

Kicking off her shoes, she padded barefoot to the sofa and stretched out. Bogart hopped onto her stomach and circled twice before settling. As Izzy's mind began to lose focus, her last conscious thought was that Vivian had the right idea—all she needed was to rest her eyes for a few minutes.

CHAPTER NINETEEN

Despite his promise, Joe didn't call the next day, or the day after, or the day after that. Izzy told herself he was busy wrapping up the cases against Lorna, but after a week, she accepted that their relationship, while friendly, had always been strictly business. Now that the Peffermans' murders were solved and the suspect arrested, she and Joe no longer had an active connection, and that was that. She experienced a brief pang of regret, but her life was busy, with one day flowing into the next like a river on its way to the ocean.

On Thanksgiving Day, Sebastian invited her and Vivian for dinner at his house. It was the first time Izzy had ever been inside the opulent, Spanish Colonial-style mansion. Their host was meticulous, and the meal deserved a Michelin star, but given the décor, she kept glancing over her shoulder, half-expecting Zorro to swing down from the second-floor interior balcony and flick a "Z" in the tablecloth with the tip of his sword.

Then there were the preparations for the reception at Cece's to introduce Izzy's photography to the public. Chantal zipped from phone calls with the caterer and local press to festooning the salon with holiday-themed décor. When Izzy offered to help, her boss replied, "Just keep the salon running. I've got this." And she did. By Thursday, every detail had been ironed out, buttoned down, and triple checked.

Late Friday morning, Izzy got a call from the photo lab that the canvases were ready.

Chantal let out a little *whoop* and checked her watch. "My next client isn't due for an hour. Let's go. I can't wait to see them!"

Since Chantal had driven to work, they took her car. Izzy stared out the window and fiddled with the strap of her purse as they merged into the stream of traffic heading north on Highway 1 toward Monterey. So much was riding on these photos. How well would the black and white images that had looked edgy and interesting on her computer screen translate to the new large-scale size? What if Chantal hated them?

Fortunately, her fears were laid to rest as soon as the shop owner carried the prints from the back room and laid them out for approval. Izzy breathed a sigh of relief. Her photos were crisp and had transferred to the large format with all details intact.

Chantal picked one up and danced around the store. "I love them. They're perfect!" She happily paid the bill, and the man helped load them in her car.

Although Izzy usually left at one o'clock, that afternoon she stuck around to help hang the pieces. When they finished, and she saw her work on the walls of the salon, pride swelled in her chest.

Her friend stood back, wiping her hands on a towel while she admired their handiwork. "You're going to be swamped with business. After tomorrow night, every shop owner in town is going to want something like this."

"I'm just glad you're happy."

Chantal turned in surprise. "Aren't you?"

Izzy had to admit, she was. Her job at Pacific Western Life had satisfied the logical, analytical side of her brain, but exploring the creative side had opened the door to a whole new world.

****

She spent the following afternoon fiddling with her hair and trying to decide what to wear. Chantal had pushed for something sexy, but short, tight dresses had always made Izzy feel tall and gangly. She decided on the mid-length, flowing chiffon sheath she'd worn to the partners' dinner at Bryce's law firm.

Bryce. She hadn't thought of him in weeks. She poked at the memories of their years together and was relieved to feel no corresponding pain. Not even a twinge.

If I could forget him so quickly and easily, I must not have really loved him.

The thought brought her comfort. Maybe Bryce had been a place-keeper, someone to mark time with until her real life — the life she was meant to live — began.

She smiled at herself in the bathroom mirror before coating her lips with a layer of eye-catching coral. She rarely wore makeup, but tonight was her night. She might as well go all out.

The crowd at Cece's was an eclectic mix of Carmel's

movers and shakers — politicians, realtors, winery owners — and they all appeared to be having a fine time mingling, chatting, and admiring Izzy's photos. Chantal was right — she'd already fielded several inquiries about future commissions.

The salon was packed elbow-to-elbow with everyone she knew in town and everyone Chantal thought she should meet. Sebastian was there, looking dapper as always, and he'd brought an *Acorn* staff photographer so Izzy could enjoy the festivities without worrying about work.

Only one person was missing. And then she saw him, pushing his way through the partiers, balancing a champagne flute in each hand. His hair looked like he'd been driving on the freeway with the windows down and his tie was askew, but she smiled anyway. "I didn't expect to see you here."

Joe handed her one of the glasses and took a long drink from the other. "I've been stuck in King City for days, working on that triple murder, but I wouldn't have missed your big evening for anything. Congratulations. This is quite a turnout."

Izzy sipped her champagne. "Chantal knows how to throw a party."

He raised his gaze to the large photographic canvases hanging just above eye level. "Your pictures turned out great. I think the one with Chantal aiming the hairdryer like a cowboy in a duel is my favorite."

"That was her idea. We had a lot of fun at the photo shoot."

His expression sobered. "I meant to call you —"

"That's okay. I understand."

"I've been concerned about you and Vivian. The case may be wrapped up, but I know it was traumatic for both of you."

Izzy tipped her head toward her neighbor, who was holding court in one corner, gesturing with a champagne glass in one hand as she regaled a circle of older ladies with the story of her visit to Beauty by the Bay. "Vivian is a strong woman. As you can see, she has rebounded remarkably."

"And you?"

She considered his question. "I'm doing well. I've been busy helping Chantal set up this mini-exhibition. If it's a success, I might host a similar event at my studio to showcase some of my other work."

Joe scanned the lively gathering. "It looks like a success to me."

She smiled. "So far, so good. I've already had a few inquiries from some of the guests."

He nodded and took another drink. "I know you didn't expect to get mixed up in two murders, but I really appreciate your help with the investigations. I hope you don't regret moving to Carmel."

She met his gaze. "Not for a second."

"Good. Do you have any plans for after the reception?"

She hadn't thought that far ahead. "Nothing particular. I expect I'll be tired and talked out."

"Do you think you'll have enough energy for dinner at Luigi's? After our lunch was interrupted by that phone call, I still owe you half a meal."

It might have been the excitement of the evening, or possibly the effects of champagne on an empty stomach, but his suggestion caused a momentary confusion. "You don't owe me anything, and besides, the cases are solved."

He leveled his gaze at her. "I'm asking you on a date,

Izzy. I think it's time we found out if we have anything in common besides murder, don't you?"

She'd never looked at their relationship from that angle, but he had a point. She downed the remainder of her champagne in a single gulp. "Um…I'd like that."

"Good. It's pretty loud in here. I'll step outside and give the restaurant a call." He eyed her glass. "When I come back, I'll bring you another glass, and maybe a few hors d'oeuvres."

She handed him her empty glass with a sheepish smile. "That's probably a good idea. Thank you."

As she watched him depart, she cast her gaze around the room, touching briefly on Chantal, Vivian, and Sebastian, each involved in animated conversation with other members of the tight-knit community. It was hard to believe that less than two months ago she had arrived in Carmel, abandoned, rejected, and half-broken. Now, for the first time in her life, she had true friends, a cozy home of her own, and a new career filled with excitement and promise.

And then there was Joe. She had no idea where their friendship might lead, but to her surprise, she was ready to find out.

ABOUT THE AUTHOR

I haven't always been a writer, but I have always embraced creativity and relished new experiences. Seeking to expand my horizons beyond Kansas City, I chose a college in upstate New York. By the time I was twenty-one I had traveled the world from Tunisia to Japan. Little did I suspect I was collecting material for future characters and stories along the way.

I began writing when my daughter entered preschool (she's now a full-fledged adult) and became addicted to the challenge of translating the living, breathing images in my mind into words. I write romance and cozy mystery because that's what I like to read. I want to give my readers the escape from the drama and tragedy of the real world we all need from time to time.

I've been married to my personal hero for more than forty years. After decades of living in the Midwest, we heeded the siren call of sun and sea and moved to the most breathtakingly beautiful place imaginable - the gorgeous central coast of California. I look forward to bringing you all the new stories this place inspires.

Made in United States
Orlando, FL
24 August 2023